The Punk and the Professor

A Novel

The Punk and the Professor

A Novel

Billy Lawrence

Apprentice House
Loyola University Maryland
Baltimore, Maryland

This book is a work of fiction and any coincidence with real life people is purely the imagination of the author.

First Edition

Printed in the United States of America

Hardcover ISBN: 978-1-62720-136-0
Paperback ISBN: 978-1-62720-137-7
E-book ISBN: 978-1-62720-138-4

Design: Apprentice House & Mary Del Plato
Editorial Development: Rachel Kingsley

Published by Apprentice House

Apprentice House
Loyola University Maryland
4501 N. Charles Street
Baltimore, MD 21210
410.617.5265 • 410.617.2198 (fax)
www.ApprenticeHouse.com
info@ApprenticeHouse.com

For All My Teachers

A stuttering little boy spells out the word butterfly for the first time.

My brother's smile.

A faded black and white photograph of six smiling friends, a world ahead of them. The Kennedy brothers on each end. Steven and Paul to my left. Gene to my right. Me in the middle.

Wrestling. Guns N' Roses. Running free on the track.

The beach. The bay. The birds.

Long Island in the shadow of the city.

The nineteen eighties crashing into the nineties.

A girl in a Catholic school dress stands there laughing and talking with her girlfriends. She doesn't see me, but I see her. She has long straight brown hair, eyes the color of a forest, and a smile that captures me. Something inside feels funny.

A horn blared and a light flashed——

—My swollen eyes stretched open. My face muscles were numb, and my lips were tight and chapped. A layer of frost covered my hair. The car approached and its window opened. I struggled to roll my window down.

"You gotta go. Can't stay here. Get on now."

"No problem. Thanks," I said.

The security guard couldn't even let me stay in the empty lot, but I didn't complain. The guy had saved my life. Another hour or so and I would have frozen to death for sure. I turned the ignition, cranked the heat, and then drove off to the safety of the twenty-four hour diner with twenty dollars in my pocket and several hours to waste before the rest of the world woke.

PREFACE

The professor steps out in front of the room with an invitation to another world. Behind him is a giant lit screen with a picture of the opening of a cave labeled along the bottom: *"The Allegory of the Cave" by Plato, Greece, 360 B.C.E.*

The professor asks,

Why do we appreciate it?

The students stare back.

Because we live it, he says.

Plato sets up a scenario where prisoners are born into the world deep down in a cave beneath the surface of the world. The prisoners are chained and face one direction— the cave wall straight ahead. The chains are so tight that they cannot even turn to their sides. They have no concept of what's behind them. All they see is the cave wall in front of them— this is all they know. This is all we know. We are the prisoners born in the cave.

Behind us sits a roaring fire. Above and beyond these flames is a platform— a kind of walkway where puppet-masters hold up puppets and statues in the form of various elements of nature— a tree, a bird, a tiger, a lamb— and they reflect onto the wall like the fake monsters one makes in a campfire. We see the shadows and believe these visions are reality. Shadows and illusions— this is all we really know sometimes, maybe most of the time.

The professor reveals a new scenario where a prisoner is unchained.

The prisoner gets up and looks around. He is now able to see the statues and puppets but is fooled once more. He thinks he is now looking at the real tree, the real bird, the real tiger, and the real lamb. We know he is staring at just another layer of reality— the puppets and statues that imitate the real thing. To see the truth he must crawl out of the cave to the surface of the planet, and there's no holding him back. The prisoner is bound to come out. Sometimes he wants to crawl out on his own, hungry, curious, eager. Sometimes he is dragged out, against his own will, for his own good.

The professor walks over to the side of the classroom and opens the blinds on the large window that spans half the length of the wall.

Look out there, he says pointing out to the far end of campus. A thick green forest seems to stretch for miles. Blue sky painted with a scatter of white fills the top of the window.

We only see what we see. When we're in the forest we see the individual trees right before us, but we can't see the whole of the forest. When we're far away we can't see the individual trees. We can't see the details of the bark and the leaves. From afar we don't know much about what those individual trees look like or anything else going on in those woods. We don't even know what's going on in the next room, do we? There is a lot we don't see. There's danger out there. There are good things too, but we can't see them either. We would need a microscope and a telescope. We can't measure them with the eye.

Our senses fool us.

The professor clarifies— *We are all in the cave. The puppet-masters are insiders, the ones who control our world. They're the ones with confidence; they're the ones selling something. But even they are inside their own caves and don't clearly see the world for what it truly is. They are the biggest fools because they think they have something over everyone else.*

The professor takes a good look at the students and then asks, *What do you think it will take to get us to see?*

The professor challenges us to remember.

Wheels turn in one student's eyes. He closes them and remembers.

PART I
The Cave

1

IT WAS A CLEAR SUNNY DAY in late May, but the inside of that school felt subterranean. Some rooms had an unobstructed window to look out of— initial joy for the view of the sky— blue all around from the bottom to the top of the window— only to be followed by the sinking recognition that plexiglass stood between us and nature. It was a glimpse of the world out there, but so difficult to break through. The plexiglass was deceiving. We were caged in that building like broken animals gone from the jungle far too long.

I sat in English class distracted by images of my brother being thrown across the room the night before. The violence was sickening, yet I tiptoed around it and it tiptoed around me. Violence and I didn't want to know each other. Not anymore. I had had my share of fights early on. All the kids I fought were bigger than me and I took them to the ground like a lion does to a water buffalo. But those fighting days were behind me. I wanted to be left alone, yet it seemed like people poke you when they know you don't want any trouble. Teachers do this sometimes.

Mrs. Lumbrera slammed her fist down on my desk.

"Mr. Tortis, what is Twain saying in paragraph four?"

"What?"

"What is he saying? What does he mean?"

"I don't know... "

"Have you read a single page of the anthology this entire year?"

"Yes."

"Yes, what? Tell me what he means."

"I don't know…you're the teacher. Why don't you tell me?"

She stood over me with her square, chiseled jaw and flexed her fists together. You would've thought this woman was going to beat me down on the spot. Her challenging demeanor warranted the worst from a disturbed student like myself, so she was lucky. Or maybe she knew deep down inside that I wasn't the crazed girlfriend-beater she had made me out to be a couple of weeks earlier in class.

In anticipation of the summer, I had shaved my head close. I went to eleventh grade English class, settled into my seat, and opened the musty anthology of American literature. Mrs. Lumbrera entered the room and sat down at her desk. The whiff of cigarette smoke sometimes followed her in from the women's room and no cheap perfume could mask it. She began taking roll. When she got down to my name she paused a moment to observe me after calling my name.

"New look? You look like a girlfriend-beater," she said.

The class snickered.

"What?" I answered.

"You look like someone who beats their girlfriend; it's that new haircut."

If I had been a good military kid, this haircut would have been the norm, and I would have been saluted with a pat on the back, but I wasn't the good kid. I was the bad one with no hope, no respect. I could've changed my style any which way and I'd still be the punk.

Welcome to paradise.

My girlfriend and I were on and off, so Mrs. Lumbrera's comments didn't sit well with me. I wanted to run down the hall opening doors, screaming, calling for recruits— out to the parking lot to open our arms to freedom and fresh air— keep running like we were in a music video with a whole crowd behind us. I blew off her statement and she resumed taking attendance. I think she was lucky. How many others thought about clocking her?

I didn't go to English class the next three days. It was something new every day with that woman. I needed a break. And like so many times before, I was once again suspended for cutting class.

After I erased the answering machine message, I showed up the next day to serve my suspension and meet the new director. Mr. Horton had been transferred into a teaching position and Mr. Kelly, the lowest on the totem pole, had taken over. The bearded man was stocky with a serious demeanor. He had just arrived at our school from Rhode Island where I heard he was a fisherman. As soon as the bell rang he ordered all the students to quiet down and stare forward. This man was serious, but he gave orders with a degree of respect.

The in-school suspension room, known as ISS, was bare and cold. Eight or nine desks faced opposing directions. Some faced the closed curtained windows. Some faced the brick walls. We were expected to sit quietly for seven hours with only one bathroom break and twenty minutes to eat lunch. If we were good, we were able to go on errands or sometimes we'd be lucky and a teacher would send for us for a period or two. This room was the beginning of the end for some of its inhabitants who would go on to make a life out of being locked up.

Throughout the first hour of the school day, Mr. Kelly went around to each of the students assigning them their work. When he got around to my desk, he handed me five sheets of paper.

"Jack, tell me something about you. A story from your life. An obstacle. Change the names of real people. At least five pages."

In my many previous suspensions, I'd sit and stare at the wall for seven hours. Mr. Horton would let us melt away in boredom if our teachers didn't send anything. Mr. Kelly's assignment could help time go faster. I had a lot to say, and I didn't know where to start, so I settled on telling him about the previous suspension, or at least what led up to it.

2

I CAME HOME to find my brother bleeding from the mouth and my mother crying in the bedroom. It was 11:30 on a Thursday. Don had left for the night. Who knows what he'd done. Who knows when he'd be back. These kinds of things happened mostly when I wasn't home or when I was upstairs sleeping. It's not that I was bigger and stronger than Don, but I guess there was something about my presence that spooked him— maybe knowing I had a crazy father of my own out there. I don't know. Any anger Don directed towards me was passive aggressive. When I wasn't around he would become another person when he was angry. I only saw a glimmer of this other Don once in a while; most of the time I would only hear about it and witness the aftermath.

My brother was sitting alone with a rag to his busted lip. He didn't want to talk, but I asked him what happened anyway.

"I bumped into the TV."

"Again?"

He threw the rag across the room. His red t-shirt was stained with sweat. His troubled red face, bent brows, and pained lips all stared back with hopelessness.

"He's a motherfucker," he said.

For a nine-year-old, JP was years ahead in so many ways, yet kept back by too many distractions. He couldn't stay still. My little brother had the energy of a marathon runner, yet he couldn't find his way to the race. No direction.

I remember once we went to the Bronx Zoo and he couldn't stop fidgeting as we waited on the long line to get in to see the monkeys. He must've been three or four, just a baby, but he bounced all over. My mother would pull him back to her every few minutes like a dog that was wandering off. At some point, he picked up a broom and shovel left behind by maintenance and started sweeping up the sidewalk. My mother yelled at him to put it down. He refused and so his father grabbed him and dragged him back into line. JP started to cry hysterically. He wanted to do what he wanted to do. It was a scene. I stood there pretending not to know them.

To deal with his hyperactivity, they pushed him out of the house.

"Go ride your bike," my stepfather would yell.

JP would go out and ride his bike all around the neighborhood, mostly in the park. Everyone in the area knew him. Crazy JP Tortis. Even though his last name wasn't the same as mine, he inherited it upon telling them who his older brother was.

As early as six he was already getting into trouble. He would have fits of wildness. One afternoon he threw his bike into the lake in front of some older kids and then went in after it. He rode the bike right out of the lake. He was so hungry for attention— a true showman.

The after-school trouble spilled into school with letters, phone calls, and his first suspension for pissing on a kid on the bus. He made my wildest days look wimpy. He was out of control, yet the only discipline he received was when he left a smudge on the wallpaper or accidentally bumped into the behemoth of a television set.

"Dude, just be careful," I told him.

What else was I supposed to do? Plot to kill my stepfather? Demand he stop the abuse? I didn't know what to do, so I went to bed.

The next morning in school a math teacher hassled me for being late in the hall. I was always feeling rushed and wondered if everyone else had this same anxiety. If I had had a number on my back or thick glasses on my face, I would have been invisible, but I had a spotlight. The spotlight screamed, "Come nail the punk for breaking yet another rule." The spotlight followed me and teachers needing a power fix were attracted to the light.

I had heard this guy was a hard-ass. We met eyes a few times in the hallway but did not know each other and never talked until this morning.

"What do you think you're doing walking this hall after the bell has rung?"

"I'm sorry. I had to return my books to my locker and had to run over to the other side and—"

"Excuses. You can't make excuses your whole life."

"Who the hell are you? Mr. Perfect?" I snapped.

"Pardon me, mister?"

"You heard me, asshole. Why don't you go pick on someone actually doing something wrong? I'm not hurting anyone."

"You're hurting me with your blatant disrespect."

"Oh, I'm sorry. Poor you. Didn't you start it?"

"Come with me." He lunged for me and yanked my arm. I shook him off and continued walking away.

"Mr. Tortis. Is there a problem?" It was Mr. Bundy calling from behind me.

"Yeah, this creep is bothering me on my way to class. My mother always told me not to talk to strangers."

"Mr. Bundy, this kid needs an attitude adjustment. His language is disgusting."

The assistant principal called me over and waved the teacher off.

"You're suspended. Two days."

"Just like that?"

"Just like that. Insubordination."

"What is that supposed to teach me?"

"Mr. Tortis!"

"What about my side of the story?"

"It doesn't matter."

I sat there in his fancy office and watched his fat hands fill out the paperwork with a heavy looking silver pen. Then he called my house and left a message about the suspension. Upon finishing the forms and being dismissed from his office, I stormed out of the doors and left school for the day. This got me an extra day in the in-school suspension room, but it didn't matter. The day was shot, and no one was going to cool me down.

I walked it off as usual, alone until I bumped into some other punks. We smoked cigarettes and small talked for a while until I got tired of them. A friend came by in a car, and I jumped in. My friend lit a pipe and then passed it to me. That first sizzle was such an escape. I knew I was going somewhere else. It wasn't always a great place, but it was always different. Sometimes it was a frenzied world of paranoia and speed. My experience on pot was different than everyone else's. It was a rush, an internal one I couldn't show because everyone else was in a relaxed lazy mood. They always say pot calms you down, but not everyone reacts to it the same way, and some pot is also sprayed with funky chemicals that alter your experience. My friends got mellow and I would be wired like I wanted to run the track. I actually dreamed about hitting the race track again, but I knew the more I smoked and the longer my life remained in turmoil, the further I got away from that other Jack.

I had embarked on the writing project immediately. By lunch, several sheets were full. I gave them to Mr. Kelly, and the man looked surprised. He told me to keep going.

"Tell me more. Show me more of this school."

3

THE ROWS were tight in the classroom. Almost thirty of us were packed into a room. Sometimes we ran out of chairs. With more than a few bad kids in a class, even the best kids could, and would, turn on the teachers. Unless a teacher had callousness in their voice, kids wouldn't back down. Some kids didn't care about anything, but they would eventually drop out or be expelled. Physical confrontations weren't that uncommon either. Frequent fights would break out in the school and teachers had to restrain students and duck punches. Some kids didn't like it when teachers put their hands on them, even if it was a simple hand on the back to calm them. A wrestling match would ensue and if teachers weren't careful they could be humiliated right there in the hallway in front of everyone. One teacher even got his arm broken. Teachers in this school had to be both smart and strong.

I grew up around a few strong women with tough city voices. The fem-strong environment of my grandmother and her sisters gave me both an appreciation and fear of women. Sometimes through the years, female teachers pissed me off, but some like Mrs. Sullivan brought me back down to Earth. Her seventh-grade social studies class was strict and rigid. You put your ass in that seat and learning happened.

I would see Mrs. Sullivan again for lunch period. My friend Dennis and I shared several classes that year including both periods with Mrs. Sullivan. We were always in trouble at lunch with the other teacher on duty, but we perked up as soon as Mrs. Sullivan stepped over to our area of the cafeteria. She had a way. She was a small woman but there was something serious in her voice. And I can't say I ever said to myself that I hated her like I did for some of the other teachers, especially most of the men.

I had more problems with male teachers. They all acted like police officers and prison guards, not teachers, not nurturers. I didn't have the macho bullshit to deal with at home because Don didn't really say much and most of his hissy fits happened while I was out. Why did I have to deal with it here? I couldn't stand the way they walked down the hall like they owned the place, how they chased after you if you didn't have a hall pass, how they hollered at you if they saw you running away down the hall.

I remember one day in Mrs. Sullivan's class we learned how slaves who had secretly learned how to read and write would forge passes to visit friends or lovers on other nearby plantations. Some would write passes to the north, all the way to freedom. If white folks saw them on the road with a pass, they assumed nothing because it was impossible for a creature that was only three-fifths human to read or write. When I asked why we had to have passes like slaves, Mrs. Sullivan retorted with a very good answer. She understood my concern, but explained that we still had freedom outside of the structured workplace. Adults have rules too, she said. Slaves didn't have any freedom at all, until after the Civil War. She explained how there was no comparison, but it didn't make me feel any better at the time. Late passes, bathroom passes, and nurse passes all seemed like an attack on my adolescent freedom. I just wanted to run free.

My biggest problem was not getting into fights, cursing out teachers, goofing around, or any of the standard suspensions, though I had experimented with all of them. My trouble was getting caught escaping or coming back from escapes. I just didn't want to be there. Popular kids in their turtle necks, jocks in their jerseys, metal heads dressed in black dirty jeans and band t-shirts like it was still the 80s, pretty boy guidos in their Z-Cavaricci pants with gold chains around their necks— I hated it all. I had tried to be all of them, but the turtlenecks choked me, the jerseys bored me, the black clothes depressed me, and I didn't have enough money for the guido costumes. None of us knew who we were. Five hundred living breathing souls with the same identity crisis.

The concrete walls of the school halls were lined with brown metal lockers. It was stuffy like a prison and I felt like I had a perpetual fever. Like the bathroom I accidentally locked myself in when I was four. All I wanted was out. I had screamed for an hour until the fire department came and broke open the lock. I didn't want to be confined ever again. I needed to move around, breathe fresh air, and get away from those florescent lights. So I cut out when I felt the urge. There was nothing like the feeling of the metal bar on the steel door moving in and then the light that hit your face as you exited the dark building.

Sometimes friends came with me. Sometimes we ran through yards and hopped fences to get away. Most of the time, we just avoided being spotted by the security van in the first place. It was a game. For some kids it was good practice. They would spend the rest of their lives on the run. Steven and Gene came with me a lot, but because of their silent dislike for one another it was one or the other. One time Paul and I left only to be rounded up with a few others by security guards and thrown in the back of a paddy wagon to be brought back to school. He never came with me again after that, but I couldn't control myself. I needed out.

Most of the time I cut out on my own. I needed the space. It wasn't about the fun and games, going to a girl's house, drinking or drugs; those all just happened to be there waiting. For me, it was the quiet and alone time I didn't get in school or at home. Out on the streets, I could finally breathe. I could walk and walk and walk. I could cool my fever.

I'd walk the streets whistling and humming songs, studying my surroundings in the dreary neighborhoods, and I envisioned a time when I would never see these streets again. Maybe I'd be a rock star or an actor far away in California and all these New York streets would be a distant memory. Everything was surreal like a dream. The jagged cracks in the sidewalks. The sharp grass of the front lawns. The white and yellow homes that all looked like one another, except for the occasional red or blue one. The neighborhoods just rolled on and on and never seemed to end. The streets were all the same. Even when I wasn't stoned and before I had even tried pot, something was strange. It was hard for me to grasp.

Many days I would just walk and smoke cigarettes. I'd go to the deli café and sit at a round table by myself with a Boston crème donut and a Yoo-hoo. I'd look around and the other tables were filled with other lonely folks, all older and many probably retired. Some looked like they were on a lunch break or like maybe they were ditching work. I felt like I should've been in work, like I was older than I really was. I guess I always rushed things and looked ahead. It was my coping mechanism to get away from where I was in the present.

My walks to nowhere usually resulted in detention or suspension. One year I spent over forty days in the ISS room, and many other weeks of after school detention and out of school suspension. The suspensions always began with a typical declaration from Mr. Bundy:

"You're being a dirt bag and you're insubordinate. I'm going to have to suspend you."

Mr. Bundy was a tall man with a giant girth. Wide eyeglasses engulfed his face and seemed connected to his bushy mustache like a Mr. Potato Head attachment. His thick dark hair was parted to the side like a politician. His chubby cheeks reminded me of a pig. His monotone voice droned on and on— and many days his morning announcement would start our day— I pledge allegiance to the flag... echoed like torture.

I slumped in my chair as he dialed the phone.

"Yes, Mrs. Tortis, this is Jack's high school principal, Mr. Bundy. Your son has been suspended for insubordination. He will serve three days in the in-school suspension room. If you would like to talk about the issue feel free to call me at the school office number. Thank you."

The good old answering machine had saved me again, at least from immediate embarrassment.

"Finish up your day and report to the suspension room tomorrow morning. Don't be late or absent because you'll get an additional day. You're dismissed."

As always I went right home and earned myself an extra day in suspension. But since no one was home, I erased the message from the answering machine and the problem would stay my problem.

I reported back to the suspension room and sat down facing the windows. Mr. Kelly arrived and took attendance. The bell rang and he began going around distributing the assignments for the day. When he got to me he smiled and shook his head.

"You really liked that assignment, eh?"

"Yes, I guess I have a lot to say."

"Have you ever thought about being a writer?"

"No, not really."

"You have real potential. You could consider journalism, but you might want to try and stay out of here if you want to go to college."

Journalism? College? These were foreign and I didn't know what to make of these suggestions. I blew them off as ridiculous.

"Yes, I'd like to stay out of here."

"All right. I read this last night and you're really taking me somewhere, but I think you're going to need to take me back to the start."

And so I started at the beginning.

4

MY MOTHER was seventeen and graduated high school five months pregnant. My father was nineteen and had dropped out at sixteen to build racecars. He still lived at home with his younger brother and sisters. Their father had taken off just after the last daughter reached her second birthday. My father wouldn't even make it to my second birthday. When I was one and a half, he packed all his belongings into a hefty bag and drove off into the night. A wife crying at the back of his head, a baby crying in the background, a rental house with no one to pay the rent or bills— all that was behind him now.

Mom moved us out of the rat-infested rental house in Bayport, and we moved into a tiny one-bedroom apartment in Bohemia. We stayed there for six months and then moved up to a bigger two-bedroom garden apartment building in Sayville. These were good times, at least how I remember them in the photo album. The Halloween parties with me dressed as Dracula. Birthday parties with my mother and aunts smoking cigarettes as little four-year-old Jack sat on their laps to blow out the candles. My mother's friend's daughter named Spring was there too. She cracked me on the back of the head with a brick one afternoon because I wouldn't play house with her. Pretty little Spring was in all these pictures until the brick incident. She was so prominent in these pictured memories, you'd think she was my sister. And then that was it, she was gone and I'd never see her again.

Her single mother remarried and pulled them off to the mysterious land of California.

When I'd ask how come I didn't have a daddy like the other kids, I was told my father was far away out in California. This story led to a mystical attachment to the state. It seemed like a lot of people were always leaving for there and I curiously wanted to see the place, especially later when I found out so many great bands came from there. As a truck driver, my father had traveled the country including California, but never really lived there. After leaving us, my father had moved back in with his mother for a period of years. At nineteen, he wasn't ready for the world yet. He lived downstairs in the basement apartment where he'd "bang his girlfriends" according to my older cousin who lived upstairs for a time. I wouldn't see my father, or even really meet him, until I was older and my mother was already remarried.

I had no memory of him, but I had met him a couple of times when he'd drop by the Fotomat where my mother worked. He came through on a motorcycle. One time while he was talking to my mother, I went over and leaned on the bike and burned the back of my leg on the hot engine. I never liked motorcycles after that, but I don't remember anything about him. He just wanted to say hello and get a glimpse of me, but I was never told he was my father. I was like a zoo animal he could come visit once in a while.

Years later I would be told wildly different stories from my father— how he desperately tried for years to track my mother down and find me, how he turned to his brother the cop to dig up my mother's location even though we were just down the block from his mother's house, even though he had stopped by my mother's place of employment. None of it really mattered.

My early years were full of rich memories with mom, like listening to Billy Joel albums or going to Fire Island on the ferry, but we had our share of adversity. Some of it I don't remember because I was too young, like the braces on my legs to help me walk or the scar on my chin from falling out of the crib. The poverty was always in the background too, but little kids don't always see this, especially if Mom is good at making the best of things.

My speech impediment couldn't be hid well though. People couldn't understand me for the longest time. The public school sent me out to an expert speech pathologist, who worked with me on a weekly basis for about a year. I can remember pushing out the word butterfly for the first time. The therapist and I celebrated. I repeated the word over and over and shouted it when my mother came to pick me up from the office.

"Butterfly, butterfly, butterfly."

It was a victory and oddly enough it's the only word I remember learning to get right.

When I was five we moved again, this time to a second-floor apartment in a house overlooking a lake in a small town in the middle of Long Island. It was a nice change and we were escaping a massive rent increase at the corporate complex. By eight years old I was beginning what seemed like a normal life— just mom and me, and a snow-white cat with blue eyes named Max. My mother tried me out with little league, but I got hit in the face with the ball and was bored the rest of the time. She also tried me out in religion classes on Saturdays. I was unimpressed with the Jesus coloring books and so I dropped out of that one too. But I had my Atari games, a good number of toys and books, an antenna with eight or nine basic channels, and my imagination. I could spend days at a time in my room alone just thinking and dreaming.

Though I was a quiet, shy kid who liked to spend time in my room lost in fantasy, I did have friends in the neighborhood. Justin lived next door with his nice looking older sister Jessica, who would come over and babysit a couple of nights a week. A couple of doors away there was this older kid named Layne. He used to tell us about how he was born with some rare problem and how his toes were purple and stuck together. Then one day he just disappeared. Rumor was he got kidnapped. We didn't think he'd really move and not say goodbye to any of us. This was a period in time when we were told not to go near any vans. Apparently, vans, white ones, were notorious for kidnapping kids in the 80s. I was always on the watch for vans. But I loved walking to school along the lake over the bridge and up the bend. Life was peaceful at the lake apartment.

Of course, things weren't as normal as I thought. My mother hid it well. This is one of her greatest parenting successes. The boyfriends on the couch were obvious, but I was oblivious to the welfare, the food stamps, the bringing me to work to one of her two jobs because she couldn't afford a babysitter. My mother was a trooper. She didn't complain.

There we were at Fotomat, a little 8 by 8 booth where people would drop off their film, my mother would file them, and then a truck would pick up the film at the end of the day. This was her full-time job. She had various part-time jobs, which included an office. I wasn't allowed at that one, but she would drag me to the booth at least three times a week during summers, or on weekends during the school year. I would walk around in circles outside the booth breathing in the smell of the nearby Long John Silvers restaurant. When I got tired of that I would take naps in the backseat of our old '71 Chevy Nova.

Mom also did housecleaning part time and brought me along. I remember going to nice houses on the north shore. My favorite was filled with plants— on the floor, tables, shelves, hanging from the ceiling— this house was a jungle. Mom would send me around watering them.

When my mother had the cash and didn't or couldn't bring me to work, she left me with various babysitters. While no one beat me up, I do remember one woman being abusive with peanut butter. I hated the stuff and still do. Something about the nutty smell makes me gag. This woman had nothing else in her entire kitchen and her job was to feed me. When I told her the peanut butter and jelly sandwich she put before me wouldn't do, she flipped out.

"What kind of kid are you? Every kid eats peanut butter and jelly. You'll eat it today because I said so."

She stuffed the sandwich in my mouth and I instantly gagged and vomited all over this woman's kitchen. I spent the rest of the afternoon on the floor locked in the woman's bathroom. When my mother picked me up, the woman complained.

"He got sick all over my house, and I would be all right with that if it wasn't intentional, but I do believe your child did this on purpose because he did not want to eat his lunch as instructed to. You really need to teach this kid better manners. I know it's difficult as a single mother and all, but…"

I never went back to that house.

Another babysitter's house was in a poor south shore town, but it seemed like the middle of the ghetto. Outside, people were fighting and yelling. Loud bass from cars in the street rattled the windows. I remember one day being thrown to the ground; loud pops were heard and glass shattered. It felt like a movie, and I walked out of there that day feeling in a daze.

I never went back to that house.

My poor single mother worked two jobs and even went to community college for some time. After a scary breakdown on a dark stretch of highway one night on her way home from college, she decided to try real estate training, but that wasn't for her. She tried training in several other fields. Welding. No. Sales. No. Corrections officer. No, not at four foot ten. Then she found a quick six-month paralegal training program. It turned out to be a for-profit gimmick, but it's how she met Don.

5

"HE LOOKS LIKE TROUBLE," they said. Despite what my aunts told her, my mother married Don. My whole world was uprooted almost overnight. There I was packing my bags, saying goodbye to friends, nine years old and crushed. In actuality, I was saying goodbye to a part of myself that wouldn't return for years. My first crush Christie was also moving, but she was going a bit farther, up to Canada. I don't know if it made me feel better or worse that she too was going somewhere. She was one of those few people in this world when I looked into her eyes I felt comfortable like I'd known her a long, long time. I'll never forget the sadness in her eyes as she stood on the sidewalk as my mother's car pulled away for the last time.

When we moved to the new town I was devastated. I missed my friends and the quiet lake neighborhood. After I moved, the whole class wrote to me at my new address and wished me good luck. I wrote back and then a few close friends wrote back one last time. There was no Internet— Who knows how I might have kept in touch and how that communication might have comforted me or maybe even made it worse. But that was it. I planned to visit them, but that never happened. You learn to move on and forget. People I had grown up with through the lower grades would go on to middle and high school and become adults I would never know. People, like my first crush, Christie in Canada, gone. While I was only nine when we left,

I wondered about her and what might have evolved out of our friendship and cute childhood crush. I wondered about others. Where are they now? Who are they now? But after a month, I realized that world was gone forever. Now I would say hello to a host of new problems.

The new apartment did not allow pets, so I had to give up my beloved cat, Max. No looking for a different apartment. This was it, even if it didn't allow Jack's pet. You would think they could at least let me keep Max as they were about to move me miles away to a new town to live with some strange man I barely knew. Making me sacrifice my pet was not the right foot to start out on. They took him away one day while I was out at my grandmother's house. I came home and that was it.

Don tried. He really did in an odd way. In the beginning, he tried to buy me with tubs of Carvel vanilla ice cream. It surely was the way to an eight-year-old kid's heart, but it stopped there. No connection— no spending time— just superficial weather talk. Even the ice cream stopped once the wedding plans were sealed.

One night six months into their relationship, they sat me down in a pizza place in some strange town we were visiting. They told me the news that they would be married in the winter, we'd be moving to the town in which we were eating pizza, and I would have a new brother in the spring. This was a fork in the road for me and I accepted it. What other choice did I have?

Don tried to be a family man. He brought us to Disney World and played the role. He went to work from nine to five and wore a suit; he tried to be a man. He was just twenty-three when he met my mother. He had just graduated from college a year before and met my mom in paralegal school. He aspired to be a lawyer someday but then life happened. He met my mother and had a baby and later bought a house. His responsibilities forced him to invest energy in his part-time car detailing business, which suddenly started to expand with lucrative car dealership accounts in the late 80s. I think sometimes this deviation from his plans ate away at him later on. He went from wanting to be a lawyer to someone who cleaned others' cars.

He provided a small but comfortable apartment home with a washer and dryer, something my mother really wanted. No more stinking laundry mats in the middle of the night or on Sunday afternoons. But there was a cost. Her relationship with me was stretched and grew more tumultuous with time as she was pulled away with new baby responsibilities, and she continued to work nights as a waitress.

In the early days, Don would be home at night while my brother and I slept. This was his time to be alone and he liked to blast rock n' roll, a trait I surely would have respected later on, though it wasn't exactly healthy for a sleeping school age child and an infant. One night my ten-year-old head awoke to the booming music of The Hooters "All You Zombies" and in my dazed half sleep I screamed like an old man for the racket to stop. It stopped and just like that I had effectively silenced Don's night music forever. I don't know why I reacted that way because I loved music. For years my mother listened to records during the day and exposed me to great music by Elton John, The Rolling Stones, and others. I loved music. Maybe I was rattled by the loud music at night or maybe it had more to do with my resentment and competition with a man who took my old life away from me.

I think he felt guilty for some time after, but later became rebellious and in an odd manner took on the persona of a kid himself. I was the adult telling him to turn his music down. Something changed in Don around this time. It was as if the silencing of his music one night stunted his adulthood and regressed him straight back into his teenage years. He was just twenty-four years old in a world I couldn't imagine being able to handle at that age.

To begin with, he was a different kind of guy— more interested in politics than sports. His voice was softer and his skin seemed years younger. His floppy light brown hair and scrawny legs didn't help his unfatherly appearance. People easily mistook him as my older brother. I guess he tried to do what he could for his image. One way of compensating for his look was driving brand new cars. His choice was a Cadillac— an old fogey kind of show-off car, but nevertheless luxurious. Every other year he upgraded and traded in the car for a new one with a different color. Some guys do that with girlfriends, but he only had one ex-girlfriend we knew of. She even came around once to visit. My mother threw her out and told her to never come back. Mom told me the woman was trying to win him back for some reason, even though she had been the one who supposedly dumped him. She said the lady had been abusive.

Cars were his passion. So it made sense that he made money doing something with cars. He was always polishing his own cars and wiping off smudges. It was a whole project every time we used his car. Afterward, he'd go through the seats adjusting seatbelt straps so they were straight, dusting off the seats with a rag, and checking the carpets for dirt. He would park his Cadillac across the street to keep it away from the neighbor's cars. One year he had a white one, one year he had a black one, and then one year he had a maroon one.

One day the first of a string of vandalism events took place. They flattened the tires on the passenger side, which faced the shrubs. On a peek out my bedroom window I thought I had seen some motion around his car, and then later I saw some kids running away, but I naively ignored it and continued with the school project I was working on. The next time it was scratches, then a busted mirror, then a stolen hood ornament, then a bent antenna. You just didn't park a car like that in our neighborhood, but he kept at it. The Cadillacs were vandalized over and over by street punks with nothing better to do than randomly destroy other people's property— something I never took part in my punkish years. Flat tires, spray paint, key scratches, none of that was fun. I didn't care to destroy someone else's property. My philosophy was don't bother anyone; after all, I didn't want to be bothered myself. Don finally gave up the Cadillacs for a real investment as he called it, a Bentley. But now he would really have to keep an eye out for the punks.

6

UNLIKE THE GENTLENESS of my old friends in the old town, it seemed like the kids in the new town were rash and rough. Take the worst kid in my old town and put him on steroids and multiply him by two. The teachers weren't so gentle either. Everything was crazier. The new school held air raid drills where a loud siren would go off and we were led out to the hallway and instructed to tuck our heads inside our knees facedown against the wall where apparently we would die more peacefully. Had my old school really ill prepared me for the nuclear attack in the final years of the Cold War by not conducting any of these drills? The new school seemed so much colder. No more carpets and decorations— just hard floors and brick walls. You'd think I'd moved to the city from the countryside, and even though it was much closer to the city, it was only twenty-two miles away in the same county— same old suburbs. But something was rotten in this town.

Right from the beginning, they gave me a hard time. The school district administrators wanted to put me back a grade from the middle of third to second. They claimed their school district was on a higher level and argued I wouldn't be able to keep up. Even though I had state test scores that put me in the top 97th percentile. Even though I had all satisfactory grades. Even though we were in the same county in the same state with the same standards of learning. Even though the old town was far nicer with lower crime and higher ranked schools. None of those factors mattered. Their decision didn't have any logic. Maybe they just wanted to punish me because they were superior and I was just some new poor punk they could toss around. I was probably just a number to them. They probably had too many kids in third and not enough in second. We didn't even fight it. I was told, "just accept it and move on." Is that a strike two or three? You take my old town, my lake, my friends, my cat, and now my grade. My mother couldn't stand up to those bullies and there were other battles to be fought. Just fitting in with the students was going to be a battle in itself, but this would be for me to deal with on my own.

In school, I was pushed around by several kids the first year. Some of the kids were ruthless. Throwing things, kicking me as they walked by my desk, knocking books out of my hands. A kid named Aaron chased me at recess and then tried to sneak up on me from behind a metal garbage barrel. I kicked the barrel to scare him off and it smacked him right in the face. Aaron held up his hands and then looked down at the blood. I was the only one suspended.

I had broken another boy's nose and this would cost me more punishment. At one point a mob of kids yelled "get him"—— only extinguished by the appearance of a teacher. The lash back lasted about a week. Kids have a short attention span.

I'll never forget the first fight I saw. A kid named Mark in the grade above me took down this other kid named Bobby. Mark pinned him to the ground and hunched over him with punches. Bobby was bloody but refused to give up at first. Mark continued to bash Bobby's head into someone's front lawn until he lay motionless. At that moment, Mark seemed like the toughest kid in the world. It was a sickening sight— two little children really— one bashing in the other's head. Bobby was so humiliated that his family took him out of school and moved away. The whole fight was apparently over something Bobby had said. I guess he misspoke. Better watch what you say around here. At least I didn't have it like Bobby.

The petty harassment went on until another new kid named Steven Roberts befriended me and chased my attackers off of the playground.

"Leave him alone," he told them, and they listened.

"Don't let them dorks bother you."

"Thanks. I'm Jack."

"I'm Steven. They don't like me either. Who cares, right?"

Steven had moved to the town the year before and had had some incidents with the kids, but they knew to leave him alone. He was a loner, but a dangerous one. He was awkward as if he were years older than he really was. If he didn't fit into the existing scheme of things he was going to start his own clan, and I was the start of it.

We found each other on the playground and realized we had an alliance. Kids immediately stopped picking on me. Though we were still outcasts, Steven and I began a path to respect. Our base of friends was limited, but it was only a matter of time.

Outside of school there was a kid in my neighborhood, who used to tell me on the street,

"I'm gonna tear your face off."

He'd tell me this right before he'd chase me for blocks until I out-ran him through bushes, yards, and across busy streets. I ran like hell. I always managed to escape even when he had the advantage of being older and having a Mongoose bike he'd stolen from Danny down the block. John was about three years older than me and obviously taller. He had messy, sandy blond hair, deep-set blue eyes, and a smirk that terrified me. He always seemed to be waiting to come out of his hiding spot in his yard. Eventually, I realized which house he lived in and got smart by walking home on the other side of the street, but that still didn't stop him.

Known in the neighborhood as Crazy John, he at least had the courtesy to ask before the chase ensued whether I wanted it now or later, my face torn off, that is. I always answered him with a scream and a run as if he were some horror movie monster, and I think we both played into the drama. Really how could someone tear a face off in broad daylight and get away with it, yet be unable to capture the face in the first place? Of course, I didn't think about this logic as he came after me like a madman. When the rush of adrenaline subsided, I always celebrated my escape. Crazy John terrorized me for an entire summer and several more months. The ordeal made me realize I wasn't such a bad runner.

One day our chase ended up right in front of Steven's house. It was heading right for the highway and who knows what would've happened if I had tried to dodge the speeding cars and trucks. Steven stepped out in front of us. He pushed me to the side and motioned John to stop. John went right for him talking smack in his face, but Steven didn't back down to the older kid. He returned the lip service and then all of a sudden the two of them were going punch for punch. Steven began to double up. For every hit John landed, Steven scored two. John's mouth was gushing and Steven's nose was running with red. John attempted to end it all by slamming Steven's head into the telephone pole in front of his own house. Steven stopped right in his tracks, grabbed the back of John's hair, and rammed his face into the pole, once, twice, three times, and one final fourth grand slam that turned John around and sent him walking home. Steven shouted at him as he walked away,

"Don't mess with him again."

Steven gave me a thumbs up, wiped the blood from his nose with his wrist, and walked right into his house. No one had fallen. Both were a bloody mess. But I and several on-lookers who had gathered from the surrounding houses all knew Crazy John had been defeated, and he had been beaten by a kid three years younger than him. John never chased me again.

One other kid had bullied me around a little— just for kicks. Paul Roma demanded I do push ups and run in circles, and I obliged. I think he had seen too many military movies. I did the pushups laughing, which angered him more. I enjoyed the exercise. It wasn't until he threatened to meet me out after school that I became concerned. That day I exited a different door and took a different way home. Outsmart the hunter. I can remember the panic, the rush as I escaped out the other side of the building, and it reminded me of bad dreams I had had of Hulk Hogan in the character of Thunderlips chasing me through the neighborhood and busting down every door I hid behind.

On one occasion, Paul's older sister even got in on it. I remember looking out the door and seeing Marie waiting outside the school clenching her fists. Once again, I found a different exit. With a big Italian family, I feared he had enough sisters and brothers to block every entrance of the school if he wanted.

One day he came to school with a cast on his arm. He had fallen and broken it. The next day I got there early and left a Mauled Paul Garbage Pail Kid card on his desk. Paul arrived and became enraged when he saw the trading card with a beat up kid who bore his name. He slapped the hard cast into the palm of his other hand threatening to get whoever it was that left the card. This was met with laughter from most of the kids in the room.

We never did fight. He didn't scare me the way Crazy John had. Paul's pursuit was more of a game to me. In a way, I antagonized him and we bickered our way into a kind of friendship.

I compared Paul's aggression to a kind of initiation that made me one of the boys. Paul would become one of the greatest friends a person could ever have— a life saver who'd take the shirt off his back for you or leave his door open when you had nowhere to go.

Paul warmed up to me even more once Steven entered the picture. We all lived on Venice Street in our town on the south shore. Steven's house was the first one on the block, a beat up old brick house. Paul's house was down toward the end near the water awkwardly plopped on a small plot of land and was among the biggest in the area. And I lived somewhere in the middle in the upstairs apartment of a brick house with a sloped driveway.

Steven and Paul took a liking to each other and started to spend time together. Paul ended up to be a pretty cool kid with all kinds of interests. He played the drums, he liked good rock music, and he drew awesome illustrations. The three of us started to hang out and it was all good times from there on. Our clan was growing.

7

AS PAUL AND STEVEN got to know each other better, I ducked out for a while with a quieter friend named Judd Reed. He wore smart looking glasses and looked like the kind of kid that would go on to build rockets. He was the spelling bee champ, who aced his tests and always had an answer. I appreciated his intellect and the break from the wildness of the other kids, though I have no recollection of how we even became friends. Every week for about six months, I went over to Judd's house where we played Transformers and talked about crazy space-age science fantasies. We also went to the movies on the weekend. It was good innocent kid fun.

Then something snapped in me one day at the end of fifth grade. Suddenly one day I didn't go to his house like I usually did. I just didn't feel like it. I strangely knew there was another road I had to take. In a sense, I knew Judd was going somewhere different too. It wasn't that he was too good for me or me too good for him; I just knew we were changing.

It was always me going to his house. His mother probably didn't trust my environment because he never came over. She must've known something. This one-sidedness helped me justify my abandonment of a best friend. I could tell Judd was hurt by my sudden estrangement. I couldn't help it though. Maybe I was just one of those wild ones like everyone else.

Judd was so far ahead of his time and didn't really belong in that rotten neighborhood. His parents knew it and pulled him out of public school after sixth grade. For the remainder of high school, Judd commuted on a train to the city to a special school for the gifted. At least two hours a day were spent on his commute with all those grown adults going to work in Manhattan. Two hours of childhood a day, gone. But at least he got out of our town.

Sixth grade for me would be a path Judd wouldn't and couldn't relate to. Nor would his mother appreciate it. I was coming out of my shell and trouble comes along with that.

My new spiked haircut was really a part of this second coming. I was sick of my moppy mess. I looked around and saw others gelling and spiking their hair back. So I went to the barber and for the first time I knew what I wanted.

"Give me a spiked haircut. You know, the Billy Idol *Rebel Yell* look," I told the man.

"I know it well," the man said.

I walked out of the shop a new kid. I went back to school the next day and kids starting talking to me instantly. It was shallow, but looks were important. A simple haircut gave me a chance to become someone new, someone confident after several years being an outsider.

In the first week of sixth grade, a nasty kid named Sean Norris said some rotten things to a pretty girl named Sue, whom all the boys pined over, myself included. I went over to his lunch table and demanded he go apologize to her. He said no, ignored me, and went back to eating his lunch. It wasn't like me to erupt but that was it— I slammed his face right into his lunch tray. Sean got up crying with tater tots in his eyes, peas and rice in his nose, and ketchup smeared all over his face like blood. He ran out of the room, and I was dragged out to sign the "black book" in the principal's office. When we got into trouble we were forced to sign the "black book" which was a journal book with a list of names that probably read back as far as the 50s of all the worst kids that ever passed through that town. Where were all those names now?

I don't regret it though. This same kid would go on to sodomize a younger boy just a couple of years later. Sean went away somewhere upstate for that one and probably never came back down. I know I didn't see him after that. Sean also just happened to be Crazy John's only friend.

The popular fraternal twin brothers Jeff and Andy Kennedy with their spiky blond haircuts became my friends. Being friends with the Kennedy brothers was a big step. Paul was already friends with them, but it was a kind of final initiation into the cool club for me and Steven. We were becoming accepted by the other kids. We were mainstream. Let the good times roll.

It was Jeff who opened up the door for me to a whole new world. Jeff was the shorter, more outgoing of the two brothers. He and I took a walk one day. For some reason, he was allowed to go home for lunch, and I had been suspended from lunch for a week for the cafeteria incident and had to go home too. It was surprising the school let two little kids walk out the front doors and leave for lunch with no parent or ride, but they had.

"You like music?" he asked as we walked.

"I love music."

"Hey, you want to come over and eat at my house? I have some records."

We walked to his house, had lunch, and he showed me the beginnings of a wicked vinyl collection.

"These are my punk albums, real classics."

He showed me a stack of albums. The Damned. The Misfits. T. Rex.

"Check out this newer one though."

Jeff put on an album and started it somewhere at the end of side one. He gave me the cover to look at. At first glance it looked like four women on the cover, but then I realized they were men wearing makeup. I didn't know what to make of it. A song called "Look What the Cat Dragged In" played and I was just as baffled by their sound. Mom had exposed me to some cool music. The Rolling Stones. Elton John. Billy Joel. Cat Stevens. But other than that older 70s music, I was really an 80s pop piano synth kind of listener. Duran Duran. Bruce Hornsby. Johnny Hates Jazz. Those were the first tapes I owned of current music. Poison's album *Look What the Cat Dragged In* was different.

"You think this is crazy? You have to hear their newest album."

He held up an album with a demon woman with a long tongue on the front cover. It was titled *Open Up and Say Ahh*.

"Have you seen any of their videos?" he asked.

"No, where?"

"MTV. Maybe next time we'll watch the videos."

I couldn't wait though. When I went home I turned on the TV and found MTV, a station I hadn't yet watched. My mother had warned me not to watch cable. Someone somewhere along the way, probably elsewhere on TV, had said that heavy metal music was the work of the devil. No one was around, so I turned on the channel and had a look for myself. After a few wild songs with long-haired men cranking guitars in the air, Poison came on with their makeup, fluorescent green lights, and fireworks. "Nothin' but a Good Time" was an anthem for young party kids. If the devil was there I couldn't see it.

We got to know each other more the rest of the week and listened to some other albums. The punk and glam rock was growing on me. After that week, Jeff introduced me to his brother Andy. He was cool and calm too. I instantly clicked with him and began hanging with him too.

As I grew more popular, my grades began to slip. My attention span struggled. It was as if I couldn't handle having friends. But I had to change. I had to be crazy. There would always be a big one and a smart one and a dirtbag one, but there needed to be a crazy one with guts. My theatrical reciting of wrestling promos and lines from *Scarface* put me on the map.

"Oh, he's so dramatic," the hall monitors would say.

I took what I saw in movies, music, and professional wrestling and regurgitated it to be funny. Sometimes it worked, sometimes it didn't, and sometimes it got me into trouble. But it always got me attention.

The world was changing for Steven and me, and our group was expanding. The Kennedy's also lived on Venice on the block right between us. We were filling in representation all the way down the street. Nothing could stop us.

8

WE PULLED UP into the long circular driveway. The lawn, where a full sized tennis court once stood in the middle, was now bright green sod. A goldfish pond was on the far side of the property and large hedges shielded the house from the street and from the neighbors on both sides. We parked in front of the giant white house, what seemed to us like a mansion— two floors, five bedrooms, four bathrooms, a sun room, a family room, an office, and a giant living room with a grand piano and a bay window overlooking the Great South Bay. In the summer their sailboat and speedboat were right outside in the canal on their personal docks. Two expensive cars were parked in the driveway out front. We walked into a kitchen and dining room overflowing with food and drink. Abundance to the brim.

The family was small, but full and loud— four great aunts, three great uncles, a few cousins, second cousins, and third cousins. The aunts were the loudest, especially when they drank. The men were quiet and reserved.

Christmas was grand like a Roman festival. The giant tree stood in the living room next to the piano. Upon arriving, all the kids would run right to the mound of gifts to seek out packages with their name on it. There was tons of food too. All my great aunts, and my grandmother, were doing quite well at this point. Aunt Judy was doing the best. By this point, she had four homes. Judy would get out of her

Jaguar and enter the house with a long fur coat, a dead animal on her head too, and big diamond rings and necklaces. All the ladies had jewelry. This was show time. The experience of being around all their flashy possessions gave me perspective. I also usually got twenty dollar bills, which wasn't a lot coming from people who flaunted their goods, but I guess I was lucky to get anything at all. My mother had years where she had to borrow money just to get a tree, and yet we were in the same room with millionaires.

Our family dynamic forced people who otherwise wouldn't associate with one another to be in the same room on holidays. This was good and bad. Good for them to see a lower class person as a fellow human being and family member, past the surface problems. Good because I got to see how other people lived and enjoyed the fruits of life, and also because I learned that money doesn't make anyone fulfilled. Bad because people thrown into a mix just don't relate, and no matter what, you can't get them to understand why your problems exist especially if you don't understand the origins yourself.

My younger cousin Courtney enjoyed piano and violin lessons and weekends on her boat. She lived with her grandmother Judy in a Bridgehampton mansion. Here I was down and out and this girl had the nerve to come crying to me at a family get together about how hard life was.

"I don't know what to do."

"About what?"

"I want to be a fashion designer."

"So? Be one."

"How? I might have to go to Miami or Beverly Hills."

"I'm sure there are designers in the Hamptons."

"Did I tell you about my dad's newest wife?"

Sure, Courtney's biological mother was a resident at the state sanitarium, and her father was a slouch who barely had a job his entire life as he waited to cash in on his mother's fortune, but Judy gave Courtney the world. I guess making the best of it is too easy.

"Listen, I don't have a pot to piss in. So I don't know what to tell you."

And she walked away.

The family didn't like Don early on. To fit in with in-laws is always a difficult task— especially if they are well off. There was a dichotomy between my poor mother and her mother and this had only increased through the years. My grandmother and her third husband Andre had hit the jackpot with his plumbing pipe invention and they shot up in status with vacations, cars, and summer homes. This success must have egged on her sons-in-law and provoked the competition. Don had his detailing and had a good thing going, compared to my uncle Russell who sank business after business. My mother's half sister Annie and her husband Russell were so bent on being successful business owners that they just about wrecked their lives over it with debt. From baked desserts to a karaoke studio, they finally settled on dry cleaning.

What were they all really trying to clean up though? What did Andre bring out in these fellows? Or was it simply that his two step-daughters had selected men who aspired to be something like Andre? Who could blame them? Both Don and Russell had suddenly given up stable nine-to-five jobs for a life that was independent, but at least Andre was the real deal— the real successful businessman— and he had worked hard for it from the ground up. My stepfather and uncle both began to superficially flaunt money they didn't have and the debts mounted. Were they actually competing with Andre? Did Don really think a collector's car and a few watches were going to match up to a million dollar house on the water? His finances were so bad one year that he picked off all my birthday cards in the mail from my aunts one year, signed the twenty-five dollar checks and deposited them. We only found out when Aunt Judy called to see why we hadn't thanked her. And did my uncle Russell really think going out to dinner several times a week to some cheap chain restaurant would match up to the fine dining my grandmother experienced? It was all probably just to make them feel better about themselves.

Don was goofy at times, but he stayed polite and tried to be social. I could tell my aunts and uncles wanted nothing to do with him. When Don would go off about this or that, some would get up and walk away. He talked too much for them. Judy would roll her eyes at him whenever he would start in. This was a tough crowd, especially if they thought he wasn't being good enough to their own, my mother.

After five or so hours, we said our goodbyes and got into my mother's Dodge to drive home. On the way, Don decided to pull off the main road and head down a side street toward the water. This was another well-to-do town miles away from my grandmother and only a couple of towns away from where we lived. Long Island was very much like my family Christmas party— A socioeconomic soup. You'd drive through one run down, scary town with bums and boozed up beggars on the street and boom— you're suddenly in a ritzy village decorated with cheerful lights with Mercedes and BMWs lined up along the cobblestone curb.

Don did a u-turn and parked along the side of the street. He rolled his window down and stuck his hand out to point across the street.

"What are we doing?" my mother asked.

"Look, everyone, that's where Captain Bob lives. You know, Captain Kangaroo!" Don announced.

I remembered the morning TV show.

A tennis court was in the front yard. Tall shrubs blocked most of the great big white house. We sat there for a minute or so staring at the house. What was Don thinking? Was he looking to show us that my mother's family members weren't the only ones with wealth? There was more of it out there.

"Look, there he is bouncing in the bushes!" Don exclaimed like a little boy. I looked but no one was there.

We laughed and my mother told him to get going.

9

HE WAS THE NEW KID at school with the pudgy face, dark skin, black curly hair, and big fierce eyes. I found Gene Muraco in the elementary school hallway crying his eyes out. He sat on the floor against the wall with his legs crouched up against him like a shield. The boy was hysterical. The boys had been picking on him for some time since he had arrived at our school, just as they had done to me when I had moved to the town. They had put me through hell— making me do pushups, chasing me around, having their older sisters wait outside, but unlike Gene, I never broke down, at least in front of them. I fought them with a vengeance or escaped out the back door. I had made it through, with the help of Steven, of course. Gene, though, was having a rough time on the road to respect, and so I had great empathy for him. This would be the foundation of our friendship.

Kneeling down next to him I assured him.

"Don't worry, it's going to be all right. They're just messin' around. They did it to me too when I moved here. They'll stop soon."

I told Gene to be strong and not to worry. I told him his frizzy hair could use a trim, but that it didn't matter too much, even though I knew my new spiked haircut had made a world of a difference. I told him it was all right to me that he looked different. His dad was half Italian and half Hawaiian, his mom was Latino, so his skin was naturally a bit darker than what everyone was used to. He stuck out as the odd guy, but maybe we needed that. I told him I thought it was cool. I told him not to fret.

Months later, Gene was feeling more at home. He was wearing gel in his hair. I had told him about a cool barber I went to up the road and he started to go. He even started to attend my backyard wrestling tournaments, which were a huge confidence builder for him. These wrestling matches had also aided me on my road to popularity. All the kids liked a place to hang.

A group of us would gather in my backyard on Saturday and Sundays to battle it out. Sometimes we had as many as twenty kids in my backyard. Steven, who was the biggest and strongest, was the world champion, of course. The other big kid in our grade never showed up. Evan Klaus didn't want the confrontation with Steven.

Battle royals were wild. A good twelve of us would rumble it out until there was one person left standing. All you had to do was stay within the boundaries and push everyone else over the line. I always eliminated kids with the use of foreign weapons: a 2x4, bulky snow boots, sand in the face, a TV remote control, a telephone cord, a folded steel chair. See any of those come out and you're going to take a step back, right over the line of elimination. There were a few times I thought they were going to kill me after these stunts.

There were two boys who always lost. They were the equivalent of the washed-up guys on TV who never won a single match in their entire careers. They called them the jobbers because they enhanced the talent of the real superstars. We would dominate these boys— pulling their hair, hoisting them into the air, slamming them on their backs. We often sent them home crying, but they always came back for more. You have to respect their determination.

Gene Muraco was not one of the losers. He was big and could hold his own in the ring with the majority of us. Wrestling with the other guys in the neighborhood was a way of proving ourselves, and Gene did it well. He would punish the two losers with sheer enjoyment. There was one memorable day when he held one of the losers straight up in the air in an upside down suplex for a whole fifteen minutes before dropping the sick screaming boy on his back. We honestly all got roughed up from time to time; I remember seeing stars a few times while wrestling Steven. We're lucky no one broke their neck.

Gene began to take on some of the other popular boys and began to make his mark on the scene. I took him on as a tag-team partner, and we went straight to the tag championship and dominated the scene for a while. Gene fought just as dirty as I did: choking, using weapons, holding opponent's pants in pins. We both did anything we could to win our matches and enjoyed being the "villains." Sometimes we would hurt someone so bad he couldn't get back up. Then we'd double-team their partner until the match was ours. Sometimes Gene and I would come out with war make-up on our faces looking like the lunatics we were; this frightened the hell out of them.

Through time, Gene and I would come to battle each other in practice matches, always non-titled of course, and private so no one would ever know the outcome. Gene and I competed during the week in his backyard, since all of the other boys were off doing basketball or baseball. Some days he got the best of me and used his weight to his advantage. Some days I used my speed and skill to outmaneuver him. There were many draws where we both lost due to time expiration or double knock out. We'd lay there exhausted, sweaty, laughing at the sky.

One day during one of our private matches in Gene's backyard, he did the unthinkable for a heavier wrestler. He perched the second ropes, which was actually a picnic bench, and he prepared to deliver a crushing elbow smash. As he leapt through the air, his big torso seemed to go into slow motion and freeze for a moment, hanging over me as I lay on the grass waiting to be crushed. Up went my foot, as wrestlers on television often do when they see a devastating elbow on the way. Gene flew at me through the air and came crashing down face first into my foot. But it wasn't his face that hurt. He had landed the wrong way on his ankle and tumbled over. His ankle instantly swelled up like a mango. He lay there on the ground before me crying as he had done a year earlier in the hallway.

"Do you want me to go get your father?" I asked him.

"No."

"Do you want me to call the hospital?"

"No."

"Is it broken?"

"No, I don't think so."

After a half an hour of crying on the grass, he stood and limped his way inside his house and I went home. Gene was the type of person to never ask for help and never admit to having a crisis; instead, he'd lay there his whole life on the grass trying to fix it all himself. He hadn't needed my help anyway; after all, it wasn't broken. A minor sprain put him on the sidelines for a few weeks and the incident was never mentioned ever again.

We were like the ultimate rock band about to begin a tear in the heart of our hazy prime. Gene was part of it now— the popular crowd. His confidence had grown. Gene had become close with one kid named Ryan Bailey, who was a little red-haired boy with a wise sense of humor. Despite the time they spent together, Gene had a cruel way of talking badly about Ryan behind his back.

One day in the Kennedy's basement, Gene ranted on how weird Ryan was and how his parents were nutcases.

"His father is a mad scientist. He lives downstairs and watches porn... His mother is a psychotic bitch and lives upstairs now that they're separated... Ryan looks like a...."

After ten minutes of verbally destroying him, we let Ryan out of the closet where he had been hiding and listening to Gene's rant. Ryan wouldn't even look at Gene for months. How anyone could talk about a true friend like that? Eventually, the kind-hearted kid forgave Gene. But I don't know how suspicion couldn't linger in the back of any of our minds after that one.

10

WHEN I WAS TEN years old, my father called one day and set up an appointment to come over and take me out for the first time. He apologized to my mother over the phone for all the years that had passed and blamed it on his work and not being able to find us. When he arrived an hour late he came up the stairs and blamed it on the traffic.

"I needed to drive on the sidewalks to get here. It's busy around here."

He had been used to the quieter way of life out east on the island, closer to where I had lived before my mother married Don. My father lived a mere couple of miles away all that time, but he was out driving trucks just like my mother's father had done. Her father had died when she was around the age when my father had just started to come around, so I guess I couldn't complain.

The man intrigued me. He was strange and wild— full of hyperbolic stories and loud laughs. The first day he took me for a drive and pointed to a shack on Sunrise Highway.

"Hey, we're home," he said and then laughed loud at the puzzled expression on my face.

He was tan like he had sat outside too long floating on a boat. He liked to fish so that's where we went a lot of the time. He'd pick me up on Sundays and we'd go to a pier, a lake, or the beach. I liked being outside. But boy did he have lousy luck because we hardly ever caught fish. I didn't mind because I didn't see the point in hooking a fish out of the water just to throw it back. His bad luck was our good luck.

My father would drive us around a lot. His Marlboro smoke drifting out his driver side window. I liked the smell. We'd stop at video arcades and fast food places. We'd stop for snack breaks at gas stations or delis that usually consisted of a Kit Kat bar and a glass bottle of Coke. We went on errands and visited all the friends he managed to make around town. He liked to talk to people. To me, it seemed tiring. He had given up driving big trucks to manage a car wash because it kept him at home where he wouldn't be so lonely like he was when he was out on the road. I liked driving around seeing different places, listening to the 80s music on the radio.

Some days he was late. A few times he just didn't show up at all. I remember waking up early on Sunday and waiting around for several hours until I gave up. By noon I was out at my friend's house or roaming the neighborhood trying to forget all about him. No phone call. No apology. No explanation. Weeks would pass and then he'd call my mother to set up another Sunday as if nothing had even happened. When I'd see him again, he'd pretend as if everything was normal. I guess I went right along with it.

11

WHEN DON UPGRADED to the Bentley, he decided to rent use of the driveway, but that didn't stop the punks. One day I heard a hissing noise. It sounded like the hiss of a leaking garden hose. I peeked out the window and didn't see anything. I went and found Don in the other room and told him I heard something funny outside. He froze and then pivoted toward the door. He took off down the stairs and out the front door. I followed right behind him. Upon exiting the house, the kid took off. The light switch had gone off in Don as it had other times, like when he went berserk on a security guard in a retail store for accusing him of stealing. Assault charges were eventually dropped. One day my brother JP was crying and my mother was yelling about something as we were driving down the road, and Don came to an abrupt stop, slammed the car into drive, yanked the keys out of the ignition, and walked home. We sat there in the middle of the road for a while until my mother decided to walk home and get the keys. You just never knew with Don.

From a distance, I watched Don capture the lone vandal. He grabbed him by the back of the head and repeatedly punched his face in until the kid could no longer stand. Don returned with blood on his hands and shirt. He looked like an axe murderer. I thought I had caught a look at the vandal when we first pursued him and then later on from down the block as I watched him crumble. I was never sure, but it looked a lot like Crazy John, in maybe what was one last failed attempt to terrorize me. Don's car was never vandalized again.

The Bentley eventually became a symbol for all that was wrong. No food in the kitchen. No allowance or lunch money. A slap in the face. We were broke. I would hear Don rant to my mother about the mounting bills, yet there was an eighty thousand dollar car in the driveway.

Sometimes it was the same dinner three or four nights in a row. Some nights I would have to go to a friend's house for dinner; I'd even bring food home for the morning. Some nights we'd go to my grandmother's to eat and I'd fill my backpack with food from her cabinets. She had lots of healthy food and some treats too. She lived right across the street from the Entenmann's family who owned a famous baked goods company, and they were always giving my grandmother donuts and cakes. It wasn't the kind of food my grandmother and Andre indulged in though, so they always gave them away to us. I was lucky because I know many don't have any food at all.

Other than basic shelter and food some of the time, one thing I could thank Don for was the part-time work he gave me as a teenager. He would bring me to jobs and put me to work cleaning cars in lots and showrooms. I would go around and shine up the rims and apply a shiny spray to the tires. I got to see all the newest cars and some old restored ones too. Don always paid me well, but it was often weeks late. This fluctuation in pay created a manic-depressive state for me. One week I'd have money in my pocket and the next one I'd be scrounging for change and wondering when and how I would eat.

Lunch money was scarce and the refrigerator would go bare for weeks, and I didn't qualify for free lunch anymore like I had when it was just my mother and me. During these times as I waited for my pay, I would have to scrounge up money in the cafeteria with what they called grubbing— standing outside the cafe door asking "got any change?" I collected five or six dollars every day, which I would use for lunch and breakfast the next morning. Some days things were just bad and no one seemed to have any extra change. There were days in high school when I had to qualify myself for free lunch by stealing. I'd wait for the line monitor to be distracted and then I'd slip the Sunny Doodles and drink into my pants and walk out pretending to have forgotten my money. It only worked with packaged junk food, but it was something to eat. Lifting cakes didn't always work because on some days they had a lady walk up and down the line as a watcher. If I couldn't find anyone with any money to lend, then I'd go hungry for the day. I would go to school with an empty stomach and was expected to learn and behave. I usually left school with a rotten stomach.

While Don didn't pay me or provide food on a consistent basis, he did provide a gigantic three thousand dollar television. He bought one of those early big screen televisions that weighed five hundred pounds and took four grown men to hoist it up the steps to our living room. Those poor guys. I found it amusing that we had such a large expensive television in such a small inexpensive apartment in the upstairs of someone else's house. It was another toy for Don. Another problem though. Too often, my brother JP would bump into it and get whooped for it. One time he smeared food on the screen with his fingers and Don went ballistic. A safe zone was established. Violate the zone and he'd get beat. I never got hit even once, but I was sure to use the remote from a distance. Maybe I was smart. Maybe he was just intimidated by the fact I had a crazy father who could pop up from out of nowhere if he needed to. Maybe hitting JP was something else, something personal, and something to do with his own feelings about himself. I wasn't about to test the theories though.

12

FOR A WHILE I felt hazy. At eleven years old I had strange bouts of odd dopey feelings. I would doze off on the living room couch after a bowl of cereal and wake to a kaleidoscope of colors swirling around on the big screen television. Except the television was turned off.

One night I awoke and I was in the TV being beaten up by professional wrestlers. I knew I wasn't dreaming or having night terrors like I had had when I was six. Sometimes in those vivid dreams, I was chased down in my neighborhood or just terribly embarrassed in front of a crowd. A psychologist later told me this was a result of some insecurity I had— perhaps my mother's busy work schedule or a missing father.

This time at eleven years old, I knew I was awake, but something different was going on. This feeling kept me from going to school on a couple of occasions. For a while, I thought it was a virus or an allergy to something, but I blew it off and hid it from my mother. I told her I was just a little dizzy.

The most memorable of these hallucinogenic states was one night around midnight. I was eleven and my little brother JP was only a toddler. He didn't wake all night, despite my screams. I had been sleeping, again on the couch after lounging around watching television. The TV was off when I awoke in terror. Something felt like it was inside my head. It was closing in chasing me from room to room. My heart pounded. I ran from room to room looking for help only to realize that no one was home. My mother was out waitressing and Don had stepped out. My yelps turned to screams. I pulled the window up in my mother's bedroom and stuck my head out into the winter night. Poking my head out from the second story window I yelled,

"Help, help."

When no one answered I just cried to the cold.

After a few minutes, I heard the front door open. The state of panic seemed to vaporize. I thought it might be my mother or Don returning, so I went to have a look. I opened up our door and peered down the hallway to the entryway. A couple out for a walk stood at the bottom of the stairs. They had heard me from the sidewalk.

"Are you ok?" they asked.

"I don't know," I replied, trembling.

"Maybe you just had a bad dream."

"Yes, I think so."

"Are your parents home?"

"No, my mother ran out for milk."

"All right, well just sit tight and wait for her. Do you want us to wait?"

"No, I'm ok. Thank you. I'm going to go back to bed."

The kind couple left and I sat there for a while at the top of the stairs with my back to the closed door. Had this been an illness? Was I crazy? Was this a panic attack? I had no idea.

It never occurred to me that some of this might have been an intentional effect I was suffering from. One night some weeks after my episode, I sat on the couch in the dark after waking up in the middle of the night. I was going to get up to go to my room when I saw the refrigerator light on. Don was leaning into the fridge with something in one hand. The other hand lowered the milk back on to the shelf. The door closed and the light disappeared. He turned around, but it was too late. He saw me. I pretended I was groggy from my nap. He too pretended he didn't know I knew that he knew I saw him.

I didn't drink milk for a while. In fact, I spilled out that container of milk and made it look like I had used it all up. I'm sure he knew. No one else used milk. My mother hated it and Don had no use for it. I used it in cereal and chocolate milk. As far as I know, I was also the only one going through these weird visuals and feelings. A couple of months passed and I started to use the milk again and never had one of those mental episodes ever again. I'll never know whether I was just some crazy person's lab experiment.

13

AFTER WRESTLING WORE OFF, everyone got into music. "Sweet Child O Mine" enraptured us during the summer of '88. We had become music freaks— denim jackets with patches, tight ripped jeans, and band t-shirts with demons and guns on the fronts. We were crazed by heavy metal in the heat of an MTV revolution of music videos and a top ten where pop music had surrendered to hard rock and metal ballads. We all grew our hair longer. Paul sketched out tattoos for all of us to choose from once we were old enough to get them (still years away). Mine was a heart with flames burning out of the top of it and a sword right down the middle. I was going to slap that one right on my left arm, and then another one above it on the shoulder (likely a girl's face), and another couple of tattoos on the other arm. We had it all worked out.

One thing we could do now at this age was pierce our ears. My mother took me for my first— one piercing through the left ear. A little while later I popped another two in the left ear after hearing someone tell me how they did it. I bought a couple of sharp pointed stud earrings at the mall, heated up the point, numbed my lobe with ice, and popped them through. They didn't look bad, considering. Later, I got my right ear pierced at the mall. I wore all kinds of studs and loops. I started to look like a real punk.

We established a band of our own and attempted to play our

instruments in Andy and Jeff's basement. I was the singer and guitarist, Andy played the bass, Jeff was rhythm guitar, Gene was our lead guitarist, and Paul was on drums. Whether it was genuine music or not was debatable. Andy and Jeff's older brother Trent said I sounded like Metallica with laryngitis. Andy, Jeff, Gene and I all had decent equipment, but we struggled to play even a single chord. The only thing we had going was Paul who actually played the drums in the school band, but he couldn't move his whole set from his house. He got through it with buckets, pots, and pans.

Andy, Jeff, Gene, Paul, and I were a band, even if it was just for a moment in time, even if we never quite made it past our first and only original song. I envisioned us as the next Guns N' Roses. I had high hopes, but we really sounded horrendous. At least we had fun.

Steven and I seemed to have our own thing going. He had actually started to fiddle around with a guitar, so he was really the original lead guitarist before Gene. But I guess he was just too much for the whole group to handle. He was better off solo. You can't group up someone like that for two long— he marched to his own beat. He and I continued to love music together though. We listened to hours of tapes, messed around on guitars, read the metal magazines from the stationary store, and talked about how crazy our favorite bands were.

Steven slept over one night and we stayed up late talking about music. Guns N' Roses was our favorite band and many of the songs on the *Appetite for Destruction* album were about drugs and addiction. Some of the band members had been in and out of rehab for heroin. I'll never forget Steven's words—

"I'll never do heroin, Jack. No Mr. Brownstone."

"Neither would I…the stuff's evil. I might be a punk, but I'm not dumb."

In the midst of our music craze, we would steal audiocassettes from TSS, a local retail store. Everyone would come along sometimes for a grand sweep of cassette raiding. Steven and Ryan were the kings of theft. They'd walk out into the parking lot of the store with cassettes in their pants, their sleeves, their hats, their socks, and who knows where else. Sometimes they would make out with as many as ten cassettes a piece. By the time I was twelve, I had built a cassette collection of three hundred, which included the entire Aerosmith catalogue. Our TSS raids contributed to at least half of my collection. Andy was uninterested in stealing, or perhaps just knew better, and would ride a bike around the store crashing into things. His crashes always made for a perfect distraction and always earned him a cassette. I think he earned himself the entire Def Leppard collection that way.

One time Steven and I went in alone. This was a mistake because there weren't enough distractions. An employee spotted Steven putting an L.A. Guns cassette down his pants and confronted him. Steven conceded and was brought away. I later joked that it must've been his choice of music that got him nabbed this time. He yelled for me to go get his uncle. Surprisingly they let me walk right out and hadn't seen me pick off a Black Sabbath cassette in the B section. I crossed the parking lot and made my way the short trip back to Steven's house. His scruffy looking, shirtless uncle opened the door and I told him what happened. He cursed and told me to hold on. He came back with a t-shirt on, busted through the screen door and hopped off the steps. I started to walk back with him, but he told me to get on.

We were lucky he was the one home. His uncle picked him up, punched him in the shoulder, and told him not to do it again. Steven listened. This was nothing compared to when his father came back into town and got angry with him. Now that Steven was bigger, he'd fight back. Imagine a twelve-year-old battling with his thirty-something father in a driveway fistfight? These two went punch for punch on the lawn. Steven was that good. But it was bloody and upsetting, and I usually had to walk away just before Steven would lose. He wasn't that good, not yet.

Steven and I had boxed a couple of times for fun. We wore real gloves, but his punches were too much to take. There was so much power behind his punches, so much emotion. I had a headache after just a few punches. It wasn't like I was a weakling either. I knocked out our friend Gary with only a few punches and he was far bigger than me. I took down Andy a couple of times in the first round too. But Steven, he'd just stare at me blankly when I hit him. He had so much fight in him.

14

AFTER A FEW YEARS in the apartment, we left for the house. Don bought a small four-bedroom house in the middle of town a few miles away from our old neighborhood by the bay. The house had a small fenced in backyard and a studio apartment above the garage. My bedroom window looked out across the street at a town baseball field where I could watch Andy hit rockets out of the park for his league team. I hated baseball, but I liked watching his games because I always wanted to see my pal put another one over the fence.

The American dream of owning a house had been achieved, yet it seemed to be more of a sinking burden on Don. The night his music ceased had been several years earlier, but loud music during the day started up once we moved into the house. His system got bigger, more expensive, and louder— rattling the shingles right off the side of the house. I could hear the bass from houses away down the street. Neighbors surely mistook this as a teenager gone mad while his parents were out. A teenager— exactly what Don was battling, not me, but himself. The teenage Don was pushing back against the adult Don and the life he had begun but was not fully committed to.

Quitting his nine to five day job as a legal assistant and abandoning his dream to be a lawyer, he propelled his small part-time business into a full-time empire of contracts. Detailing cars at the dealerships worked well for both the adult and teenager inside— sleep late until

2 pm— be home for dinner— go to work at 8 pm after the dealer is closed and no one is there to look over you— and stay out until the early parts of the morning. Later I would learn from an older sister of a friend how Don's late nights "working" had evolved into partying, all confirmed by the fights my mother would have with him screaming over STDs, women's perfume, and bottles of pills. He no longer had much of a stepfather role— that he threw away for the role of the out of control older brother. We were about fifteen years apart in age, but far closer in other ways. I think there were times when he was far more out of control than I ever was. One morning I opened the door to leave for school and he was just coming in from a long night out. He stood there surprised, embarrassed, in a quiet daze. I said good morning and went my way. Other mornings he slipped in the door while I was upstairs getting ready, but I heard.

Don tried to find control. When he bought the house, he gained a garage as a sanctuary to store his possessions in. There were several hardcore locks on the doors and we didn't go in there. But we knew what was on the other side: the Bentley, a collection of Rolex watches and other jewels, and a pistol he showed us once. His man-cave treasures and a safe in the bathroom closet were odd because we didn't really have any money and most of the time the cupboard in the kitchen was bare. And we weren't truly a family that could trust one another, not with so many secrets stored away.

After just half a year living at the house, my mother left Don. We packed up one night while he was out at work and drove off to my grandmother's house where we hid for several days. Don called my grandmother, but she told him my mother needed some time and would call in a few days. After a week, my mother called him and told him where we were. My mother threatened to leave him. He asked her to think it over for a while. Her mother and Andre offered to buy her a house if she got away from him. Mom was in a crux.

Staying as my grandmother's guests in her great big house on the water was an everyday reminder of what we didn't have. Tension seemed to be growing in this house now too. JP was bouncing off the walls. Poor Andre was working more hours, probably to get a break from us. To get away from it all, I walked the streets in her ritzy neighborhood whistling and listening to my cassette Walkman. Sometimes a fog would come in and spook up the neighborhood.

My teacher Mr. Flannery actually lived in the next town over from where my grandmother lived and he offered to pick me up in the mornings. He pulled up to this great big house in his shitty old VW and picked me up for the thirty-minute commute to school. It was still early because he had prep time before the students arrived, so he'd drop me off at Gene's house. Gene and I would sit and talk as he finished getting ready and then we'd walk to school together.

It was good but strange to be back in the old neighborhood down by the shore on the south side. I hadn't been gone that long, but just a few months feels like a lifetime when you're a teen. Some days I would go back to Gene's house after school, especially if it was a Friday. On Friday nights his father and sister would go out and we'd have the house to make as much noise as we wanted. We'd set the room up as if it were a stadium stage. Wearing sunglasses and wigs, we'd put on a lip synching air guitar show in the mirror that no one could rival. We'd work our way through the entire *Appetite for Destruction* album. Sweat, laughs, and fun— memories no one can take from you.

Something saddened me about the separation and I started crying one day in the car with my mom. I told her I missed Don. Maybe it was the fear of having to leave all my new friends just when I started to fit in. It had taken so long and now I would have to start all over. She pulled me closer and hugged me and told me it would be all right.

Of course, I was being selfish. If Don was not treating her right, she had every right to leave, and we would find our way.

Most of my friends came from broken homes. Paul lived with his father. Gene lived with his father. Steven lived with his mother, but his estranged father would pop in. Ryan lived with both, but they were divorced and lived on different floors of the house. Many others only lived with their mother, as I had for most of my childhood. Andy and Jeff were the only ones with both parents together and their parents were a lot older. Maybe all parents ought to start waiting until they're older.

In the end, we spent two cold winter months away at my grand-mother's house and then my mother took him back and agreed to come home. Don had apologized and blamed his recent aggression on a head cold and bad medicine that clouded his mind. We moved back in and went on as if nothing had happened. It was good to be back in my bedroom with the smell of fresh carpets and a small space to call my own, at least for a little more time.

15

RUNNING gave me a sense of freedom. My elementary school days out on the track in gym class previously consisted of socializing with Gene. The teacher didn't care how slow we went, as long as we were moving. Some of us moped like zombies because we couldn't run— Gene. Some of us turtled along because we didn't care about gym and wanted to be with our friends— Me.

Gene and I would talk and joke around as kids flew past us. What was the rush? Evan Klaus, the school athlete, was the winner every time. What was the point? He was equal in size to Steven, a bit taller, not as stocky, but he had more speed. Steven would be the football guy and Evan would be the basketball guy. Tall, slim, and fast, Evan was popular with the girls, even though he was shy and his mother wouldn't let him hang out with any. He took out his insecurities on anyone smaller than him. A classic dick. He thought he deserved respect just for being gifted with looks and physique.

It was a new year. I was back in the house after two months living out of a suitcase. On the first day back to gym class, I decided right there on the field I was going to run. It was an urge that came over me and I didn't know why, but I couldn't ignore it. I had to go. I had to leave Gene behind.

"I'm going to run this one, Gene."

"Whaaaat?"

"Yeah, I just feel like running."

"Runnin' with the devil!" he shouted in a high heavy metal voice while making the metal horns with his fingers to send me along.

I took off.

Moving my way around the field I caught up to fourth place, then third, then second. Right behind Evan, I kept at it. He seemed to slow a bit and dropped back just in front of me to my right. He nodded his head forward motioning to the finish line.

"What do you think you're doing, Jack? You trying to run?"

"Yeah, I'm running."

"You think you can run? You think you can beat me after all of this? You cool now?"

"Yeah," I huffed.

"Come on, puss. Run, run, run," he taunted.

We rounded the turn into the final hundred yards.

"You can't beat me, Tortis."

Something kicked on inside me. I couldn't control it. My eyes steered forward. My legs were flying out in front of me and something inside pushed hard. I took off and left Evan in the dust by at least forty yards. The expected winner was too busy talking it up. I found I had a gift for speed and a hunger for winning. I had crossed the finish line and defeated the usual winner.

Everyone was shocked and congratulated me. If my new spiky haircut hadn't done it. If my walks home with Jeff and connecting with other popular kids hadn't done it. If my backyard wrestling tournaments hadn't done it. My winning run over Evan would bring me to a whole new level of status.

The mile was mine. The hundred yard dash. The four-forty. Why stop with one race? The sit-ups, push ups, obstacle course. I crushed them all too.

I had never really won anything, so the contests were a high. There was something about seeing everyone behind me that intrigued me. I started to train after school and on weekends. I was obsessed.

Evan was suddenly second place. So quickly, he had lost everything he had been good at to a smaller kid he had tried to push around.

I wondered what my victories did to Gene. Had I abandoned him? Did he understand? I was doing something good, something healthy, something I had fallen in love with. Drag myself around in the dirt with Gene or run free with the wind in my face?

At the end of the year in June, I qualified for my age group to represent my school in the district jamboree. I would jump on a bus to go to another school to compete against kids from several other schools. Evan had gone the last several years. Now it was my turn.

I whipped everyone in the fifty, one hundred, and four hundred forty yard races. I lost sit-ups and pull-ups by two each. Tied an obstacle course. Lost some silly climb the rope contest. Easily won the push-ups. The final contest was the grand mile run. It went just like my first race against Evan.

From the middle of the pack, I made my way up to fourth place. On the second lap, number three got winded. On the beginning of lap four, I slipped into second place. This kid named Owen was in the lead by half a lap. I came out of nowhere.

Overdrive kicked in. I felt a burn, a fire inside, and adrenaline raced through my body. Just around the bend I went whipping past Owen and raced him hard to the finish line. I won the mile by fifteen yards. For a kid who had been in the lead the whole mile race, this had to be an upset. That was my strategy though. Stun him. Upset him. And it worked.

At the end of the jamboree, we all gathered in the gym. When the teachers announced Owen as the winner of my age category, I thought they were kidding with me. Owen went up and grabbed the trophy and held it up smiling to the flash of a camera. This had to be a mistake. They would still call my name, I thought. But they never did.

I had won five contests, tied in one, and lost three. Even if Owen had won the three I lost and tied with me in the obstacle course, the math didn't add up. How does the kid who loses more contests go home with the trophy? I went up to one of the teachers and told them this must be a mistake.

"Oh, don't be a sore loser now."

That teacher laughed me off. I went to another teacher.

"No, I'm sorry, they got it all figured out correctly. Math doesn't lie. Some of the contests are worth more points."

Points? What kind of funny math were they doing here?

"So shouldn't the mile and the major races be worth more?"

I was waved along, so I went to one more teacher. When I told her how many contests I had won, she stood there with a blank expression that turned to guilt.

"Sorry, it's too late."

I was devastated.

When my mother asked how the day went, I told her I got ripped off. She just thought I was being a sore loser and that was the end of it. No witnesses to testify for me. No one stood up for what was right. To think parents and teachers would let such a thing happen. To think they would favor another kid, a well-off kid over the poor kid from the south shore. Of course, Owen's mother, a teacher somewhere in the district, was one of the officials that day. I saw her give her son a big hug and they walked off with the trophy. My eyes burned.

A year or so later, Owen lost his sister in a car wreck. When I heard the news I felt terrible. And as expected, it really messed him up. All ill feelings I had about the jamboree receded and seemed insignificant in the bigger picture. Give the kid ten trophies for all I care. I wouldn't wish that kind of loss on anyone. Despite the corruption that day, I'm glad they gave him the trophy, even if he hadn't really won it.

16

STEVEN WAS OVER one day hanging out playing Nintendo. JP was in and out of my room jacked up on too much sugar or something in the shit food we were eating. Steven picked him up and gave him a wedgie and hung him from his underwear on a plant hook. Of course, Steven held his arms out to catch him when his underwear began to tear. JP was so wild that he both laughed and cried. My poor brother, JP.

Gene would push him around too. One day he hung JP from his feet over the stairs at my house. I didn't appreciate that kind of stunt and scolded Gene for being irresponsible. If he had slipped, my brother surely would have been seriously injured if not dead from that kind of height. Gene was lucky. He often joked around in cruel ways when someone else had the potential to be hurt. He did other stupid things like blowing pot smoke in the face of people's pets. None of it was funny when it was done against such defenseless victims. Steven did everything in good fun but never crossed the line like Gene.

Now that we were in junior high, drugs that had once existed in *Metal Edge* magazine were now a reality. It all started with cigarettes. If you were open to them, then you had the balls to do other things, and of course being in the crowd with kids who smoked made it more likely you'd eventually encounter someone who'd propose,

"Hey, you all wanna get stoned? You know, smoke a joint?"

And you would pretend you did it a hundred times before and say,

"All right, man, if you got it."

The older kid would spark up the rolled paper joint and pass it to you. You'd suck it in the way the older kid did, but you'd cough like crazy for some reason. Within minutes you'd be full of giggles you just couldn't shake.

We all went through it. For me, it was Don's sister's friend Simon. He had gotten me stoned with a clip of a joint when I was thirteen. We'd bump into each other out walking the streets. Since he was twenty-one, he had also picked up alcohol for me a few times. One day Simon gave me a full joint and told me to share it with my friends.

For Steven, Ryan, and Gene, I was that kid who made the proposal to get stoned for the first time. Andy was there that day too, but he declined and left to go play basketball. Paul was into a girl, and Jeff was into skate boarding, so their first time would be deferred. Steven, Ryan, Gene, and I went to the Catholic school parking lot down the road from the junior high. We sat on the curb and lit the joint, our very first full joint. We coughed hard.

"Take it in easy," I told them.

No one ever understands until they have that first cough. You also never again feel the way you felt the first few times getting stoned. Maybe that's why people end up smoking so much— they chase that initial bliss. The silly giggles. Coughs turn to laughs and laughs turn to coughs.

We were on a new path. For some of us this was exactly what those old folks in suits called it, the gateway drug. But if it hadn't been pot, it would've been something else and if it hadn't been me, it would've been someone else offering them their first high. So I'm glad we got to share this together.

Steven and I didn't smoke anything that night in my room. In fact, we always had such real down to Earth conversations about life. He only clowned around when we were out with other friends. One on one, he was as mellow as they come, most of the time.

Early the next morning, my father came to get me. He pulled up in his truck. Steven and I climbed up. We laughed and hollered all the way to Steven's house to drop him off. My father pulled the horn as we drove away and I waved to Steven.

The next day in school, Steven told me how great my dad was. I told him I didn't call him my dad, and that he was more like a father who came around once in a while. He had a point though. I could have had it so much worse— a criminal, complete abandonment, or someone like Steven's dad who stuck around and abused them. Someone in my family had told me I was lucky my father wasn't around, for my own safety.

My father wasn't the greatest, but he wasn't the worst. Steven's father might have been. He was always in and out of work. He would disappear for months, sometimes to his other home at the county jail. When he was home there were months where he would lay around in his underwear drinking and looking scruffy like the stereotypical drunk. Steven's mother always worked long hours. It was all on her. She drove a beat up old Chevy and smoked Camels, which added to her raspy voice and aged skin. Her sister lived with them in the house. So did the grandfather, grandmother, and his uncle for a time. The grandfather died at some point in late elementary school. The grandmother lived out her years in a back room with daily visits from a public health aide from the state. They all smoked outside now that the emphysema had kicked in on grandma.

Later that same month, Steven's uncle, the one who picked him up from TSS the day he got caught stealing, hitched a ride to a bad neighborhood just outside of our town to buy drugs. He did his last speedball, swallowed a bottle of Valium, tied a rope around his neck in a back alley, and hanged himself from a hook on a brick wall. There was no chance of saving him. Steven was devastated by this news. They all thought it was murder, but Steven knew it was suicide. He told me his uncle had talked about how shitty life was. The family couldn't afford a funeral, so they just had a get together at the house. I went but left early when the drinking and fighting erupted.

17

AROUND THE SECOND YEAR in the new house, Don hired a tattooed man with long hair named Edwin Duggan to help detail cars at night. The business was growing and he had several accounts every night. The new house had a small studio apartment in it to the side at the back entrance. When we bought the house, the apartment had been badly damaged and abused by an older crazy church lady with four cats. The clean up took weeks, but Don finally managed to remodel the place and got it back into rentable shape. For the first year, a young woman lived in the one room apartment. Her boyfriend eventually moved in and at the end of the lease they decided to leave for a bigger apartment. This is when Edwin moved in.

"Call me Win," he said.

I had already met and worked with Win for several months when he moved in. I was fourteen and he was thirty-eight, though he looked years older. I was entering one of the worst phases of my life, and Win seemed to complement this dark phase. I wore black, he wore black. I smoked cigarettes, he smoked cigarettes. I smoked marijuana, he smoked marijuana. I liked rock n roll, he liked rock n roll. Who could argue with so much in common? Age didn't matter much, at least not to us.

We worked at the dealership at night. On our days off, or after school, I spent time with him smoking and listening to old 70s rock.

I'll never forget the first night. We had a couple of cheap beers and then he broke out the deck of cards. We played blackjack and listened to an old Alice Cooper record for what seemed like hours. One song titled "Eighteen" really captured the way I felt about being a boy and a man at the same time. Stuck in the middle. Wanting to be ahead of where I was.

"No More Mr. Nice Guy" came on and he offered to cook us up a juicy flank steak.

After dinner, Win changed the record and broke out the glass bong.

"You ever smoke?" he asked.

I had been getting joints from Don's sister's friend Simon every once in a while, but then he disappeared. I heard he went off to jail for stealing prescriptions from the pharmacy he worked at. But this would be the first time I smoked a bong. It felt a little crackish to me, but I went with it. Win helped light it and told me to suck on the smoke. I sucked it in and coughed. The smoke hurt, but I felt the rush. The next time he reminded me to go easier on the inhalation. The Steve Miller Band *Greatest Hits* side two ended and Win got up and changed the record.

After a few hits each, we lit cigarettes and zoned out to *Led Zeppelin III*. To hear the rumbling of "Immigrant Song" for the first time, stoned and fourteen, did amazing things. The song was manic and woke something up inside. The entire album was fantastic. Music was a common bond we had, perhaps the only true link. He introduced me to so many good groups like The Doors, but he was skeptical of some of the music I listened to. He thought some of it was too wild, that some new bands glorified heroin. He dug the song "Mr. Brownstone" though because he thought it was a warning about the dangers of drugs and street life, but he thought the singer had an attitude. Maybe he just saw himself.

At midnight, my mother came up the three steps to the apartment to knock on the door to tell me it was time to come home. I was zonked out and the place was good and smoky. Did she even wonder what the hell I was doing in there with an older man? I told her I'd be right there, and Win closed the door and we instantly began laughing, the giddy kind of stoned laughing. This man had become my friend.

18

VIOLENCE FLOATED through the halls and grounds of my school. Deadly weapons weren't too much of an issue, but Emilio Pearcy was expelled for having a blade, so it did happen on occasion. Most kids weren't afraid to throw chairs or any other piece of furniture that wasn't bolted to the floor. Fights would erupt in the halls, classrooms, and cafeteria. The gym locker room was a vulnerable spot because you could get attacked while changing. One kid was beaten by three others with his pants still down. Of course, there were after-school fights too, which promised a little more time before someone broke it up. On the steps of the school, on the lawns of nearby homes, in front of the deli—fights were rampant.

I practiced my defense craft by boxing or wrestling my friends. Gary and Andy were first round knockouts. Syd was a tie. Brad was a ten-second drop. I hadn't bothered boxing Steven in a long time now. If I couldn't beat Steven in a boxing or wrestling match, it didn't matter. This only put him higher on the list of dangerous and I was still better than most. All of the kids I beat in street fights were taller than me by at least four inches, which made a lot of people wonder. I was the small crazy one. I had "Eye of the Tiger" looped in my head.

We lived in the shadows of the biggest city in the world. The town was located on the south shore of Long Island, a thirty-minute train ride from the city. When you live in a shadow of a giant you struggle to find your own identity. Everyone was a tough guy. Imagine thousands of people with a Napoleon complex. Real city people didn't need to act like tough guys.

This fight mentality of "who is tougher" was the world we lived in. It was a fight for survival and though it didn't consume us, it was always in the back drop— waiting for us behind the bank after school, at parties, in backyards, and on the streets.

My fight against Jim Hirsch was nerve racking. I was tough but he was much bigger than me with a good five-inch advantage. The fight drew a large crowd out in front of the bank next to the school. A circle formed around us and we threw up our hands. I moved in like a savage. I walked right into a large left jab. His long reach surprised me. I stopped, wiped my mouth, and became angered at the little bit of blood on my fingers. I went crazy on him and let out a wild scream and barrage of punches— most of them missed, but a few rocked him back. I backed him to the edge of the crowd, launched in, and took hold of him in a side headlock. With all of my strength, I brought this big kid off his feet and slammed him over my back onto the concrete and landed right on top of him. I could hear all the oohs and ahhs around me. With my left arm still locked around his neck, I crashed a fury of punches onto the top of his head. Then I stood and kicked him a couple of times as he got to his knees.

"Back it up."

The principal was on his way through the crowd. Jim got up and ran off and I flashed my fists to the crowd. The principal grabbed me and escorted me away from the crowd. I told him I had been attacked and fought back out of defense. No trouble at all. He walked me around the building on one of his security rounds and then let me go. I had asked, "Do you really think a little kid like me is going to pick a fight with a big kid?" The principal saw the logic.

Jacked up on a liter of this cola stuff called Jolt that boasted "twice the caffeine," along with some weed, which often gave me the opposite effect and sped me up, I went out to the parking lot behind the stores in the village. We were taking on a couple of kids from another town to avenge a kid whose cousin had been beaten up after being jumped by several kids. It was an easy beat down on our turf. I once again took on a guy bigger than me. He swung and missed. I hit him with a right hand across the jaw, then a left blow to the ribs, and then a quick and powerful right uppercut. He swung a low roundhouse right but I jumped back and he missed. He lunged for me out of desperation and I wrapped my arm around his neck into a side headlock and flipped him over my shoulder. When he tried to get up I blasted him with a right hand and that was it. The aggressive onslaught had begun to send these boys into retreat mode. As they climbed into the car to drive away, one of our guys jumped on the car hood and started to kick at the windshield. He jumped off just before they gunned the engine and drove off.

There were a few other group fights like this, and many more fights between two competing males. Girl fights weren't any prettier though. They'd tear each apart with nails like claws, punching, kicking, biting, and choking. Renee Gambino was ruthless. She had dark scary eyes and long straight black hair like a witch. She pointed to one girl at the top of the steps of the bank and ascended up the stairs after her. The poor girl tried to walk away, but Renee yanked her by her hair and started to bash away at her face. She didn't stop, even after the blood. The fight was stopped just in time as Renee was about to smash the girl's face into the concrete steps. She was blood-thirsty.

I didn't sit and watch too many of these, and I didn't fight as much as some of the others. I also liked a good even fight. Once it was on the ground it was over. I didn't like to get into that kind of rolling around or beating up on someone. But others, both boys and girls, got into it on the ground. They didn't think they were done until you were crying and bleeding and no longer looked like the person you were when the fight began. These fights were hard to watch. I never understood why you would keep punching someone when they were down and out; it seemed barbaric, but it also seemed like the ultimate display of insecurity. As if knocking them down wasn't enough to build your own confidence, confidence that someone else had usually stolen.

The worst was when older kids came back and got involved. What were these seventeen, or nineteen, or twenty-three year olds doing at their old school, of which most of them had left without a diploma? Two of these older guys started to pop up in eighth grade. Neil was a tall lanky dark-haired kid who looked like a young Eric Roberts. He had a popular younger sister he tagged along with and often ended up in my circle. We were kids with nowhere to go except Main Street in the village, so of course it wasn't hard to find us. Then there was Mo Mo, a long time legendary town loser on the path to becoming a career criminal. Neil was twenty, but Mo Mo, who knows? He was a full-grown man. Best guess— early twenties. Rumor had him in and out of jail. He walked like a gangster and had the scars to show he had no fear.

One day Neil and Mo Mo ended up in the same place. Mo Mo didn't like having another older kid around and didn't like "the way" he looked at him. He went right up to him and started to shove him. Neil was about a foot and a half taller than Mo Mo, but it didn't matter. Neil backed away and just as it looked like he was going to run, he got clocked in the face with a fist. Mo Mo leapt off the ground with another two punches. Neil spun and fell flat on his face. Mo Mo threw a final kick to Neil's back and then strutted off with his friends. Neil never showed his face again. Of course, Mo Mo eventually went to jail and we never saw him around again either.

When I finally got around to fighting Evan in a circle on the sidewalk, all those years of competitive jockeying ended in less than a minute. I heard he had been talking about me and a few others and

I told someone he'd better watch it. He heard about my warning. We bumped into each other on the stairs and he asked,

"So I heard you want to fight me after school?"

"Let's do it," I responded.

We met in the village and both had a number of our friends behind us. Other bloodthirsty spectators showed up. He stood there, still far taller than me, but still slower. I advanced and knocked him back with a few punches. I missed a couple and felt nothing but air. In the corner of my eye I noticed something wrapped around his right hand. Distracted, I rushed in, but it was too late. I spun, dizzy, the sky above turned fuzzy, and I froze in place knowing something was wrong. Upon hitting me, Evan threw what appeared to be something wrapped in a cloth to his friend and the friend quickly left the scene. In fact, as soon as he hit me all his friends scattered, all knowing something I didn't, something I wouldn't expect from an honors student and jock. But this was an honors jock with a vendetta. Now I knew what those track and field wins had done to him psychologically.

Evan stood there holding his broken hand, the result when someone hits another at just the right angle with brass knuckles. But now he would have to contend with Steven who saw the whole episode with his own eyes. The two biggest kids from our neighborhood had always stayed away from one another— Now here they were. My clash with Evan brought Steven to my defense. Evan had essentially tried to bully me again as he had done that day on the race track, and this time he avoided defeat by cheating. There would be an embarrassing price for that. Steven knocked Evan back with several punches. That was all Evan needed. He turned to run. Steven ran after him and blasted him a few more times in the back of the head as he fled the scene.

Steven walked me home. I was still shaky and my head began to swell. A couple of hours later I went to the hospital to be examined. Besides the bulging bump, everything checked out okay, but the nurse was sure to note,

"I find it hard to believe any teenage punch could do that damage alone. Did you file a report with the police?"

As long as the bump would heal, I would get along fine without bringing in the authorities. Evan would have to live with knowing what he did.

19

IT HAPPENED in Rachel's bed, but not with Rachel. Time alone with Jane, while Rachel's parents were on vacation, took weeks of planning. We had no worries of interruption and Rachel just waited downstairs. I climbed out my second story window, leapt off the roof, and then went over to Rachel's house. The candles were already lit. We got out the oils and strawberry flavored something. The satin sheets we bought were on the bed. I hit on side A of Alice Cooper's album *Trash* on cassette tape. Songs like "Poison" and "Spark in the Dark" got us going. There was a click and side B started in with "Bed of Nails." It felt like I was going down a slide head-first. Jane and I slid against each other until that explosive first-time empty into the latex. Look at a fourteen-year-old and it doesn't even seem possible. But it is.

In first grade, I was scolded by my principal for chasing little Krista around and lifting up her skirt on the playground. Where did I get this from? Was it TV? Family? School? Nature? Despite being a good kid in the old town, I guess I hadn't always been appropriate around girls. But it wasn't until later in second grade when I overheard a friend talking about humping.

"Oh, you don't know what humping is?" he said.

"No."

"It's when the guy gets on the girl's back and does it, you know, like an animal."

"Oh yeah, I know that," I said envisioning a guy on a girl's shoulders along for a piggyback ride. I thought of Krista and me engaged in this circus act.

My first concept of real sex didn't come until fourth grade, so where did this first-grade skirt interest on the playground come from? This desire to see what was underneath. What was I looking for underneath Krista's skirt? Who taught me this? I was infatuated with her. I can still remember her blond hair in pigtails and big bright blue eyes. When I lifted her dress that day on the playground, something else had come out of my mouth. I had apparently said something to her, not anything terribly graphic, but nothing worth repeating. Where did I get this concept?

My first real girlfriend Jane Martelli and I were abnormally intimate for our age. Maybe it was TV or the movies or just the adults we were around. We wanted to be so much older, but we weren't and that made us dependent on others. Her sisters' boyfriends bought us the beer and hard liquor when we wanted to party. When her sisters and mom were out working, we had some time alone at her house. We'd spend hours together and it just felt natural.

One day I was kissing Jane goodbye in the hallway before class and wrapped my arms around her when suddenly I felt a violent tug at my arm. We stepped back and saw Mr. Grahm, one of the gym teachers.

"This is disgusting behavior," he said angrily.

"What do you mean?" I asked.

"Young man, you're coming with me."

Mr. Grahm pulled me by the arm and dragged me to the principal's office, as Jane dejectedly looked on.

"You can't do things like that here. This is a public space," he said.

"I was kissing my girlfriend goodbye. It's called love and affection, man."

"I don't care, it's wrong," he said as he pushed me into Mr. Bundy's office.

"What's the trouble this time?" the assistant principal asked.

"I caught this young fellow getting sexual on his girlfriend in the hall. When I told him it was improper he gave me a hard time."

"What? First of all, we weren't 'getting sexual' and second of all, Mr. Grahm didn't give me a chance to give him a hard time," I objected.

"Mr. Grahm says so and it's his word over yours. I wish I could trust you but with your record I can't," replied Mr. Bundy. "Next time, you're suspended from school. Get out."

There was this other girl named Danica in my first-period seventh-grade math class. She sat two seats ahead of me in the next row, so my view of her back was perfect. I stared at her all class and pictured her sitting there in the classroom in her underwear. Then my mind unclipped her bra. Then her panties. Her long black hair fell around her shoulders and on her back. Then she'd stand up and it was hormones through the roof. This was my math. Every day for the first week of school I repeated this fantasy of a stranger who I had never even talked to. Of course, I imagined talking to her, walking her home, and going to the mall with her. In the real world, I met someone else, and I wonder what might have happened if I never got to my last class of the day where Jane was. After that grade, I didn't see Danica around anymore.

I had walked into English class the first day of the school year to find Andy Kennedy and some others there. But then there she was. The first day I didn't know what to make of her. I was speechless. The second day I was curious. The third day I was hooked. Jane walked up to the front of the room to get a bathroom pass and my eyes followed her every move. She had a carefree attitude that both bothered me and aroused me. She carried a confidence I didn't see in other girls our age. Her smile was almost devious. Her thick chocolate colored hair. The whiteness of her bare skin. A smell I couldn't get enough of. Her deep brown eyes— I felt like I knew those eyes for a thousand years. Everything about her paralyzed me.

After three weeks of getting to know each other in class, we started dating. Our first kiss was in the rain at the train station like a cliché Hollywood movie, a tragedy in the making. It was the fall of 1989, the end of a fun decadent decade. We wanted to hang on to the 80s, but it was inevitably slipping away. We were slipping away even as we were just beginning.

20

WIN LIVED AN ISOLATED LIFE. Besides me, he didn't have family or many friends. He had an evangelical sister, who lived a few miles away, but they didn't get along so well. The only friends Win had were bar friends, and for the sake of money and health he told me he stayed away from the bars these days. That winter I started to hang out with him a couple of nights a week in his apartment. Over some beers one night, he told me about his wild bar days, spent mostly in our town bars. Rumor was our town actually held a record for most pubs within a square mile, as if that were something to be proud of. Most of these pubs had hard crowds— not the kind of civilized place you'd go on a date. He talked of fights, arrests, all kinds of trouble. He spoke highly of one friend in particular.

"Dee Dee, she was my best friend. We did everything together. So many nights we got each other through rough times."

"So where is she now?"

"But but… she fell off the wagon."

He paused for a moment and then continued,

"She overdosed four years ago."

Win was choked up. He ran his fingers through his red beard as if it held some kind of magic support.

Win went off the deep end with guilt. He told me this is when those wild nights at the town bars turned into sad, angry nights. The depression and anger he felt just about destroyed his life and cost him a fourth of a lung. Doctors said he had some kind of lung damage. Of course, he continued to smoke cigarettes and weed even after the operation, but he slowed down. After his hospitalization, he promised himself and the spirit of Dee Dee he would get a grip on his life.

Win had been a postal carrier for twenty-two years. Even in his worst times, he marched on and got his work done. But he grew tired of it. Just before his hospitalization, he had a breakdown one day and went postal and threw a chair across the room. Things weren't the same when he returned from leave, so he quit his position and went to work for my stepfather. In fact, the first time I ever saw him he still had his postal uniform on. He had come over to meet Don and interview for the job. But by the time he had returned for the first night of work, his proper blue uniform had morphed into a biker meets hippie uniform of black jeans, dangling chain from a belt, and black t-shirt with flannel shirt. His pack of Marlboros fit nicely in his shirt left pocket. His long reddish brown hair was still tied back, but his trimmed reddish beard had grown longer, which helped cover up the gash in his left cheek from a bar fight.

Some time after becoming friends I asked him,

"Did you wear these clothes on the weekends when you were a postal worker?"

"You kiddin' me? As soon as I got home I tore off that uniform."

"Was it a tough job?"

"Well, it was a good job, but I changed. I needed a change. Nothing wrong with that," he said as he balanced a lit cigarette between his thin yellow fingers and brought the ash down to the tray. "We all change and nothing's forever."

Win began buying cigarettes for me. He got 'buy one get two free' specials that I didn't have access to. I could walk into any deli or gas station and buy smokes, but the good deals were too far away. He went to smoke shops and interstate gas stations that had package discounts and he would hook me up with them because he knew I needed my work money for food, clothes, and spending. I felt bad though and I also didn't want to feel like I owed anyone, so sometimes I'd leave cash on the seat in his kitchen.

One day Win took me for a ride in his van and we pulled into an open parking lot. He turned the ignition off and turned to me.

"You ready to drive?"

"Ah, yeah, okay, sure."

He got out and walked around to the passenger door and I just jumped over to the driver's seat. He walked me through what to do and I started up the old van. I started to drive along the edge of the lot and he just instructed me what to do and where to go.

"You know, fathers are supposed to do these things?"

"Did you have one?" I asked.

"Yes, but he didn't do these kinds of things. He should have."

I drove along a little while longer and then pulled over and put it in park.

"You can keep going if you want."

"No, it's all right. We can go."

I didn't want to owe anyone. And I didn't want anyone to think they were being a father figure to a punk like me.

Win also began driving me to school. I suppose he was helping my mother out, though I never got rides from her or Don anyway. The walk was two miles and I enjoyed it many days. I guess Win thought if he drove me I wouldn't be tempted to cut out. I had at the time already been suspended for truancy a few days and he knew that. He helped get me to school, but after a while I told him it was all right. I was starting to feel strange getting dropped off by this older bearded man in his beat up van. I felt like the other kids were going to start thinking he was my father or someone. I didn't have a father to drop me off like some of the other kids and I wasn't going to start having one now.

21

WE WERE JUST KIDS. We experimented. We smoked. We did some drugs and got drunk on an eclectic variety of alcohol. We blasted 80s hair metal. We loved and laughed. We kissed in the rain. We stole from stores.

We entered the grocery store wild-eyed and hungry. Aisle by aisle we filled plastic bags that were crumbled up in our pockets when we entered. Soda, chips, a steak, TV dinners, even some dog food. It was a rush. Jane, Rachel, and I filled those sacks and then walked right out the front doors and walked home. Nobody in the world was going to get in our way. After several shots of booze, none of us were in our right minds. Good thing Jane wasn't crazier than she was, because I was so crazy over her I probably would've done anything at that point in time.

But for the rest of the school year and into the summer we really tried to slow down and chill. Back at her house, Jane and I would occasionally get into a kiss as Rachel looked away and smoked her cigarette. Sometimes Rachel would just get up and leave. Jane and I would laugh and continue on. I liked Rachel and she came to like me, though she was extremely jealous of me in the beginning and competed for Jane's attention. Every time Jane and I fought, I sensed Rachel was in her glory.

Rachel was good looking and smart. Her family lived a step up from Jane and me. Honestly, I don't know why she pined over Jane the way she did. It should've been the other way around. There were a few times when I forgot about the competition for Jane's attention and thought about getting with her. One time I ran into Rachel's house to get something from her— I don't remember what because I just remember the skimpy nightgown she was wearing. Jane and I were on the way to the beach with her older sister. Rachel couldn't come with us, so Jane's sister stopped at her house. I ran in to get whatever it was while Jane and her sister waited in the car. Rachel had just woken up out of bed. Her hair was messy, but she looked good. I checked her out and she smirked. For a moment I envisioned an alternative universe— no girlfriend waiting outside in a car. Me and Rachel on her kitchen table, and then on the stairs leading up to her room, and then on to her bed in the sheets, the very bed that Jane and I had spent a night in. There we were in her kitchen frozen for a moment looking at each other, maybe both thinking about the same thing. Then we snapped out of it and said goodbye.

Another time Rachel came inside my house to get something after Jane had left. Again, I have no memory of what that something was that left us there alone, but I remember standing close to each other. We stared for a frozen moment again, just like the time in her kitchen. Her legs were accentuated by the tight spandex shorts she had on, and her straight brown hair made me wild. This could have been it. But then I heard my mother yell up to see if I was home. There were moments when I wondered what might have been if we hadn't been so taken by and so loyal to Jane.

The summer of 1990 got quiet. I'd see Win twice a week at the dealership and one other night. Andy and Jeff had taken off to Florida for the summer. I made it a point to see Gene and Steve about every two weeks, though separately since they didn't get along so well. I also saw Paul a few times that summer. But most days and nights were spent with Jane. We even worked together during the day at the high school painting and cleaning for the maintenance team. We didn't tell anyone because we were embarrassed, but it was decent pay for us at the time. It paid for our food and cigarettes. And once in a while we'd sneak off into one of the bathrooms.

For two weeks, my family shipped me off to North Carolina. For a long time, my great aunt Gloria had wanted to send me to this nature camp out in the middle of the woods to nurture my love for nature. She finally went and paid for it. She wasn't as wealthy as her sisters, and cancer had struck her recently, but she made it a priority. I obliged. I was sure to tell my mother how much I hated the idea, but I was polite to Gloria.

Whisked off to this strange place on an airplane for the first time, I was a teenager worried about missing a party, a crush, a romance, a breakup, a fight— something I expected to happen while I was away. Of course, not much happened. Life goes on. At first, all I could do was think about Jane and my friends back home. My small comfortable world.

The first night there I called my mother and asked her to send me home from this terrible place. She wouldn't, so I dealt with it. The kid in the bunk above me hated it even more and would go off to smoke his cigarettes by himself. In a way he made me feel like it wasn't so bad. After all, I had no desire to smoke out there in the woods. The air was too fresh and clean. And then there was this girl with dark blond hair who grabbed my attention. If I were feeling rotten and hiding out by myself, I'd miss seeing her at events. We said hello to each other on the fifth day and she told me with a cute accent she was from Tennessee. I think that was the extent, but it didn't matter. I just liked seeing her. Day by day, the place grew on me.

For two weeks in the Carolina woods, we walked out to the lake every morning in the darkness. When the sun started to inch up and give us just enough light, we'd jump off the wooden dock into the cold lake. Near naked boys and girls swimming in nature under an escalating sun. Our chills dissipated, warmness spread by our jittering joy. In the afternoons on the trail, the spruce smell hit our faces as the guide waved us along to "find our souls." And then it was time to go home and lose those souls all over again within our walls. When I got back and went over to Jane's house, she stopped and looked at me, and said,

"You seem different."

22

WE WERE ALL LOOKING to be saved with something. For me, it was music and Jane. When TSS closed down, we all joked around that it was surely because of the music department losses. Gene and I continued our greed across the street at a new store called Caldor, but everyone else went off to other hobbies, some better, some worse. Since compact discs had just come out, Gene and I decided to begin a CD collection. If record companies were going to take tapes away from us, we'd strike back. One day after school, we went to Caldor to load up on CDs as we had done several times before. As we walked toward the exit I heard a voice.

"Going somewhere guys?"

We could somehow tell just by the tone of the voice, it was a genuine security guard.

"Run," I said to Gene.

"No," he replied and I hesitated with my escape for a moment to look at him in awe. Why would he hold us back like that? I thought of that day out on the track when I left Gene behind and beat Evan for the first time. I needed to run again.

I sped out into the parking lot. I flung the CDs out of my pants at the agents in pursuit, but it didn't do any good. A big muscle-head guard grabbed me by the back of my shirt, clenched a headlock around my neck, and then threw me to the pavement. The man lifted me, threw my hands behind my back and walked me inside. A woman came up behind him yelling into a radio, documenting the incident play by play. He brought me back into the store and past the whole line of front cash registers filled with people checking out— with my hands twisted behind my back like a criminal and my T-shirt torn and hanging off of me in shreds. It was humiliating enough to never steal anything again. I always knew what we were doing was wrong, but we excused it with some kind of anarchist anti-corporate rationale.

"They're not going to lose anything," we'd say.

Inside the security office, as I waited for my mother to come and pick me up, I became acquainted with the store's brand new security system. The wall was lined with monitors showing different parts of the store and rotating the view every few minutes. A guard zoomed in on a young girl bending over— amazing technology, but certainly evil in the hands of a pervert.

Obviously, they had captured me on the camera placing the CDs in my pants, but what about Gene? He had simply slipped out the doors and strolled off into the parking lot unharmed the way I had when Steven was caught. We were all having our turns.

Gene made me want to desert him rather than sink with him. And then he deserted me. Had Steven felt this way about me? We had never talked about it and he didn't seem mad at me. Should I have taken the fall with both Steven and Gene? Maybe if I hadn't run we wouldn't have been caught. Maybe we both would have been caught anyway, but maybe it would've strengthened our friendship.

Football saved Steven for a while. I decided to join him and give it a try. Steven, David Pace, Ricky Sharpe, and I were the team stars. I was the smaller, faster one. Get the ball to me and I'd run it right up the field. David was a hulk. He was a bit bigger than Steven but better in school. The all around good guy, he protected his friends, as Steven did, but there was something even more paternal yet authoritarian about David. Steven was authoritative, but he didn't try to control any of us. Steven versus David was the ultimate fantasy fight. I admit I envisioned it, but hoped something that tragic wouldn't happen. It luckily didn't. It was like they knew how costly it would be to each other, so they avoided it out of silent respect.

Ricky Sharpe had a careless way about him. He just didn't care about anything. He'd curse a teacher out. He'd curse his own mother out.

The first time I heard of him, some kid asked me if I knew who he was.

"I saw him punch the shit out of some kid. He's tough," the kid told me.

"I've never heard of him."

When I met Ricky at football the following year, I was unsure about his unorthodox look. He was only a little bigger than me, but not much bigger than any of the other kids I had beaten up. Ricky looked older than most of us though. He had the beginnings of facial hair and had bags, even wrinkles, under his vacant eyes. His clothes were beat up and droopy. He wore a backward cap. He was thuggish and clashed with what most high school jocks looked like.

It was a cold fall day. We had made plans to watch football at Ricky's house. Of course, that included a pre-game practice in front of the house in the street. Patches of ice still plagued the street, and snow on the grass from the first snowfall made the day brighter than it was. There were eight of us. The ball went back and forth. No tackles, just a firm double pat on the back would do. Toward the end of the game, I nabbed Ricky with a tag on the back, but we slid on the ice and couldn't stop. We were going too fast. He crashed into the underbelly of a parked car and I landed on top of him. I popped up to my feet and saw he was banged up and struggling for a grip. I gave him my hand, but he waved me off. The wind had been knocked out of him.

"You all right?" I asked. "I'm sorry about that one. It got away from us."

"Fuck, man," he said angrily.

Ricky struggled to his knees and tried to shake it off. He sat on the sideline for a little while to get his air back. He seemed defeated for the rest of the day and had trouble looking me in the eye. We all watched the game that day in his bare 70s styled living room. His mother and older brother were out for the day so we took over the house as a football party often does. I couldn't care less about the teams, the stats, and the players compared to some of the other guys that day, but I made the best of the game and enjoyed it. I was astonished by the way other guys got sucked into it. I got bored and sleepy; I'd rather be playing the sport than watching others throw around a ball. Watching sports was time-consuming too. I wanted to do other things like play guitar, hang with girls, and just feel good, but I guess watching other people have fun made them feel good.

We called ourselves the "four horsemen," but it wouldn't last long.

"Come on, we're not messing around. Get with it," one coach would yell.

"Get up. You look like you're taking a shit," the other coach would yell.

The condescending insults on my teammates from the fat coaches annoyed me. Who were they? They couldn't move like us. Even the big kids were agile. No one needed to be constantly scolded. There was no fun in that. I didn't want to see others mistreated all in the name of the game. Being called a rat bastard punk didn't improve my game.

David and Steven stayed on and had a great first season. I walked off the field one day several weeks into the season and never went back. Ricky wasn't too far behind me. I tried out football because football players got more respect than runners, but I never really had a love for the game and at the time no real understanding of it. With no real love for any sports and with a new girlfriend and friends like Win, my career as an athlete didn't stand a chance. I wasn't going to be a professional or even college football player, especially as kids got bigger and I stayed the same size, reassured by the height of my parents. I was going to use my time constructively from here on out— hang with my girlfriend, drink with friends, and work for money.

I hung out at Jane's house almost every day after I quit football— it was like I had time to make up. The place was a mess. Overflowing ashtrays the size of hubcaps lay on the floor, smoke hovered in the air, old beer and soda cans just sat out scattered around, three or four cats crept around, and a couple of dogs took up the space in the middle with a couple of occasional accidents from the older one. I'd often clean the place up because apparently no one else was going to do it. But it made me feel good. It made me feel like I was helping out and being a part of something. And her mother appreciated the company around the house, didn't mind the cleaning, and didn't mind the partying either.

On New Year's Eve we started a drinking campaign at noon. By four o'clock we were hung-over. By seven, Jane's mother was home from work with the ingredients for rum and cokes, and we started all over again. Hello, 1991. My mother eventually came looking for me at some point after midnight. Through the laughing and music, we heard a knock on the metal screen door. I laughed as my mother stood on their stoop and smoke poured out of the front door into her face as beer bottles rolled around the floor at my feet and people in the house shouted happy new year into the cold winter air. It was outrageous really.

23

I WAS BECOMING A SMOKER. In the days of no tobacco regulation, I was able to walk into a deli and buy a pack of cigarettes for two dollars at thirteen years old. For the first couple of years it was only on and off, a pack here and there, sometimes as many as six months would pass before I would buy another one, especially when I was in fitness mode. Hanging with Win, Gene, and Jane surprisingly didn't keep me entirely away from running. Even quitting football hadn't yet squashed my love for running and working out. For ten weeks out of the year, I was a fitness freak and not the kind that was out to just look good like most of the vain posers in my town. I loved the feeling inside when I would run several miles just for fun. Not because some fat coach ordered me to. Not because I was whipping Evan's ass in a race in gym class, though that was satisfactory too. I just loved the wind in my face. I loved the freedom.

My great aunt Gloria died on a cold day in January. This would only motivate me more the following season. I would run in her memory. Breathe the air in and blow it out to remind me of her shallow lung cancer breaths the last time I saw her at the hospital but also of the fresh North Carolina morning air she had sent me into the previous summer.

I signed up for track in the spring of middle school both years. Some of my best school memories were on that track. On the track team I went nearly undefeated, only losing to a few older taller kids with beards from other towns. But I also enjoyed being a very successful anchor on an undefeated relay team. In the school field day competitions, I was undefeated at the one hundred, four hundred forty, and the mile. Evan was in the dust, and Jamboree champ Owen was nowhere to be seen. In my hand, I clutched a good luck crystal Gloria had given me.

My wins were lonely though— like the old cliché about the loneliness of the long distance runner. I didn't see much of Win or Gene during these ten weeks. Even Jane and I saw each other less. Other than my close old friends, hardly anyone congratulated me. No one else said "nice going." No pat on the back from my teammates. None of my teachers, no adults, not even my slouch of a coach Mr. Flinder had much to say. And this guy had been my on and off gym teacher since fourth grade. This apathy just about killed my love for running.

As soon as the track season ended I was right back to my old ways. Pretty soon I was smoking a pack a day. I can't even point to exactly when I got hooked. One day out in the field in late June after school and after track season had ended I was hanging with a bunch of other punks. I spotted Coach Flinder. He looked over and I curled the cigarette up in my cupped hand as the smoke leaked from the sides of my mouth. He looked away. That was it. Not a word. Not another look.

No "you're hanging out with the wrong people."

No "come back and be a track star."

Nothing.

He turned away and disowned me— washed his hands of me too easily. Most of my teachers were like this too— no ability or desire to talk, really talk, or connect to their troubled teenage students. We were plagued, infected with loserism, and there was no saving us.

24

THERE WERE FOUR WEIRD MOMENTS with Edwin that led to my estrangement from him by the end of spring 1991. The first was when he put on an old 70s porno film one night. He only played it for a few minutes, just to show me there were VHS tapes out there like this. The women had 70s hairstyles, unusually big breasts, and a bush of hair between their legs. The men were fat with big mustaches. He told me it was all right if I ever wanted to come over and watch one while he wasn't home. I never did. Even if I had wanted to watch old hairy people in their thirties and forties having sex, I wouldn't want to in his small apartment, even if he wasn't there. I was content with Jane and the bra section of Mom's JC Penny catalogue.

The second moment occurred as we were eating a steak. A strange tasteless white powder was lightly sprinkled on top of the meat. After we finished eating, he told me a story about how a friend had played a trick on him once and laced something with a substance that made it difficult to get an erection for a while. Of course, I thought about the powder and asked,

"You didn't... did you?"

"I guess you'll find out," he said chuckling.

Right back to the JC Penny catalogue the next day, I wanted to see if it was true. I tried and tried, but I couldn't. I don't know if it was psychosomatic, but I couldn't get an erection for several days after that steak dinner. I was weirded out and stayed away from Win for about a week. My distance must have warned him, because that never happened again.

The third weird moment came when he oddly placed his hand on my lap one night. I was sitting down in his living room and he reached over and just placed his hand there for a moment. He leaned in and said, "You're a special kid, Jack. Don't forget it. You can do whatever you want." I looked at him with puzzlement and he took his hand away. A few minutes later I excused myself. I didn't think his gesture was sexual and didn't think he intended to do much more, but it was awkward enough. Maybe he just genuinely wanted to inspire me, but I wondered about my little brother JP. He would go up and curiously check out the odd man living across the way in the apartment up three steps. Win would invite him in. I hoped he hadn't put his hand on my brother's lap too. JP wouldn't have been able to fight him off the way I could. I told JP not to go visit him anymore because the man was kooky, and he stopped going.

The fourth and final weird moment was when he showed up at my girlfriend's house to tell me it was time to come home. He looked nervous. I thought someone had died or fallen ill.

"Jack, your mom is looking for you. We'd better go."

"So why is she sending you out?"

"Because she's busy with your brother."

I told him to go home alone and that I would be there soon. After he drove off, I left on foot.

The next day he pulled me aside on my way out to walk to school.

"Listen, Jack, I don't think that girl's any good for you. She's going to tear you up."

"Well, I think I can manage my girlfriend myself. I love this girl."

"You probably don't really love her. You're too young to fall in love."

Here was the guy giving me cigarettes and drugs telling me I was too young to fall in love.

"That's a Motley Crue song," I told him and pushed him aside. "And don't tell me what to do."

I didn't talk to him for a week.

When the summer began, I needed independence from both Win's weirdness and Don's unpredictable pay schedule. I found this independence in a job at the local deli during the day and then office cleaning at night.

My neighbor Gerard Difranco waved me over one day.

"Hey, Jack, I know you do work for your stepfather, but do you know anyone looking for work?"

"Ah yeah, how about me?"

It was perfect. He drove us to the offices on Tuesday, Thursday, and Friday nights. My Friday nights were shot, but it was nice money. I didn't mind emptying garbage cans— around a hundred in a night while Gerard cleaned the bathrooms and dusted. I really learned how to work for my money. I also got a glimpse of the high-class world through the people who worked in the real estate office we cleaned. Mr. Luger was the president of a wealthy real estate firm. His office was grand. Glass tops on rich wood furniture, a giant leather chair rimmed with gold, and a giant eagle sculpture sat on one of the tables. He had pictures of himself with the governor and other important people in another world I had no concept of. It was a trip going in there to empty his garbage and I always saved it for last.

After a week, Win knocked on the door and my mother called me down and told me he wanted to see me. He asked me to go fishing. I agreed. He asked me to come over and talk for awhile too, but I told him I needed to take care of some things. Didn't my mother and Don wonder what was going on with this guy? Why would you allow your teenage son, or even worse your smaller child, to go visit with a strange man in a smoky apartment? Mom did ask at some point what he and I did and if everything was all right, and I told her not to worry. But what if I had been lying? What if he had threatened me with a blade? I wondered if Don would've been all right with us going next door to visit Jeffrey Dahmer. One day though I saw my mother and Win get into something. She said something to him and he flipped. Just couldn't believe it. Cursed her and walked away. She shook her head and walked inside.

When the fishing day came around, I had slept out at Andy's house and didn't make it back in time. I did so on purpose because I didn't want to deal with the guy telling me this or that while being out on a boat with him. Win went fishing alone. From there on, Win and I simply avoided each other around the yard. He started to spend more time locked up inside, and I was always out at Jane's house anyway. I may have been young, and we may have been wild, but I knew caring about someone was not doing anyone harm, even if I ended up with a broken heart later on. It didn't compare to the weirdness of the world Win exposed me to.

25

GIRLFRIENDS TAKE UP TIME and many of my old friends seemed to scatter in their own directions. Gene and I would occasionally get together when I was feeling down. I knew I was down because every time I was with Gene I would get sloppy drunk on Dewar's scotch whiskey blend. Usually, I ended up sick and vomiting in his backyard.

I tried to blend these two worlds of love and darkness as best as possible.

I met Gene at the train station on a Saturday in July. Despite the summer warmth, he was wearing a long black trench coat.

"Hey," he said opening his coat to reveal a bottle of scotch whiskey blend he'd stolen from his father's liquor cabinet.

"Glasses too?" I inquired.

"Fuck no. What do you think I'm some kind of classy guy?"

We walked along under the raised above-the-ground tracks. Trains occasionally passed overhead as we walked under the bridge. After about ten minutes we reached a break in the chain link fence. Someone had torn open the fence with wire cutters a long time ago. We looked around and then climbed in and headed up the hill to where the land met the tracks. Along the path was a graffitied brick wall that grew smaller and smaller until the narrow path widened into an opening just aside the tracks. Rock bands, dead love, youth angst in acronyms like FTW (fuck the world) welcomed us.

At the end of the brick wall we sat down on top and opened the bottle. It was two o'clock in the afternoon. Gene surprised me with shot glasses.

"You lied!" I said as I took the soda and beer chasers out of a bag.

The girls arrived at around three thirty and we were already on our way to a bad place.

Eventually, we all ended up on the tracks. Gene got along with Jane's friend Rachel fine enough. He had her pissing her pants with laughter. Jane and I slobbered each other with whiskey kisses. We were entering our second year together, and everything was still exciting. The youthful feel of a fresh kiss, my arms wrapped around her hips, and then a rumble that told us the train was coming. Gene and Rachel jumped off the tracks back onto the path. Jane and I stayed. I grabbed on to her waistband and snug my fingers into the back of her pants. Her nails ran down my back. Her big brown eyes lit up. The train honked and was getting closer.

"Get the fuck out of there," yelled Rachel.

"You're fucking crazy," yelled Gene.

"Guys please…" pleaded Rachel.

The ground thundered, we tossed the shot glasses onto the tracks and jumped off the platform of rocks back onto the path. We hit the ground on our sides with our arms around each other and our heads up facing the train. The wind hit us in the faces, we screamed, and in a few moments just like a climax, it was all over.

We got up, chugged the rest of the bottle, and staggered down the path. I left the empty bottle standing there on display with the label forward. Jane stopped to write our names on the wall with a black marker— *Jack and Jane 4 ever*— and then we carried on.

"Riding the night train, brother," I said to Gene.

Jane's house was only three blocks away from the tracks, but it felt like twenty blocks when you're that wasted. I fell only a couple of houses away from hers— face first to the sidewalk. My lip was bloody, and I had chipped a tooth and scraped the side of my cheek. It looked like I had been in a fight and lost badly. I pulled myself up laughing and spitting blood. Gene walked ahead.

The house was a disaster as usual. Empty beer cans on the floor. Cats running for cover. A couple of dogs barking and jumping around. The sofa was torn like a wrestling ring turnbuckle with stuffing over-flowing onto the filthy wood floor. The old television was crooked on a flimsy cart. Pictures of Jane and her two older sisters and one younger brother were on the far wall, also crooked and from a time that seemed long before the corruption of innocence.

Within an hour I was at the toilet. Jane was right behind me. I had started a chain reaction. She couldn't even wait for me to pull my head out. Just as I was getting out what seemed like the last of it, she threw up right on top of my head. The smell of her putrid vomit trig-gered another wave of nausea in me and we shared a few heaves before it was over. I stumbled back into the living room and fell right in the middle of the room. My body lay in cigarette ashes since no one in the house actually used an astray; ashtrays were only used for putting the cigarette out and even then they sometimes used old beer cans. I swam in the ashes— my body now blackened. After a while, I stopped and could no longer move. I couldn't feel. Rachel shook me. I mumbled and she told me I looked green.

When Jane came back out feeling better, she joined Rachel in her worries about my deteriorating condition. Gene sat there and even-tually got up.

"It looks like the party's over. He needs to go to sleep and I'm going now."

"What if he dies, you fuck?" asked Jane.

He laughed and said, "You're fucking crazy. Just let him sleep."

Let him sleep? I was practically dead. He might as well have left me on the tracks up the hill.

I couldn't sleep. I lay there half conscious shaking with the chills. They considered calling an ambulance. Jane called upstairs to her oldest sister Winona and her boyfriend Kevin. They had their own private space upstairs and hadn't heard any of the commotion. Kevin came down and realized my condition.

"He's shitfaced," he declared. "It's getting late and we need to get him home. We can't have him pass out here all night."

They certainly didn't need me dying on them.

Kevin wasn't a very big guy, but the thin rock-star-looking guy picked me right up and threw me over his shoulder, flipped his hair back, and carried me out to his old Trans Am where he dumped me in the backseat. He patted me on the back and said,

"It's not far, so just hold on."

Jane's head was spinning again so she went to bed. Rachel needed a ride home, so she jumped in and held me steady in the backseat.

The ten-minute ride felt like we were in a dune buggy. I bounced all over as Rachel held me. Kevin was calm and cool as he drove me home. When we got home he went up and knocked on my front door to tell my mother he'd be bringing me up to bed. I couldn't make it on my own. I was completely out of it, so he carried me up the steps cradled in his arms. After depositing me in the bed, he went downstairs and told my mother that I had been out with a friend and showed up at Jane's house like that. My mother thanked him, said goodbye, and then came upstairs to check on me. She left a metal pot by my head and a glass of water and then closed the door.

I had visions that night. Speeding cars and trains. Tied to the tracks. Clouds floating overhead. Rain gently misting on my face. A river flowing beside me. A mudslide. I had filled the pot with vomit, pissed myself and shit the bed by the time I awoke at four o'clock the next day. I had narrowly escaped death by alcohol poisoning. I was only fourteen years old.

26

MY MOHAWK was scary for a while. I had started to buzz my head punk style just as my father started to come around more and wanted to introduce me to more of the people in his life. Sure, why not wait until your kid is a full-blown punk? One day my stepmother scoffed:

"Who lets him do that to himself? My kid would never look like that."

They told me to wait in the car while they ran in to get the food for take out. She refused to be seen in public with a kid that looked as scary as I did. I guess I don't blame her, but good thing we didn't have to live with one another under the same roof.

The next time he picked me up I had graduated to the straight razor. I don't know what gave me the idea, but it seemed crazy enough. Crazy was always a good objective in my town. The back of my head had little nicks and scabs. On the top of my head remained a short strip. Sometimes I even colored it blonde, blue, or green. I looked truly psychotic for a period of time— Taxi Driver style. Apparently, my stepmother was frightened by the way I looked. As if I were going to rob them, wreck their house, and become violent— exactly what her own younger brother was doing to her family at the time despite looking like a regular working-class guy. I really couldn't blame her though. She didn't know me. Most of my family didn't know me.

For a while, my father would pick me up and we'd spend the day alone driving around. On a couple of occasions he seemed apologetic for being gone so long, but he also seemed to evade responsibility.

"You know, women change when they get older and get married. They get fat…"

"Has your new wife gone through these changes yet?" I asked.

He sidestepped the issue and resorted to his stories about trying to find me for several years as if I had been abducted to some far away land.

Soon enough, my stepmother softened up to me. Maybe she felt bad. My hair toned down to just a regular buzz cut like every other teenager on Long Island. She bought me a couple of drinks at the beach bar. I sat with her and her good-looking friend while we waited for my father to return from somewhere. Feed booze to the already troubled kid? What was she trying to do?

My father later asked me, "You know your stepmother's Mustang?"

"Yeah, it's a cool car."

"Well, we're going to give it to you when you get your license. I think she'll be wanting a new car soon, so it works out."

"Wow, thanks!"

The red Mustang was a late eighties model, nothing special, but I'd be more than happy to drive it. This was something to look forward to. I was beginning to like the benefits of having a father and another side to the family.

A few months after I stopped talking to Win, he brought home a new kid. This strange twelve-year-old kid was in trouble and was kicked out of the house by his stepfather. He had been in and out of juvenile detention several times already. Win's newly adopted friend lived with him for about four months. In that time, Win had tried to mentor him; I suppose the way he had tried with me. Took him out to

drive his van in a parking lot. Probably. Cigarettes and alcohol. Most
certainly. Maybe even put his hand on his lap and told him he was
special. I had hoped I had misread him, I hoped his mentoring of me
was innocent, I hoped this wasn't the way it looked to most other normal adults, like the intentions of a pedophile setting up a victim, but I
could never be sure. He hadn't gone past the hand on the lap with me,
but that kid was younger and also lived with him in the same close
quarters of a studio apartment. It didn't look good. In no time, the kid
was out of control lashing out at Win and stealing money from him.
Soon he was gone and Win's life was in shambles.

When I was still friends with him, Win had complained about
Don not paying him on time, which Don was notorious for. Win's
resentment toward Don began to grow. In a way, Don seemed to take
ownership of Win's life. Win worked for Don and lived under his
roof, the same way I did. Win used to say that Don was a control freak
trying to be a dictator over my mother, JP, and me. It was apparent
how Win felt about his boss and landlord, but how had he fallen into
this situation without wondering who Don was? And how did Don
really feel about his employee and renter? Was Don in some strange
way resentful of Win for spending time with me or being a bad influence on me, or was he hoping the guy would mess me up?

After the adopted kid fled, Win packed his stuff and fled. He
hadn't worked for Don for some time and hadn't bothered to pay the
last month's rent. He hadn't come out of the house for weeks. The
place was a disaster. Cat shit all over, cigarette ashes, burns in the rug,
and black filth a quarter of an inch thick covered all the surfaces. It
was a complete waste land. I wondered what the hell had happened
in there.

I found myself back with Gene again as the summer came to a
close. My boss at the deli asked if I could DJ his parties for the rest of
the summer. I brought along Gene. Tom's family owned the popular

town deli where I worked during the day. Every Saturday night in August he threw a party right there in the fenced in yard of the deli. Tom was in his early twenties, so Gene and I were out of our league with the older crowd, but we made great DJs. Probably everyone came over to us at some point in the night to thank us for the great tunes. Gene played the heavy metal tracks. I played the punk and rock tracks and the ballads. There we were having the time of our life. Most nights we would drink a beer or two, some nights we would smoke a little pot, but getting messed up wasn't the highlight like usual. There was no excess, no self-destruction, no negative talk, no depression. Maybe it was because of Tom's optimistic attitude and his laid back environment. It was all about being happy, being ourselves, doing what we love. That was our moment.

And then the summer was over. The new school year was beginning. High school had arrived. Unlike other kids my age, my work money was becoming necessary if I wanted to wear decent fitting clothes and have spending money for food. Working would teach me independence— something some adults don't ever learn— something I am thankful for— but it also put a lot of strain on my childhood and schooling.

The deli job could not continue since they were closed at night. Tom at the deli was going off to join the military too, which surprised me and Gene. We didn't take him for the type, but I knew he was getting out of something here at home. The summer parties made sense now.

I still had the office cleaning. Other kids would be home sleeping and I was out emptying garbage cans until two a.m. some nights. I was making money that most parents just give their kids for basic necessities. I saw so many kids getting hand outs and they'd go out and spend it on the town. I wish I had had that luxury.

I was missing my Friday nights, and I felt depressed after a while. The job was lonely too. I thought I could get a more social job during normal hours and maybe just keep Tuesday nights with Gerard, but he wanted someone for all three nights. He understood though and welcomed me back if I should change my mind. I took a job delivering newspapers. The pay was far less, but at least I would still be free of Don. I had worked since the age of eleven and the need was only getting greater now that high school was before us.

27

RENEE REPLACED RACHEL. She was more like Jane— Wild and careless. Jane had grown bored with Rachel. We were in high school now and things would inevitably change. Rachel didn't like Renee and warned Jane that she was going to get into trouble with her. She expressed this same concern to another mutual friend and it got back to Jane. She didn't like the talk. She called Rachel up one day and threatened to fight her. Just like that, I thought. A childhood friendship thrown away for some girl you don't even know? I asked her this and she told me to shut up.

Rachel didn't back down. She told Jane to meet her after school to talk things out. Jane brought along a number of spectators looking to see a fight. Renee Gambino was one of them— there to supervise the destruction of a friendship. They met face to face on the racetrack outside in the back of the school. Jane tried to bully her around at first, but Rachel yelled back. She wouldn't back down, even when Jane started to throw punches.

Jane overpowered her. She tore at Rachel's long hair, dragged her to the ground and ripped some of her clothing away. She pulled at her lace underwear, her flesh, her hips, her legs, her freckled back. In the early moments of the struggle there was something that turned on the male pig in me. But then the fight began. Once on top of her, Jane lashed into her, bloody knuckled, over and over, pounding her face.

Renee egged on Jane and taunted Rachel.

"Yeah, Jane, kick that bitch's ass. Where's your big mouth now, Rachel?"

Jane continued to beat on her.

"Get up and fight, you whore," shouted Renee.

I grimaced from afar and called for an end.

"Jane, that's enough. Come on."

She didn't stop and told me to shut up. The crying was dreadful. Renee kept taunting Rachel. I stared down her other girlfriends and they finally got the hint and pulled Jane away. All that bloody pounding on her former best friend of so many years, just because Rachel had said something true— how Jane was starting to fall in with the wrong people and was turning into someone different, someone meaner, someone a little angrier at the world, bitter over her own misfortunes of poverty, family drug addiction, an abandoned overworked mother, and a father who moved away and got rich. One of her sister's ex-boyfriends had punched her sister on the way out before being picked up for prison. It was all just terrible. Jane didn't have it easy, but I couldn't understand how she could take it out on the one girl who had had her back in this world. They grew up together, but that was that. This deception got me thinking about watching my own back.

Jane and I broke up more times than I can recall. I took the break ups like a champion defeated for my title. I sulked, but I enjoyed the cat and mouse drama of getting back together. I'd go and listen to 80s ballads and it was a real high. The ride was turbulent, filled with nasty fights, passionate forgiveness, and then more nasty fights that included breaking the gifts we gave to one another. She took hammers to jewelry. Andy and I took turns breaking an acoustic guitar she gave me over each other's backs like the wrestler Honky Tonk Man used to do. Of course, nothing compared to the night I took a frying pan on the head, and I even forgave her after that. Such dysfunction at such a young age; we were both missing a great deal from home.

It wasn't too long after Rachel's exile that Jane said goodbye to me for good too. She was heading in a different direction. It was October, and we had had a nice run for two years from September to September. It all reminded me of a Neil Diamond song I used to hear, and I was crushed, but who the hell stays together that long from that age to begin with? I tried to forget the good times, the kissing in the rain, the afternoon naps, the look of her deep eyes, the smell of her skin, the way my hands would get lost in her long thick hair. It was better off now. I had stopped stealing and was tired of the drinking and fighting. I guess I was changing too. We had been on and off for too long— indecisive, young and stupid, but with our entire lives ahead of us.

A month later her mother suddenly packed them up and retreated for California— another person from my life gone to that state. I bumped into her mother at the town deli the week before their departure and she invited me to their big going away bash that Saturday night, but I couldn't bring myself to go. That part of my life was over. I couldn't go back. But I always wondered and wished her well. For years the wondering would become a sensation. That moment of a surreal disappointment in a store or restaurant when I spotted her, only to realize it was someone else. Jane was gone.

28

WE MARCHED down the street. Blood on our hands, in our hair, in our mouths, from another battle. Our eyes were bloodshot from the smoke and booze at the house party, which had erupted into chaos when a fight broke out between two rival groups. The house belonged to the parents of some dumb kid who wanted a fast ticket to popularity, and it was smashed up pretty good. Holes in walls, furniture cracked in half, doors splintered. The cops chased off any of the remaining kids and called in the paramedics to pick up the injured.

Some nights we brought destruction out into the public. One night in October a large group of us went to a nightclub a few towns away. The building pounded with bass, then our faces were pounded with fists, and then our fists pounded other faces. The wildest brawl erupted. I wasn't even close to the center or the cause, but I still got clocked. People from my town were right in the middle with a rival town. Knives came out on both sides. One friend got his forehead slashed. Several people were sliced and poked. Cinder blocks were thrown through windows. No one died, but just a little spilled blood was enough. This was only a club of sixteen to twenty-year-olds. We were all just kids, just children, but we acted like barbarians. The club closed down that night, with the owners unable to recover insurance for the brawl damage.

I saw Gene tear someone's bottom lip down as he elbowed another in the face, just before a bigger guy landed a right hand and knocked him out cold. I woke him up and dragged him away to the side. He was able to stand after a few minutes. When a gunshot went off, we bolted for the exit and climbed right out one of the broken panels missing a window. The wide open parking lot had more potential for danger, so Gene and I slipped off and ran fast. Some stupid guido roid rage wasn't worth a life-long scar or worse.

These were typical nights for kids from our town, and now that I didn't have the shield of a girlfriend I was seeing a whole new side. We weren't even the worst kids. The worst ones were robbing drug stores, shooting drugs, or already locked up. We were just a step away from the popular jocks. Many of us intermingled with various crowds. In the end it didn't matter. Most of us were going to be laborers in the service industry. No matter what you did when you were young, how good you were, how hard you worked, your stinking parents and their place in society pulled you back down to this toilet of a neighborhood. The crabs in the bucket pull you back in. That's just how it goes. Many good, quiet kids in elementary school became roaring tyrants and drug fiends in high school. Many more fell off the back of the truck after high school. Some waited and went to college to learn how to be alcoholics. But we're all the same. Whether you got a star on your English paper or you knocked a kid out. Whether you did drugs now or later. It seemed like the whole town was programmed for sameness.

Some got out through the years. A pop star from the 80s. A couple of television actors. A famous hockey player. None of them ever looked back. Others moved away, but they're all scarred. Forever branded. Don't drink the water there, or eat the food, or breathe the air. This town is diseased. There's a coldness there. Such a darkness too— dark like a cave.

29

WE WERE CALLED THE "GENERALS" yet we were the majority. The top ten percent were the only ones worth teaching to, maybe because they could be controlled easier. As long as we passed with Ds or dropped out, the administrator's numbers wouldn't be affected. We were left to fend for ourselves, and success only meant staying out of jail or off drugs. Our educations didn't matter. We didn't matter.

Our high school was built around divisions and had a tracking system of classification. If you were poor and fell into the lower end of the tracking system, the generals, you had it the worst with all the bullies and misfits running the halls and ruining the classrooms. Generals were situated in the back end of the school with access to more doors leading out to the parking lot— practically pushed out those doors.

The Regents population located in the middle section of the school was probably half okay and half screwed up. Regents graduates either went straight to state college or straight to the dumping grounds of American mediocrity to spend the rest of their life recovering from post-high-school-loss-of-popularity-depression.

The kids in the very small honors population positioned right at the front of the building were the only ones who had high hopes. They were the only ones set to go to college, even helped with their applications by teachers, usually the best teachers.

We were the poor, the disadvantaged from broken homes, or the ones with just one bad test score, which is what originally landed me in the general population. After succumbing to one bad state test score in math at the end of elementary school, the trajectory was set. I was ruined.

Math sank my ship. One bad math teacher in third grade was a domino effect and I never caught up, even despite being in the top ninety-seventh percentile of reading and writing skills— but it didn't matter if I was a prodigy of language, the number scores are what mattered most, even more than getting me the help I needed.

Numbers weren't my thing. They made me feel dizzy. As far back as second grade, I can remember struggling and using flash cards. After I got the multiplication tables down, it was on to a battle over division. By the time I got to high school math, it was all just was a crapshoot. It was strange that I never did well with numbers because I love to figure things out. I even like to work out budgets. I love science, which sometimes relies on math. I like to look at percentages and graphs and charts. But as soon as you ask me to do something with numbers that seem disconnected from my real world, I'm lost.

I had a math teacher who flew through lessons and I couldn't keep up. It got to the point where I just skipped class. This didn't make for a good grade on the exam. My math deficiencies grew as time went on. My English teacher wouldn't even teach. He sat there with a newspaper, as did several other teachers throughout my time in high school. I guess they thought why bother with kids who are already so far behind and don't care. It was like having a substitute teacher every day. Yet I sometimes mysteriously passed the classes.

We were from this bottom class, yet some kids discriminated just as much as those on the school board and administration, just as much as those "best" teachers who didn't want the bad kids because they couldn't learn, and just as much as those cranky old folks in the community who voted down our budget on several occasions because they didn't want to invest in public education. I heard this kind of crap all the time:

"What are you a fuckin' faggot?"

"Niggers are crack heads!"

"Cheap Jews."

"Girls are whores."

The rotten language went on and on. Maybe the school officials were looking to protect the other kids from bigots, but not all generals were hateful.

Gene had his moments.

One day he even went off, "those spics are…"

"Wait a minute, aren't you…?" I asked.

"No, man, it's different."

Gene seemed to have a problem with everyone now that we were in high school. Had he forgotten the way others had treated him for looking different when he moved to our town? Did he forget that he wasn't German or Irish, or enough Italian to be considered Italian? I wondered if maybe this was just his way of venting by projecting how he felt about himself. My friend of misery.

I tried to distance myself.

Terrible behaviors were deeply ingrained in the psyche of the town. It was all passed on generation to generation. To think, such division right in the backyard of the most diverse place in the world. There was still pent up tension from the city neighborhoods in the 50s. Even my own family members didn't have high regard for others.

"Don't go that way; that's a Negro neighborhood," my Aunt Judy would say as we drove through the city on our way back to the island.

All these surrounding sentiments made me more afraid than anything else. We were told: Stay away from black towns. You'll get robbed and beat up. Watch out for gays. They'll sodomize you and bend you over. Beware of women. They'll steal your soul.

Despite my fears, I felt a connection to the blacks in the next town over. I knew many were no different. Poor. Dysfunctional. Oppressed. Uneducated families. I too felt different, segregated, even enslaved, though I could never compare my suburban angst to the heritage of slavery or the generations who faced extreme adversity. If I was starting at home base, many of them were starting from the dug out, or even the parking lot.

In the locker room or on the street, I'd hear other kids accentuate those two words: nigger and faggot. It made me cringe sometimes, especially when there was a "fucking" in front of them, which made it all so angrier sounding. Did they have to use those words? Would they say them in public in front of a black or gay person?

It was as if the boys in my town were brought up with some cultish superstition to stay away from anyone who wasn't white, Italian, Irish, or German. Certainly don't let them know you're gay unless you want to be bullied until the end of time. Yet most of them wore crosses around their necks. If you questioned religion though, heads usually turned with disapproval, and then they quickly returned to sucking on a bong or beer.

Our town had been built by Germans and had a significant population of Germans and Italians with a lower segment of Jewish, Polish, and English, and hardly any Hispanics. We only had a few blacks in our school and they mostly kept to themselves. One was a smart kid in the grade below me and the one in my grade was a jock, and I just never crossed paths with them. The people in the town next to us to the west were mostly Hispanic and the town to the north was all black. The town to the east was wealthier and white. We were the monkey in the middle. The segregated communities only added to the decades-long racial tension on Long Island.

Parents here named their kids after mobsters, either on purpose as a tribute or unknowingly just deciding on another standard Italian-American name. But what do you do with yourself when your full

name is also the name of a popular dead or imprisoned mafia gangster? Those parents were disabling their children from the get-go. It's
all funny there in your little town on your little island, but what do
they do if they want to go somewhere else in this world? They get
Godfather quotes thrown at them the rest of their life.

I remember one woman in a store telling me with a huff how I
didn't look Italian enough to be from there. She was tan with a big
nose and jet-black hair and she spoke in an unbelievable accent.

"Where ya from, honey?"

"What?"

"What neighbahood ya from?"

"Here."

She shook her head and took my dollar for the orange soda.

"The Germans a' tall and blond, and we Italians a' darka. Ya not
eitha."

"No, I'm actually Italian."

Even though my mother's side was Italian, I guess my lighter
brown hair made me look more like my father's side.

"Maybe a qawter. Ya one of the newbies."

"My mother's parents came over from Italy and Sicily. My family's
been in New York a while."

"Not this town though. Ya Irish too?"

"No, I'm French and English on my father's side."

"Dat explains it. I don't see too many of those."

She handed me my change.

"Don't sweat it, honey. Ya not one of those monkeys or chicos."

I walked out of the deli finished with the genealogy inquisition
wondering what line of questioning Gene would have received.

The first time Gene ever came to my house, my stepfather asked
who he was. Don warned, "That kid looks like trouble."

Why, because he has darker skin and thicker hair?

How does someone look like trouble?

Maybe Gene was just a confused kid reflecting the world, a world that mistreated him.

30

THE WORLD AFTER JANE was difficult at first. I had lost time, and kids my age were moving in new directions. But it was a new year in a new place.

I went to sign up for the track team. It had been so long and I wanted another shot. I had already regretted giving up my love of running for girls and smoking. Maybe I could redeem myself. I could give up the smokes and start over. I knew I still had it in me.

When I arrived at the gym I saw the crowd gathered around a clipboard on a table. On the other side of the table, Mr. Grahm, the anti-kissing junior high gym teacher, sat overseeing the high school sign ups. I went in and pulled aside a classmate.

"What happened to Coach Bissell?"

"Oh, he couldn't coach the fall team this year."

"Why not?"

"I don't know. It kind of sucks though. He was a lot cooler than Mr. Grahm."

"Yeah, you're telling me," I snarled as I exited the gym and walked on to my next class. I shouldn't have let him stand in my way, but I did. I didn't want to deal with the guy. Running was over, at least on the track.

One morning in September a gang of us left school to go party at a girl's house. Her name was Kara and she was in the grade below me. They broke out the liquor and weed at nine o'clock a.m. and before we knew it the house was an orgy of sex and drugs. Kara was suddenly stretched out naked on the living room table where we all licked ice cubes off her overly developed fifteen-year-old breasts and the rest of her voluptuous body. Before we knew it, she was in the bathroom with some kid, and then another, and there I was next on line. The door opened and I scurried in before someone else could push me out of the way.

"Hey, Kara. What's going on?"

I was surprised to see her now partially clothed and smiling.

"Having fun today?" she asked.

"I guess. What about you?"

"I am."

She pulled me close to her chest and drew me to her neck.

"I'm not going all the way with everyone. Just a little feel."

She felt around the front of my pants and unzipped me.

"You know I don't really want Nicky Ulrich to come in here."

I felt her lips.

"Just say you're done and they'll go away."

"Yeah, he just skeeves me out."

I felt her tongue.

"You do what you want," I told her as the banging on the door started in. This was obviously a merry go round and it was my turn to get off.

"Hey, they're not going to stop banging."

"Well..." she stood up and reached into her purse on the ledge, grabbed a pencil and paper, and starting writing. "I hope you'll call me."

I took her number and wondered if the others got her number.

"Ah, yeah, I will."

"Do me a favor? Tell them I'll be out in a little while."

"Sure thing."

I opened the door and the other kids were hungry and looking to get in, including Nicky Ulrich. I quickly closed the door behind me and heard the lock click from the inside.

"Hey, guys, sorry, show's over. Nothing going on in there anyway."

There was some hollering and complaining, but the line broke up and the kids went back to drinking and smoking. Most of us spent the morning in Kara's dining room drinking beer out of fancy china. An hour or so after the bathroom scenario, a few of us wondered where Kara was. One kid was suspicious that another boy was getting lucky with her. So we went to check it out. We couldn't find her anywhere in the house, but then someone noticed a door to the basement. We tiptoed down the stairs and when we got to the bottom we found her riding Louie on a chair. Any crazy chance that I'd call her was ruined upon seeing her jump off of Louie. He shouted for us to get out of there as they gathered up their clothes and retreated to a bedroom upstairs for privacy where apparently another boy joined them. Kara's friend Darlene, who was having sex in another room for a couple of hours, eventually came out looking like she had just run the treadmill at the gym. She was red and sweaty, and it was awkward for us. A year later she would be a teen mom.

By noon most of us departed. There was nothing else to do there. The house was sad. Kara had lost her father only a year before. Had he lived, I don't think she would have been holding a rite to passage ceremony for the boys. No one ever talked about that day after that, but I'm sure no one forgot it.

The rest of October was spent with some metal heads, smoking and selling them weed. Darrell Johnson was the main guy I hung around with. He had long brown hair and his scary looking older brother was in a hardcore band. His house was a creepy old haunted looking thing near the train station. His mother worked a lot and his father was absent. They had a pink-haired freaky looking younger sister too, whom they guarded and shielded from the world.

One of Darrell's friends was this big looming guy named Vick Hutter who reminded me of the Frankenstein monster. He miraculously had a hot girlfriend named Alyssa who he dragged around everywhere. She was constantly being scolded by him, grabbed by the wrists, yelled at, finger in the face. It was terrible. She was battered before she was even out of puberty.

Some girls my age were abused, both verbally and physically. Some of the girls seemed to like the verbal tough talk game. I don't know how many liked the sexual harassment though, like the slaps on the ass. Of course, none liked to be hit. Some girls dropped kids their age and went with older ones, some as old as their late twenties, which was both creepy and illegal, and sometimes this worked out better, but sometimes worse. The jock girls were in a better place though, at least until they sprouted out of their shells in their later years. I would hear all kinds of stories about prude and innocent Sofia doing this guy or that guy in between a line of coke at a city dance club. Maybe they were just stories, but I knew some had to be true. Occasionally there were girls like Alyssa, where it was apparent they were being manhandled.

Vick would sometimes show up without her, like when he knocked on my house door at seven on a Saturday morning looking for weed. I had been out the night before and groggily dragged myself down to get the door.

"What's the matter?"

"You got a twenty bag?"

"This early? You pulled me out of bed for this? And came to my house? Why didn't you wait and beep me later?"

"Sorry man, I needed it for today. We're going fishing. Wanna come?"

I went and got him the twenty bag, took the cash, and decided selling little baggies of pot was a nuisance. I would finish up my stock of pot and then spread the word around that I no longer sold. I had taken over while the star quarterback had gone back to his season and because quite frankly the paper route wasn't cutting it.

Later that day, I took the rest of my selling stock of ten-dollar baggies and went out to make the rounds. I visited all the main spots where kids hung out and unloaded my stock throughout the day. The weather had turned dark and I slipped into the local youth center for some shelter from the rain. Nirvana had just hit the airwaves and was playing in the background. There was Jeff as I stepped into the back room. He was spending a lot of time here at this point with new skater friends. It was great to see him. We joked around for a little while until another kid came over and asked to talk to me in private.

"You have any weed left? Some guy's outside asking if anyone has any?"

"Some guy? Does anyone know him?"

"No, I don't think so."

I went out to have a look myself. The man looked like he was in his late twenties. I went up to him. He said hello and shook my hand.

"Hey, you have some pot I could buy?"

"Oh, no. I don't. I was going to ask you the same thing, man. I heard some kid had some, but he left a while ago, don't know his name, don't know if he'll be back."

"Oh, okay. You sure?"

"Yeah, sorry, man. Good luck."

The man went off. My grip on the bag of pot in my pocket loosened. He was either a desperate adult with lost pot connections hoping to capture some nostalgia or he was a narc looking to wreck my life and shake me down for info to nab others. I had heard stories of undercover cops. I wasn't going to take a chance and destroy the rest of my life, especially on the day I decided to quit selling drugs. Someone would happily take over. There was no shortage of drug dealers in this town. I went back into the youth center and hung with Jeff for a little while longer before moving on to my next spot. By the end of the day I was free of the burden.

Of course, there had been another part of me that didn't want anything to do with customers like Vick Hutter. His treatment of Alyssa was disturbing and escalating to a dangerous place. Six months later, when the serious physical abuse started, her parents caught on and forbid him to go near their daughter. Shortly after, he took the family hostage with a huge butcher knife until a neighbor shot him in the leg and incapacitated him. We learned all of this via Channel Twelve News right in Gene's living room one afternoon. Ryan called us on the phone to tell us.

"Yo, you got to turn on the local news right away."

Our jaws dropped but we weren't surprised. Gene knew Vick too and had gotten into a scuffle with him over something stupid. We both celebrated that day. Abusive control freaks like Vick Hutter are never really liked by others. I was glad none of my close friends, even Gene with his secret pent up anger, never took part in anything close to this kind of crazy. Knowing a really bad person does put things in perspective. Upon hearing the news, we sparked up a joint and wished Alyssa and her family the best.

It seemed like I was back in the saddle after Jane, but the trail was rugged. My life went from friend to friend, crowd to crowd. I was searching for something. Just when I started to get close to someone, something about them scared me off. Maybe this was normal. Maybe Paul, Andy, Jeff, Steven, and Gene were all going through the same exact thing. Or maybe this was just the way I was handling high school, while Paul dated hot girls, Andy lost himself in hoops, Jeff hung with skaters, Steven became obsessed with football for half the year, and Gene got angry. Andy, Jeff, Steven, and Paul had these activities that kept them constructive. For Gene and me it was a shot in the dark.

31

RANDY MCKINNEY was "the driver" and we all somehow trusted him to get us through our highs alive. He'd roll up a joint or two and cruise around town all day in his white Camaro. His long straight hair reminded me of a Native American for some reason. I recall him telling us about his native heritage once, but we really didn't know much about the guy, other than he was two years older and a senior in high school. He was a metal head at heart but by the time I met him he had become a fan of rap. The first Cypress Hill album was a favorite in his car for some time. The album lyrics rapped of smoking bongs, packing a sawed-off shotgun, and fighting police as if these were everyday societal activities. Admittedly, I laughed at most of the lyrics, but there were also times when we were high and this album really took us to a cold place. Lyrics about killing people and having gunfights with law enforcement don't always make for a feel good mood.

Randy also had a sense of adventure. Going for drives to new places was something he loved to do. He loved to drive around the airport, which had a long circular road that seemed like a racetrack. There was a rhythm to his drives and when you were stoned out it seemed almost like you left the ground. The pumped up bass of the music rattled you and seemed to compete with your heartbeat. He drove around at frightening speeds, sometimes topping one hundred miles per hour, sometimes swerving in and out of traffic, even trees, yet he never got pulled over, never got a ticket, never got into an accident. We probably should've been dead or arrested.

I met Randy on a cold rainy day in November through a friend named Armando, who was one of the younger drug dealers my age, but from the next town over. We were looking to score some pot and Armando's regular source dried up that week.

"I know the perfect guy to help us. You're going to dig him."

Randy pulled up in his white Camaro, opened the passenger door, and waved us in.

"Come on, let's go get banged out," he said.

Randy would drive us around and we would contribute some cash. We spent our days driving around, picking up different people, taking them on a high ride, and then depositing them for another round of subjects. I brought Steven and Gene into the rides, but on different occasions, since they didn't mesh so well.

There were a couple of times Randy had ditched his car to steal another with Armando. They would steal another Camaro or a Firebird and beat it up for an hour or two and then abandon it on the side of the road. I felt uneasy about those days and ducked out early.

There were some days where I would be the shotgun passenger in the front, or "co-captain" as we called it. This person usually stayed around for longer intervals and watched several people come and go from the back seat. Armando was a co-captain for a while. After a while, I didn't see him again. He went on doing his thing in his own town. Co-captains came and went. That's just how these circles worked.

Randy would eventually clean house at some point in the day and break the news that he had to go home or go to work. His home life and work place was a mystery. We also never saw the guy get gas, which was puzzling. An eight cylinder American sports car racing around town, even exploring other towns, yet he never ran out of gas? And with all the traffic in and out of his car and all the pot smoking, the car always remained so fresh and clean with a whiff of vanilla in the air. It also seemed like Randy rarely went to class, yet he graduated on time in June. I couldn't imagine this work ethic lasting into the real world though.

Ricky Sharpe and I met up again through Randy McKinney. Although it had only been around a year, we were both already a world away from our days in football.

Randy pulled up to a corner and put it in park.

"You want to go test drive a new car?"

"Yeah, sure, why not? Can you?" I asked.

"Yeah, hold on here, guys. I'll be right back."

Randy walked across the street and up the block to the main highway to the dealership. He had us wait in his car around the corner and then picked us up in the borrowed car about ten minutes later. Why and how a dealership just let a kid with long hair and bloodshot eyes take a brand new car was beyond me, but I didn't ask any questions. There we were speeding around in a new shiny black Camaro for over an hour, though it felt like hours. He beat the shit out of the car, spinning the tires, doing donuts in a lot, and power breaking. We stopped in the middle of our trip to smoke a blunt behind some shrubs on the side of the road and then to take a piss at Ricky's house. We went in the back door and his mother was home when we went in. She stunk like vodka and it was 11:30 in the morning. The bottle sat on the kitchen counter. She said hello.

"What are you doing out of school so soon, Ricky?"

"Oh, we're just out for lunch, ma."

"You boys be good now."

We made our way through his house to a hallway. We took turns in the bathroom. Ricky shouted goodbye to his mother and she returned the goodbye. On our way out the front door, we heard a door from the top of the stairs open.

"Ricky!"

"Yeah?"

"You take that fuckin' garbage out?"

"Yeah, what the fuck?"

"You giving me an attitude?"

"No, Dustin."

"Then I better not hear it in your voice."

"All right, sorry."

"Get the fuck out of here!"

Randy and I looked at each other with disbelief. This was Ricky's older brother, who in his late twenties still lived at home upstairs from his mother and younger brother. The guy was a loser and a bully, perhaps the source of some of Ricky's angst. I might not have been the best older brother, but I never ordered around my little brother like a master.

Randy drove us back to the dealer, left us at his car, returned it and then walked back to get us. I remember sitting there with Ricky silently waiting for Randy to return and not wanting to bring up his brother. He was irritated and rambled aggressively about fighting, "fuck this one, fuck that one, fuck the police." The anger just boiled inside of him. Ricky made Gene look like a lightweight in comparison, a real angel.

Randy returned and we got in and drove off. The next time I'd see Ricky, he'd be my enemy, on the wrong side making war with others, and on a road to self-destruction.

32

MOST KIDS ENVIED him. Vinnie had it all for a guy only in high school. He drove a shiny black BMW and had the best clothes money could buy. He had money, or at least his parents did, which meant he did too for the time being. Vinnie was also a wresting champion and one of the school's toughest. No one dared to mess with him. Appearance was not a problem in Vinnie's life either. His tall, slender but shredded-build, dark eyes and keen smile stole many of the girl's hearts away. The guy seemed to have it all.

Vinnie the wrestler approached me one day on my walk home from school. I was surprised at the time, maybe even scared, because seniors didn't normally talk to freshmen. By the way he had called me over to him I could tell it was non-threatening though.

"Hey," he said.

"Hey, you're Vinnie right?" I replied.

"Yup that's me, you've heard of me."

He asked me my name and I introduced myself.

"How are those freshmen girls?" he asked with curiosity.

"Oh, they're alright, but it's the girls in your grade who are the best. The ones in junior high are something to look forward to next year too."

Vinnie laughed his head off,

"Looking ahead are ya, Jack? You got the right attitude."

"Hey, do you wrestle?" he then asked.

"No, I used to in junior high; now I just go to the gym."

I tried out wrestling, but I quit it to take martial arts. I quit that too.

"Cool, maybe I'll see you in there after the season is over with. Hey, you should go to the meet this Friday night," he suggested.

"Yeah, that would be cool."

"All right, I'll see you around," he said patting me on the shoulder.

"Ok, it was cool meeting you man, good luck Friday."

Friday night I went to Vinnie's wrestling meet. Andy was shocked when Vinnie flashed me a wave as he stepped out onto the mat.

"You know that guy?"

"Yeah, he's from my new neighborhood."

Vinnie's opponent resembled a rag doll. Back and forth he threw the poor victim about. Vinnie lifted his enemy way up in the air and then crushed him to the mat. I had never seen such a display of power.

The entire team that year was brutally good with several county and state champions. Rumor had it half the team was doing speed or steroids, but maybe they were just naturally crazy. Ric was a state champion. He would scoop guys up and toss them off the mat. A short stocky kid named Mitch was tough as hell too. He'd shoot for his opponent's leg, tuck it in, and then lift them high into the air just before slamming them to the mat. Since these guys were all different weight classes, it was hard to tell who was the best. A good six of them were near undefeated that year, and it seemed wrong that most of them didn't even bother to go to college.

From that night on Vinnie would nod his head to me in the hallway at school with a wide smile. Once in a while I would be standing with a group of friends and he'd stop to squeeze my bicep with a grin.

"Nice work, Jack!" he would always say.

It seemed my high school network was widening, but as my popularity increased I felt more and more drained. The more people who surrounded me the lonelier I felt. Did I even want to know all these people? Especially these particular people? And why did some of them want to know me?

I was a big jerk for a few months after Jane. I would start dating a girl and then suddenly disappear on her or stop calling. I realized the thrill of the chase was the part I enjoyed the most. Some of them were great girls too. Smart ones. Pretty ones. Sexy ones. Older ones. Younger ones.

The one that stung the most was a younger girl named Nancy. I would go down to the middle school to pick her up like I was some kind of serious long term boyfriend like the older guys I saw picking up the hot girls in my grade. I'd go to her house when she would stay home sick and her mother was out. We kissed, touched a little, and stared at each other for hours on the living room couch. She was so clean and smelled so fresh. She was a great student, smart and creative. She was sweet and soft-spoken. Innocent. Full of goodness. Really seemed to care about getting to know me. But I was just some hot-shot, done and bored after a few weeks. She was a goldmine and there I was closing up the passage. What a loss. I wasn't ready. I didn't feel worthy. I was still hurting.

33

EVERYTHING was in slow motion. My vision was blurred as I plucked my legs out of the back of the Camaro. I marched like a battery operated robot running out of juice. I wobbled in the back door. Everyone was asleep. I carried myself, even seemed to float through the dark of the kitchen and living room. I was the Tin Man with rusty parts. While my joints creaked and muscles shivered, my mind raced. I was stuck in this dichotomy world of slow distorted movement versus fast night-train-paced thinking. The voices swirled around my head like a whirlpool. I climbed the staircase, my face inches from the carpet. Step by step, I pulled myself up like a thirst-deprived rock climber in the desert. I clawed my way into my bed like a drunk. Except I wasn't drunk. I was ripped high on PCP, otherwise known as angel dust—or animal trank—or aurora borealis—or DOA. Whatever you want to call it. It was the only time I ever did it. I would've known because no one forgets it. I didn't mean to do it, of course.

Randy had picked me up for one of our ritualistic drives. Steven was with him and apparently had just joined him because his hair was still wet. We were all ready for a Friday night. The night air was fresh. The vanilla air freshener was fresh. The gas was full. Just the three of us out on a journey. The plan was to find some action— friends, girls, more drugs, whatever we came across. It was nine o'clock and we set out for a ride.

Once out on the highway, Randy sparked a joint, took a hit, and then passed it to Steven. My old friend worked on it a little and then passed it back to me. This time was different. The taste was a little off. I still tasted marijuana. I still smelled marijuana. But this joint had a different smell, a little like burning plastic, burning skin, burning metal after a flaming car wreck. We smoked it and passed it back and forth, as Randy took us north to Sweet Hollow Road. This was a local Long Island site loaded with urban legends about hauntings from a white lady ghost named Mary and the ghosts of children who supposedly died in a bus crash. Then there was the ghost of a police officer who pulled you over, asked you where you were going, and then returned to his car. If you were brave enough to watch him return to his car you supposedly saw the shotgun blast in his back. Another legend claimed an old closed down insane asylum rested up on a hill and if you broke down or stopped, you'd be captured and confined there by the lunatics, or ghosts of lunatics. Of course, the 2.2 miles of winding dark road is merely a residential neighborhood lined with trees and a county park bordering on two main highways and Walt Whitman High School. You would see all of this normality if you drove through it during the day. But at night this place crept out generations of kids. It didn't help when they were on drugs. It really didn't help to be on this sinister drug.

As we crossed the intersection of Old Country Road and made our way onto Sweet Hollow Road, Randy joked that the lunatics were coming for us. Steven reassured us that we'd be ok.

"We'll just shoot them," Steven said casually.

After a minute of silence, I asked.

"What did you say?"

"We'll shoot them," he repeated.

"How? With what?"

"With my gun."

"He doesn't have a gun," chimed in Randy.

"Yes, I do. Look, I'll take it out."

"No, no," I screamed. "Put it away. Put the gun away."

I seemed to panic at the thought of having a weapon in the car.

"Hide it. Don't use it. Keep it away," I pleaded.

"All right, all right, all right," Steven answered.

"Promise me."

"All right, I promise."

I had grown hysterical and paranoid. In the midst of this madness, Randy stopped the car just on the other side of the bridge underneath the Northern State Parkway.

"You know, they say three boys committed suicide by hanging themselves off this overpass," Randy said.

The number occurred to me and I was freaked out.

"That's fucked up, Randy. There are three of us tonight," I said.

"It's bullshit," Steven said. "Another myth."

"They say you can see the three bodies hanging sometimes," Randy said.

"Then let's get the hell out of here," I suggested.

"What was in this shit tonight?" Steven asked.

"I think the guy laced it with dust," Randy said.

"Dust?" I asked.

"Yeah, PCP, it's weird stuff, right?" Randy said.

"That's screwed up. What guy? Did you know?" asked Steven.

"No man, I had no idea. Just hold on," he said and hit the gas.

I think Steven was a little mad at him, but brushed it off to live in the moment. That's what he always seemed to do. I wasn't any different tonight. I didn't know what to think.

On every twist and turn of the road, I grimaced at the sight of an oak tree coming at me. The ride was a rollercoaster. Streaming colored lights raced past us. My eyes bulged. My forehead was sweaty. My mouth was dry as a desert. We reached the end of the road and I was relieved, but only for a moment. Upon exiting the dark winding road, I realized the road emptied out onto a busy lit up highway. Now we needed to get through this. Randy turned onto Jericho Turnpike and picked up speed. He miraculously swerved in and out of traffic as usual. We went several miles before turning onto the big lit up route 231 drag. This was the highway where all the kids (and some odd adults) would cruise and tailgate in parking lots facing the road as if they were on display like a product in a store for a lover or fighter to come bite into. We wouldn't be setting up shop like these folks, but we certainly needed a rest area.

Randy pulled into a parking lot in front of a small strip of dark stores closed for the night. A big red sign with a scary man's face was staring at us. We pulled into an open spot right between two parked cars. Randy killed the ignition, slipped his seat back, and jammed the door locked with the back of his hand. I had never seen it until now. The man had met his limit. Randy actually appeared incapacitated to drive. The drugs had kicked in. Steven was banged out in the passenger seat groaning, too high to move, let alone lock his door. I sat in the back behind Steven trying to close my eyes and ignored the kids partying in the parking lot all around us. The blurry lights. The laughter. The strange looks. We must have looked like pathetic junkies. We must have been the laughing stock of the highway for a few minutes until they began to ignore us. The kids carried on with whatever they were busy with in their parking lot on a Friday night. No one around here seemed to have a purpose. High or not. Dusted or not.

After about what felt like twenty minutes of zoning out, Randy sat up, started the car, and said let's go. He was heading home. There was nothing left to do tonight. No strength left. We had lost our spirit by midnight. Who knows how long we had really sat in that parking lot— probably an hour. The drug had sapped our souls. I wondered if we would make it home safely.

"You ok?" I mumbled from the back.

"Yeah, we'll get there, I think" he answered.

Had he known about the dust? Had he done it himself? Probably not likely, but possible. How he drove us home is beyond me. He had a tolerance unlike anyone, yet even this night he was tested. The ride was a slow motion blur. He slowly and cautiously made his way back to our homes. It felt like Randy was dragging us home at twenty-five miles per hour. Steven was first on the way and then me.

We never talked about that night ever again. It was as if our lives were tainted and something had strangely been taken away.

34

AT A PARTY one night, a wasted Ricky Sharpe started a fight with me. First he talked smack about several other people who couldn't defend themselves. He suddenly remembered the incident at his house when I had tackled him and he slid under a car. He was riled up and challenged me. He looked infantile and aimless, but that's what made him dangerous. I was ready to have it, but Vinnie the wrestler stepped in and told the guy to get lost.

"Leave the party, get out of here, you dirtbag."

Vinnie waved him off and the kid listened to him, no questions asked. Party's over. Ricky had been ousted from the inner circle. Vinnie had beaten this guy just as bad as the opponents we had seen him beat out on the wrestling mat, but this time with even less effort and mere words.

This acquaintance had become someone to look up to, yet when Vinnie saw me on the street and asked me to come hang at his house I felt awkward and said I had to be somewhere. Vinnie would be going off to college in the fall, so I knew I couldn't rely on him as a bodyguard, but I still hoped his protective act had gained and not lost me some credibility. I thanked him and wished him the best.

The next time I saw Ricky was a few weeks later and I was leaving another party with Gene and a friend named Matt and he was on his way in. When he saw me his head dropped. Not a word, but his indifference towards others continued to build. He beat up a couple of kids with cheapshots when they weren't looking. He was down tying his shoes and then punched one kid out of nowhere. He bullied a few other kids in and after school and they usually just walked or ran away.

One day he picked a fight with the wrong person. No one even recalls what the reason was. Did he look at him the "wrong" way? Did he say something? It was doubtful that David Pace, the mellow and humble big guy in our grade, did anything to Ricky. But then again Ricky was ultra sensitive. Maybe he was just jealous of David's football success. It was Ricky who challenged David to a fight. David accepted and was not going be pushed around by this kid.

They faced each other out in the parking lot and a circle of us surrounded them to see the battle and to block people on the outside from seeing into the violence. David told him one last time,

"I've got no problem with you, but if you want to fight, let's do it."

"Yeah, well I got a problem with you," Ricky replied.

Maybe he was just trying to gain some credibility by beating the biggest kid in our grade. That wouldn't happen though.

Ricky threw the first punch. David just stood there and stared at him. Ricky threw another one. Nothing. David shook his head and threw a cluster of rock solid fists at Ricky. The kid fell backwards, but then came back for more. David cracked him again and Ricky lost his balance and fell over. The kid still got up and went for David again. David picked him up and slammed him on the ground. Ricky tried to get back up for more, so David got on top of him and pummeled him a couple of more times.

"I don't want to fight you. Are you done yet?" David asked.

"No, fuck you."

David hit him again a few times.

"Are you done?"

Ricky shook his head from side to side and still struggled to get up. David punched him three more times. That had to be it.

"Are we finished?"

Ricky managed to whisper a yeah. That was it. The humble big guy had done the job. The villain, who had picked on and even ambushed so many others, had been beaten. It really had been a battle of good and bad. I quietly celebrated the justice.

About a month later Ricky got up his confidence again and challenged a new Latino kid named Jose. This was a disaster too. Jose proved to be far tougher than anyone had expected. Their cafeteria fistfight was nasty and Ricky was bloodied up bad. This was no way to redeem yourself after losing to the toughest guy in the grade. Ricky dropped out not long after the fight with Jose. His suspensions had been excessive and he was already a year behind with barely any credits. He graduated to a darker world.

His first arrest was for beating up his girlfriend. She was just another person to take it out on. Everybody had heard about how she had been bruised up by Ricky, but we didn't know whether she or a close friend had called the police. She was just too good for him. She couldn't be dragged into his world. Once everyone saw her black-eye, there was no way Ricky was going to show his sorry face around town. The few degenerates who still associated with him were on their way down too.

One stupid brother, an absent father, and maybe a few other screwed up adults had made him this way. They had shaped him and trained him to hate himself and the world around him. But if you want to survive you learn to rebel from the cycle, be different from those who made you. I guess some kids are just too out of control though. I wondered if he had ever had a chance at all.

35

ONE NIGHT Corey Hall took us for a ride. Gene and I joined Randy and Corey in his father's Buick. Corey was our age but had dropped out at fourteen to be a mechanic. The problem was he couldn't hold a job. Drugs had this kid by the balls and he ended up working on junked cars out of his father's driveway. At this point, he was trying to just stick with weed. So we all chipped in and took a ride to Bushwick and picked up a bag. Corey pulled over and Randy and I got out and walked down three steps to a big metal door. He knocked three times and after about a minute a slot opened in the door. Dark eyes appeared. A Jamaican accent asked us what we wanted. We slipped twenty-five dollars in the slot and ordered Chocolate Thai marijuana, which has a choco-smokey taste and smooth high. Two minutes later, a packed out bag was pushed out the slot and we were on our way. Back in the car Randy rolled up a few dubes.

This was an anomaly for Randy to be out of his car, out of the driver's seat. It was the only time I ever hung with him in this situation. Later on, he'd make this a habit— maybe he was tired of driving, maybe something happened, maybe it was the dust, maybe he wanted to drink. But tonight he would end up back in the driver's seat. Once we were all rolled up, Corey hit the road and we sparked up the joints. We had two lit and going all at once with the windows up. Just when you got done with one, another one was passed your way. In no time we were all stoned out and Corey was back on the highway crossing bridges, weaving in and out traffic, and leaving New York. By the time we all realized what was happening, we were nearing Stamford.

"What the fuck!" we all said as a sign welcomed us to Connecticut.

"I'm so tired of my life, guys. I just want to get out of here for awhile," Corey said.

He was driving very fast and crying.

"Whoa, man. You got to get this car back by one or your dad's going to flip and put you back in rehab," Randy reminded him.

"Don't take me out of New York, man. Let's head back home," said Gene.

"I just hate this shit," Corey said starting to moan.

The car started to swerve. My side of the car came close to the guardrail.

"I hate my life," he cried.

"Pull over dude. Let me drive us home," suggested Randy. "I'll get us back all right."

Corey finally broke, pulled off an exit, rolled into a gas station, and got out. He pulled at his hair and screamed at the sky.

"The last time they put him in rehab was for stealing the gold crucifix over his mother's bed. He sold it for crack," Randy informed us just before getting out to make the switch to the driver's seat.

"What was his mother doing with a gold crucifix over her bed?" I asked and Gene and I laughed.

Randy got in the driver's seat and Corey managed to calm down in the passenger seat. I think he even fell asleep at one point as Randy sped home. The bass in the music carried us home, as I gripped the seat and watched the lights go by. We made it back to Long Island from Connecticut in under an hour. Of course, we zoomed in and out of traffic like in the movies. This was the Randy I knew, not the dusted out one who barely got us home a few weeks earlier. He seemed so cool and confident in what he was doing. We could've been killed for sure. We were lucky. He was lucky, perhaps. Randy once again returned us safely and got Corey home on time. I never saw Corey again after that. Another face that disappeared. He either cleaned himself up or fell off the deep end, though I'm pretty sure it was the latter. That's just what happened to a lot of kids around there.

36

NO ONE VISITED YOU in the suspension room once you were in the upper grades. In junior high, my history teacher, Mrs. Ravitch, called me out into the hallway.

"Sweetie Jack, what happened?"

"I don't know. Nothing really."

"Well, you wouldn't have been suspended then."

"It was stupid. Some other kids went out to smoke. I just happened to be there."

"You weren't smoking?"

"No, but Mr. Bundy accused me of smoking. Then when I tried to tell him why I was out there he told me I was being insubordinate. I hate that word, insubordinate. I might as well have been smoking"

"So what were you doing out there?"

"I just wanted some fresh air. The field is nice in October."

"Yes, it's a beautiful month and I think you should be allowed fresh air whenever you need it, but you know we have to do what we need to. Oh, sweet Jack."

"Thanks for visiting."

"Now don't break any hearts today, ok?"

"All right."

Mrs. Ravitch patted me on the back and led me back into the suspension room. That was middle school. Mrs. Ravitch stayed behind in the middle school. Mr. Bundy unfortunately followed. In fact, he followed our class almost every year except for two grades where we had Mr. Panzram and Mr. O'Connor.

Nicky Ulrich was one kid teachers didn't care whether he disappeared and never came back to their class. I can't blame them entirely. His disorderly behavior and a crippling emotional disability with aggressive "acting out" made him a difficult kid to deal with. While most of his aggression was self-destructive, Nicky was known to initiate fights with other kids, and get quite verbally abusive with female peers. This made him difficult for us to deal with too, but he never started in with me. I had let him stay the night a couple of times when he couldn't go back to a bad situation at home. His life made me feel better about mine, for sure. He was clingy though; I had to shake him after a while because the kid was needy.

Nicky's suspension resume included numerous in-school suspensions for disrupting classes. He was known for throwing items at teachers, bothering other students, and cutting class (often a relief for his teachers). His out-of-school suspension record included numerous suspensions for excessive class cutting, missing detentions, and physical conflicts with teachers and students. These out of school suspensions were also a relief for faculty.

Nicky's truancy was certainly not so he could stay home with an abusive stepfather, or an alcoholic mother. Nicky's escape from school was an escape into the streets or to a friend's house where he was free from his parents but also free from the expectations that school put on him. Already having indulged in alcohol, LSD, and prescription drugs, Nicky's drift from education only pushed him a step closer to being addicted to harder street drugs, and ultimately a life of crime and prison. Nicky's offenses began to pile up, so when he started a riot of chair throwing in the suspension room that day, it was the last straw for the school district. Chairs, blood, screaming— it was a horror show. I ducked out fast and didn't want anything to do with that prison practice— what I considered a warm up for the big time. I wouldn't see Nicky Ulrich ever again. It's like he vanished off the face of the Earth, like so many others.

I was nothing like some of these kids. I just wanted to be left alone. My offenses were for not being there in class. Isn't that better than being there and causing a problem? There was a world of a difference between the two types of school trouble. But the principals didn't see it that way. We were all just the hopeless generals.

One day I spotted Mr. Bundy in the convenience store in a daze in front of the snack shelf. He already had several packages in his hands and was deciding on one more treat to get his fix. Maybe it was emotional. Maybe it was pre-diabetes. But whatever it was, he wasn't a very happy healthy guy. He was rather grouchy, and I wondered if there had ever been a time when he was just a sensitive good-hearted teacher who later turned to the dark side when he became an assistant principal and got a nice raise. After all, he couldn't be a nice guy if he was going to play prison guard.

Of course, I heard once from a friend's parent who went to high school with him that he was the same old tough guy jock he had always been.

"He always had an attitude," she said.

And here he was always telling me about my bad attitude.

Mr. Bundy was one of the coaches of the varsity football team now, so the jocks kissed his ass— they had to. To him, I was just another dirtbag. He didn't give me the time of the day, even when I was doing good like during sophomore year when I tried to stay out of trouble. The jocks got a nod or a good morning. I got a cold stare that read "I'm watching you and waiting for your next screw up. And I know you'll do it."

37

I NEEDED TO WORK. I had delivered newspapers for a while in my neighborhood, but it was pennies. I grew tired of the early weekend mornings riding my bike in the rain and snow, and occasionally falling off and landing in the mud. It was embarrassing crap work. I couldn't go back to work for my stepfather because the tension was growing at home. Gerard had found a replacement and I couldn't ask him to fire another kid. And selling ten-dollar pot baggies out my backdoor was more of a hassle than anything else. I felt compelled to work. With no real allowance, or even lunch money on most days, I needed the basics. I should have been worrying about grades, or sports, or school activities, but I didn't have that home grounding. Work not only put money in my pocket, which made me feel independent and powerful, but it also gave me more of a purpose and kept me out of trouble.

My friends Matt and Syd worked at The Chicken Shack, a fast food fried chicken take-out joint on Main Street. Matt was a hard worker. Syd was a crazy guy. We had hung out for a couple of years, even boxed each other for fun on an icy Sunday morning in March. Just the two of us and our boxing gloves in the park across the street from my house. We were beaten and bloodied up to an official tie by the time a few others showed up to watch.

Matt and Syd had worked there for several years, but Syd was leaving. He needed out. He didn't say why at the time, but he encouraged me to take his spot. I later found out the coke was getting to him. Emotional drug-induced outbursts that led him to piss in the mashed potatoes were only going to get him fired and sued. I took his spot, minus the coke and piss.

Matt sent me in and I applied for Syd's job. A quiet laid-back guy named Kenny hired me. He warned me of the other two owners and their wild approaches to management.

I was lucky to get a third-tier position. Matt was a hard worker and had a second-tier position for more pay and responsibilities. A quiet older kid named Wally was a first-tier, the only one at that level and a step away from becoming the manager and co-owner of a new store. There was a fourth-tier below me and they did the shit work.

My job consisted of cutting the birds and preparing them for cooking. The first part of my job was to prepare the chickens, which would come defeathered, headless, and ice cold in boxes of a dozen. Matt showed me how. He stuck his hand inside the chicken and pulled out the lump of stored fat.

"Technically, we're supposed to wash each bird, but come on, we don't have time for that," he explained. "You want to get into a groove here and knock out as many boxes as you can."

Matt spread the bird on the cutting board and clipped off the stubby tail to begin the process. Next he cut right down the middle from the top splitting the bird into two. Then he chopped the wing followed by the thigh of one half and then the other. He did this all under eight seconds. His rapid cutting got him cut a few times, but luckily he held onto all his fingers. If it meant I was going to go a little slower, I wasn't going to risk injury.

I tried my first chicken and cut the bird down the middle. Then I whacked off the wing. The leg always required a good strong chop; if you were weak the first time you'd have to give another chop and that took off an extra couple of seconds. Next I repeated the same process to the other side of the icy bird.

"Nice one," Matt said. I felt ready.

"For skinless," he explained, "You need to rip the skin down when you separate the bird in half. Just pull it from top to bottom and peel it off like a girl's underwear."

He demonstrated with a new bird. Skinless was a "healthier" option for customers, but we made only one tray of skinless to every ten regular. I tried one out and stuck my fingers into the grooved edge along the top of the bird and peeled the skin from the top right down to the bottom. I just did what I did and didn't think much about it.

"You're a madman," Matt said.

When we were done cutting and had enough bird parts to fill a metal tray, we did the breading. We filled the metal trays with cheap breading. Then we buried each chicken part in it until each one was thoroughly covered. We stored the finished trays of breaded chicken in an ice locker. When the staff cooking that night needed new chicken to dump in the deep fryer, they called on the support staff in the back room to deliver one of those fresh trays.

For the second half of the night, we either went up front to cook or we stayed in the back as support. The back room support had its advantages. There wasn't as much pressure back there and customers weren't watching us as they waited for their take out. I could sometimes slip out for a smoke, but was careful not to get caught by one of the owners, one of which was always on shift. Kenny only worked once a week on Thursdays and every other Sunday. Mario, the eldest and most powerful of the three owners, worked two to three days. He was a serious tough guy with an attitude. When he was on shift we just kept quiet and worked as fast as possible. Most of my shifts were managed by the third and newest owner, Phil Scarpa.

Phil would slip off to the bathroom, lock himself away for ten minutes, and then come out racing around like a lunatic. Everything went into high speed. Chickens were cooked, orders were packaged up, customers were rung up and sent on their way. He'd yell orders while shaking all the baskets, checking all the ovens, bagging a few orders, it seemed all at once in a rapid succession of movements. He barked orders and got snappy at everyone else for not being able to keep up with his coke induced pace.

It didn't take me long to figure out Phil. He was a thirty-two-year old man with an Elvis Presley haircut working in a fast food chicken joint, unmarried, still living with his mother, no real future to speak of, and a nasty cocaine habit, yet he talked down to people like they were peasants. As long as we worked there, we were in his world. This was his stage.

I got Gene a much-needed job. It was a fourth-tier position, but it was independence from his father, and it was better than scrounging off of me. His bad attitude didn't mix well with Phil though. He quit after only a couple of weeks and said the job was too messy.

"Messier than the job you don't have somewhere else?" I asked.

"Dude, the place is gross and they had me throwing boxes out in the bee infested dumpster. I'm not going to get stung by a swarm of bees for a couple of hundred dollars a week."

So he had a point. I couldn't blame him. If he didn't need to work in high school, then why do it? I had the need though. If I wanted new clothes or spending money, if I wanted to save for a car, or most importantly feed myself, it was going to be up to me.

I bumped into Armando and got him Gene's vacant spot. He was finally looking for honest work, but he endured all kinds of racist jokes for months. Phil would sing and dance and call him Rico Suave. Armando lasted about four months before he blew his cool and quit. I couldn't blame him. Back to selling drugs and crime, but no one could say he didn't try.

The fourth tier guys like Armando cleaned up after me. The excess chicken fat, the slimy skin, the stubby tails. Some kids couldn't hack this job after an hour. One kid severed a finger cleaning a cleaver on his first night, maybe even on purpose as an exit. One guy slid on grease and smacked his head on the table. Others threw down their aprons in disgust.

One chubby boy with what seemed like a British accent got sick at the sight of the chickens and kept crying to go home. He was hired to work the back and it was a bloody disaster. The boy kept slipping on the back room floor, which got very slippery with fat and slimy juices from the chicken and oil. You needed good balance to do well back there and this kid kept going down, flat on his back, under the sink, into a pile of boxes. On his first and last day, he fell so hard he whacked his head. He wobbled to his feet and went and told Phil he was nauseous. Maybe he was, but Phil ragged on him for the whole half hour as he waited for his mother to come pick him up.

"I'm nauseous...I'm going to vomit. I think I should go home."

"Keep working, you pansy. We need you tonight," answered Phil.

The boy's mother came down the next day to yell at Phil.

"You made my Chrissy cry and wouldn't let him come home."

"Let him? He could've walked out. No one had him tied down, lady."

"I feel nauseous. I need to go home," Phil kept saying in a fake British accent mocking the boy. He mocked the lady and imitated her complaints for weeks. "You made my Chrissy cry." Confrontations like this were funny, but they put Phil in a rambunctious mood.

Phil was often everywhere all at once. From the front room he'd race to the back room. He'd be harassing the cashiers otherwise known as "counter girls" and then in the next moment he'd be harassing you in the back room. There wasn't a person who escaped his verbal abuse. Even customers got it. One customer was talking to Phil one day about some random thing he cared nothing about and there he was motioning a jerk off to us behind the guy's back. When the guy said goodbye, Phil responded with a loud, quick, jumbled,

"All-right-have-a-good-night-all-right-you-fuckin'-asshole-great-see-you-soon."

Another customer was saying goodbye and Phil pulled the same thing.

"All-right-fuckin'-asshole-see-you-later-dick."

How did these folks not hear what he was saying? Were they just in denial that an adult business owner could say such outlandish things to innocent, friendly, paying customers? It was hilarious when it wasn't being done to us.

He never really disrespected me; just some jokes here and there. If I was working fast, he'd joke in a loud yell, "Easy, my man!!" If I asked for a favor or my nightly meal, he'd joke, "Easy there." He'd poke fun at my shaved head and said I looked like Robert Deniro in Taxi Driver. "You lookin' at me?" I inherited a funny nickname "Billy Jack" because he said I also reminded him of the title character in the film Billy Jack— about a rebellious good guy fighting for justice up against adversity in a tragic situation. The comparison was an unusual compliment coming from Phil.

But the counter girls— they got it bad. Counter girls came and went because if Phil wasn't sexually harassing them, he was telling the boys to. The verbal abuse sometimes escalated to physical abuse, all just natural fun and kicks according to Phil. He called them "counter hos" as he slapped them on their asses and plucked their bra straps. He and the boys coaxed one girl to strip down and sit on the back table. They told her to be sexy and so she did a few poses in different positions. Once she was completely naked they all laughed at her and sent her to the bathroom crying.

If you were Syd, your abuse was pure peer pressure. Do this to a counter girl. Do this to the stripper (occasionally hired by them and brought in the back room after closing). Do some shots with me. Do some coke with me. Go stick your penis in the mashed potatoes. It all got to be too much for Syd and of course there I was taking his spot and fighting to avoid the after-hours scene. "My girlfriend's waiting for me" was the perfect excuse. You can't argue with a guy who has a girlfriend waiting.

38

TIME AND SPACE froze all around me. It was like a surreal dream.

I remembered back to eighth grade when I was walking home down Main Street past the Catholic school, down the block from the junior high. Andy stopped me and pointed to a girl.

"Hey, that's Evan's girlfriend."

A girl in a Catholic school dress stood there laughing and talking with her girlfriends. She didn't see us, but I saw her. She had long straight brown hair and a smile that captured my heart. Something inside felt funny.

"No, they're not together anymore," Paul said.

"She's too good for him," I added.

She was fun and full of life. What a difference from most of the girls I had ever known. The scene was uncanny. But talking to her hadn't even crossed my mind. Even if I hadn't been with Jane at the time, I probably didn't have the guts to cross the other side of the fence and enter that other world of a Catholic schoolyard. The disbelief that Evan could get a girl like this was swept away by the disbelief that such a girl even existed in this town. So we carried on.

That was the first time I had ever seen Elizabeth. Here I was now, over a year later. In December of ninth grade, a mutual friend named Jon was over my house and brought up her name. Jon was the kind of cool kid no one had a problem with. He lived a few blocks from her. He asked me if I knew her.

"Yeah, Evan's ex?"

"Yeah, sort of, from like eighth grade," he said.

"I'm calling her right now. I swear you're going to marry this girl."

Jon called her, talked to her for a few minutes, handed me the phone, and then left. She and I talked for hours about all the same people we knew and began to discover all the moments we had missed meeting one another, being in all the same places at the wrong time. How she was bussed over to my elementary school for extra help on some days and actually sat with Steven in the learning center. How she knew the Kennedy brothers from the town beaches. How she briefly dated my old racing buddy Evan. How a friend of hers brought her over to the house of a girl named Jane and the girl talked about her wonderful boyfriend who had just left minutes before their arrival. And how I had walked into the Catholic school dance with Andy the month after breaking up with Jane only to be discovered and tossed out for not being a student only moments before Elizabeth arrived with her girlfriends. There were so many close calls, yet we had never met.

Elizabeth told me her school class schedule for January and I realized I had just switched into her social studies class because of a time conflict. Perfect fate.

On the first day back to school in January, I was talking to Armando outside during lunch. He had dropped by our school to visit and probably recruit some pot smokers, but I wasn't going to get smashed before meeting Elizabeth in social studies class that day. I was about to tell him to call me during the weekend and someone tapped us on the back.

"You two know each other?"

It was Elizabeth.

"You two know each other?" Armando repeated.

"You two know each other too?" I added.

"Armando's like an older brother, but I hope he's being good and not being a bad influence." She gave him a look.

"Come on, sis. Go easy on me. I think it's the other way around."

"Yeah, sure." I said laughing.

"We went to Catholic school together until he left for the other town."

"Oh, I see the connection, of course."

The pre-bell rang.

"Gotta go, Armando. Give me a buzz," I said.

"Will do," he said. "Nice seeing you, sis."

"Bye Armando," she said.

We turned and walked into school together for the first time.

"So we've finally met," I said.

"Now what?" she asked looking into my eyes with such an overwhelming stare.

She left me there in a moment trying to find the right words to say and there were none.

Ninth-grade social studies class is where we got to know each other a bit more. Our teacher did nothing but read the paper most days. The class was pandemonium. I sat behind Elizabeth stringing her long brown hair with my fingers. The flirting was monumental, but she played hard to get.

"Come on and be my girlfriend," I'd say on a daily basis for about two months.

"Maybe," she'd reply.

In the hallways I now felt like I saw her all the time, whereas before we met I don't think I had ever seen her in the halls. It was as if she just appeared from out of nowhere. I asked her if she was real, or just visiting? She'd laugh.

"When are you going to go out with me?"

"Someday," she'd reply.

Elizabeth and I also realized we were friends with some of the same girls. I had spent many days with Leela and her friends Heather and Marissa. It just so happened that they were friends with Elizabeth. They celebrated when they found out we had started talking. Friday nights at Leela's house brought us closer. We spent the rest of ninth grade pulling all-nighters and partying.

Leela always lit up the room. She was cheery and her face had a glow to it. Her older brother Jimmy was one of the funniest guys I ever met. He'd stop in and hang out with us and tell wild stories about escapades with his friends or his latest love disaster. Their divorced mother worked double shifts as a waitress at a local seafood restaurant and she was never home. She'd stop in to say hello and get a change of clothes before heading over to her boyfriend's place where she spent most of her time. The house was pretty much all Leela and Jimmy's. But they took good care of it.

Sometimes I brought along Steven, Andy, or Gene. We would bring beer or wine coolers we got from someone's older brother or sister. Some of us would smoke cigarettes until the place was fogged out. We'd be coughing and waving the smoke out of our faces. Leela would eventually open a window and we'd just drink more to ease our sore throats. It was a good time.

One night in May we all walked down to the local park by Leela's house. It was a beautiful night and summer was nearing. We climbed the monkey bars with our beers and wine coolers. We sat on swings and swung back and forth. We lay in the sand looking up at the starry sky. The childhood memories on a playground we all have. We were no different now, but adulthood was growing closer and something was slipping away.

At some point, Elizabeth and I took a walk out to the field under the stars.

"Tell me about your parents," she said. And so we sat on a log and I told her all about my mother and our years alone, and Don's arrival, and my introduction to a long lost father.

"Besides Jane, have you ever lost anyone you love?" she asked.

"My great aunt Gloria, my grandmother's sister. She died last year of lung cancer. She finally got to send me to nature camp during the summer before eighth grade. I hated it at first. It was in the middle of nowhere in the woods of North Carolina, and I felt like I was missing so much back at home."

"How long was it?"

"Two weeks."

Elizabeth laughed.

"Yeah, I know. But thinking back now, it was a great time. The first few nights were miserable, but then my camp counselor took us out on a nature walk. He called it a spirit walk. We saw all kinds of birds and critters, smelled all kinds of woodsy scents, and then when we were good and deep in the woods he lit a candle. We all made a wish and he blew it out. As corny as it sounds, it was life changing."

"That must have made Gloria feel good."

"Yes, I hope so. I don't know if she ever really knew how much I loved that experience. She was in and out of the hospital at the time."

"Well, I'm sure she did. She sounds like someone I would've really liked."

"Yes, you remind me of her a bit."

"How?"

"You're adventurous and mystical. What other girl would stay out all night with me in a park? Jeez, and here we are smoking cigarettes. Gloria smoked for twenty years and then quit for fifteen and the cancer still got her. We're going to need to quit this crap."

"I agree. It's a deal."

"What about you? What's your story?" I asked.

"Well, I'm a recovering former Catholic school girl."

"I know. Did the nuns get you?"

"Yes, almost, but I was too smart for them. They'd tell me to wash off the makeup and then it'd be back on ten minutes later. The socks were supposed to be up to my knees. Nope. There was something wrong with mine because they wouldn't stay up."

She cracked me up.

"So is that why you joined us this year in public school?"

"Yes, and no. My mother grew tired of the place and we just had too many bad experiences with them. My dad couldn't fight it anymore."

"Your family is actually still together? That's a rare thing these days around here."

"Yes. I have a mom and a dad— an older sister and three younger brothers. You're going to love them."

"I'm sure I will if they're anything like you."

After a while, we looked around and realized it had been a while since we saw the others. When we got back to the playground we found the others had moved on. We had been left alone.

39

CHANGES WERE HAPPENING. One day Randy picked me up to show me his new car. By now I had been spending much of my time with others and he had a new group of followers. I guess he couldn't entertain the same people all the time and expect the same thrill. Eventually, I imagined he ran out of willing participants altogether, at least our age.

Randy had changed. His long straight hair was short and spiky now eventually morphing into the trendy buzz cuts everyone else had. His white Camaro was now a fire red Pontiac Firebird. He was living the high life. He had given up paper joints for a metal pipe or glass bowl. On a few occasions, I bumped into him out with others. He was drunk in the passenger seat of someone else's car— an unusual place to see Randy McKinney.

That last day, Randy and I drove around for a little while, but it wouldn't be an hours long smoke fest like the old days. I took a few hits of a joint and then stopped. I felt satisfied.

"No, I'm cool, man," I said and waved off the joint. I knew he was wondering what was wrong with me.

Even though he didn't say it, his initial reaction was "What? Smoke some more. Come on." I could tell by the flash that went across his face.

That initial look turned to awkwardness and then to play it off cool— "Your choice, man. More for me."

By this point in time, Armando had dropped off the scene. We dropped by Steven's house, but he wasn't there. This disappointment coupled with my odd discomfort in his new car and melancholy for his old one soured the mood. That day was my first and only time in Randy's new car. We had both changed and we knew it. I never saw the guy again.

After the night on dust, Steven and I grew distant for a time. But this was normal. At least for us. We all circled around. For months we'd spend every weekend with the same best friend, and then suddenly it was on to a new one. Space... And then we'd return home to the same old childhood friends, the south shore boys: Andy, Jeff, Paul, Steven, and Gene. People like Randy disappeared, but we always found our way back around.

Steven and I found each other again at the end of ninth grade in one of our many cycles. We started our year together and there we were ending it.

In June, Leela threw several big parties at her house. We downed our beers and spent the night smoking pot and dozens of cigarettes. We were with mostly girls— Leela, Marissa, Heather, Angela, a few others, and of course Elizabeth. Steven didn't get involved with any of the single girls. Maybe they sensed his trouble. For me, this had been a year of losing love, doing drugs, selling drugs, buying drugs through a slot in a door in Bushwick, and then finding new love. Elizabeth wasn't happy with my drug use. To be honest, I too was feeling worn down by the partying. One night in early June, she challenged me,

"If you're not attached then flush it."

I opened the bag, let the green clumps fall to the water and then flushed the toilet. It was more of a symbolic action. I showed her, and myself, that I wasn't attached. I was free. I would go some time before I smoked again and it would never be the same. I was caught up in love.

When I met Elizabeth, a new world had opened up. She was full of mystery, excitement, and joy. Elizabeth's family was warm and welcoming. I stayed for dinner and celebrated holidays and birthdays. I didn't have this at home. They lived south of the highway near the water but on the other side of the canal opposite from where I grew up. This was the better side of town. It seemed like all the families on her block were still together, unlike my side of town where we all came from broken homes.

Things were really getting better for me. Steven was getting worse though and experimenting with new things I didn't want to be a part of. I was lucky Elizabeth came into my life when she had. I probably would've ended up in some bad place.

It seemed like those nights with her and all our friends at Leela's house would last forever. But they didn't. That summer Leela and Marissa decided to drop out of high school. They seemed to drop out of everything— gone from the world. They'd fall into new circles with some guys from the next town. Elizabeth and I took our own path— the way of a quiet couple looking for peace from wilder times. It was just as well. We would walk around town together and explore. We'd hang out at her house watching movies or sit by the bay watching the water.

In a party one night in early July before Leela and Marissa decided to end high school and not return to tenth grade, we all got together for what seemed like a final bash. We partied all night, first at Leela's, then out onto the streets. Elizabeth and I lost them at some point around four a.m. and ended up by ourselves, separated from the pack like we had a couple of months earlier, almost abandoned, but maybe saved. We walked back to the park across the street from my house and had a seat on a bench.

"Well, it looks like the scene is changing," she said.

"It's just you and me, babe."

"Maybe it's a good time to make some new resolutions."

"Like doing better in school and keeping our heads straight? Yeah, that sounds great. I'm tired of living this way,"

"Here's to a brand new year ahead," she said and fist bumped me.

"We're going to do great things together."

"I know it."

We had spent the morning kissing, talking, and laughing. The sun had risen. It seemed like we didn't have enough time to say all we wanted to say. At around seven o'clock I walked her to her friend Angela's house, her sleep-over alibi, where she would call her mother for a ride home. Angela opened the door.

"Elizabeth, you look like you just saw a ghost."

"Is that what it looks like?"

She kissed me goodbye and I walked home as the summer day began. It was Fourth of July, Independence Day, and we were free from something.

40

TENTH GRADE began. On the first day of school, I felt a tap on my shoulder. I turned around to see Mr. Panzram, the tenth-grade principal. Mr. Bundy only managed the ninth and eleventh grades, so I would now have to contend with Mr. Panzram. The man had a gray mustache and his Kojak head was so shiny you could see yourself on it.

He spoke in a slurred, nasally, and almost impeded manner. The man sounded drunk.

"I know your reputation. Don't think for a second you're going to give me any trouble. If you think otherwise you might as well drop out now."

"I'm really not a bad guy."

"Well, that's not what your reputation says and you certainly don't look innocent. Just watch yourself."

I nodded and walked on to class as I fought a growing pain inside my stomach. As the weeks progressed, and I tried to ignore Mr. Panzram's suspicious eyes in the hallway, I had also developed a stomach ailment. I didn't know where this trouble came from. Maybe my body was in shock. I wasn't smoking pot anymore and I was keeping my head clear. Someone once told me if you quit anything after doing it for a long time, your body reacts as if it were a fish out of water. Maybe that's all it was. Some days my stomach problems prevented me from even going to school. I'd get out the door and turn around.

On so many days my cramps were unbearable and I sat curled over at my desk in class. Many days I was in and out of the bathroom with the runs. The harsh pains in my stomach forced me to the nurse's bathroom, the only toilet in the school with a door. All of the boy's rooms had the doors removed from the stalls. When the nurse's restroom was occupied with some other sickly student, I was forced to walk home in agony. If I couldn't make it far enough to reach the house I'd stop along the way at the deli or gas station. The gas station was filthy but at least it had a door, and unlike the nurse's office, ten girls wouldn't be waiting outside the hollow door as you pooped the hell out of the toilet.

One day in mid September I left school in distress and stopped at the deli where I could privately use a toilet. Upon washing up, I stepped outside to find Mr. Panzram waiting for me.

"So you think you can just leave school and go to the deli? Surprise!" he said smiling. His smile quickly faded to an angry expression and he muttered, "You're suspended."

I tried to explain, but there was no use. Mr. Panzram simply got back into his car and drove off down the road, leaving me there to drag myself home in frustration.

When I returned to regular classes after three days in ISS, I tried my hardest to fight off the stomach pains. Cutting a class here and there seemed to be the only way to escape the pain. Mr. Panzram eventually caught up with me and slapped me with yet another suspension.

"I knew it wasn't too hard to break a person like you. Bound to mess up."

"No, I'm not going in there again. It's not fair," I protested.

"Fine, you'll have three days out-of-school suspension instead for insubordination."

For three days I walked the streets of the town. Out on my perpetual walk, I brought a notebook to write in, to try to clear my head of the fogginess. I wondered why I was having these cramps, why I was feeling dizzy. I wondered if there was something in the milk again. I roamed around town occasionally stopping to smoke a cigarette with another punk I'd run into. Some of them were off into some bad things like breaking into cars or doing smack, so I made the smoke break quick and moved on. Some kids were just like me though, wandering and digging deep.

After three days of solitude, I returned to school. The issue was embarrassing so I didn't get into it with Elizabeth. I promised her I wouldn't mess around anymore and would get serious about our plan to do well. I was already looking like a screw up, but she was patient. I knew I couldn't keep getting suspended so I started to keep a bottle of Pepto-Bismol in my backpack and started to use the faculty men's room. It was clean and had doors on the stalls, and was far less risky than leaving the building. I stopped having cereal for breakfast and surprisingly felt much better. I was slow to put the pieces together, but what do you expect out of a kid who's brainwashed from an early age that milk does a body good and school is a great place to be. We're all fed such illusions.

41

MY BROTHER JP was eight when he was first locked up. We took a family trip upstate to visit him in a facility named Tryon. It was a mid level security facility in the middle of rural farmland. Just down the road from a Llama farm, behind barbed wire and a secured brick building, my little brother lived for six months with some of the most deranged kids in New York State. He was there because our school district reported him for truancy. As if putting him among the worst criminals, drug addicts, and psychologically ill kids would suddenly convert him into the teacher's pet. He didn't want to go to school because he couldn't pay attention and felt inadequate, and teachers only made him feel worse. Those were the reasons, the real causes they needed to work on, but the state just threw kids away.

We sat with him on steel benches in a plain metal room. JP was thoroughly happy to see us. He was so young and already locked into a terrible cycle of incarceration, freedom, incarceration, freedom. He was now part of the system and we didn't even know it then. There he was with arsonists, burglars, sexual deviants, attempted murderers and he hadn't even been in a physical fight with anyone. Thousands of kids are incarcerated in America for all of those crimes, yet mixed in with them are the misguided or abused ones like JP.

The Sunday visit was thirty minutes. We were allowed to share chocolate and candy but nothing else. There wasn't much to say; what do you say in a situation like this?

"Hey remember the time we went to the Bronx Zoo and you wouldn't stop crying and the line went on and on and Mom had to keep yelling at you and throw in an occasional spank?"

Really, what do you say at a time like this?

A loud bell rang when our time was up. I hugged him goodbye and he reached out to us as he was pulled away back to his cell. We were ushered out of the room. He cried, "Don't leave me" but we didn't have a choice. He was property of the state now.

I never treated my brother the best. He needed attention and wasn't getting it at home. Don didn't know how to talk to him like a human being and my mother would get fed up with him and tell him to go out on his bike. When he came to me, I was just a rotten teenager who wanted to be with his friends, but I also wanted to get away from that house. If I was home my door was often locked shut and music drowned out any knocks or calls.

Perhaps I subconsciously resented my brother. He was the reason I was snatched from a peaceful life in the old town and dragged to the new one where I was bullied. His arrival changed my whole world. I didn't consciously blame him for anything at the time, but my actions showed an underlying psychological resentment I wasn't even aware of.

At home one day while he was locked away I thought of him and dug out a family video of a trip to Pennsylvania a couple of years before. We were visiting one of my Aunt Judy's vacation homes. JP was outside just being a kid spinning the tire swing and two of my great aunts were scolding him as if he were torching the whole god damn house up in flames.

"What is he doing? What is he doing?" asked Aunt Sandra.

"Rotten kid," Aunt Judy could be heard saying in the video.

As if being a happy kid having fun was so rotten. Sometimes I think they tried to make him rotten because they didn't like his father.

Maybe they were rotten.

42

ELIZABETH AND I had plans to go out, but I needed to walk up to the Chicken Shack to pick up my weekly pay. She agreed to go with me. We walked up to the shopping center on the main highway and I suggested we get something to eat while we were out. We sat on the stools at the counter and ate a quick lunch. Phil was respectful to Elizabeth calling her Billy Jack's little lady. He was on good behavior with my guest. None of the counter girls got harassed and the calm scene contradicted my stories. He wore cool blue jeans and our uniform bright blue polo with a chicken logo on the left breast. His high black hair glistened as he bounced back and forth between the cooker and counter. He loved to multi-task—cook—bag and hand it off like a baton in a race. This was his race and realm.

After we ate we left. I was pleasantly surprised at the calmness Elizabeth had brought to the scene. We started to walk, but suddenly got stuck in the middle of a torrential downpour.

"Run for it," I yelled.

We ran home, stopping for a breath and a kiss every so often. Gallons of water dropped on us in minutes. It rained so hard it hurt. We ran holding hands. We were soaked when we got back to my house. The perfect excuse to get comfortable.

Elizabeth and I were trying to do the right thing in school. We stuck together tight. She was my rock. Most of tenth grade was quiet and my grades were far better, though it seemed some teachers, Mr. Bundy, and now Mr. Panzram still occasionally picked on me and judged me based on my reputation. With only a few suspensions early on in the year due to my stomach issues, I had learned to cope with the ailment. I kept my mouth shut the rest of the year, went to class, and did as instructed.

I had a couple of great classes that year too. Ms. Marsolice was a great science teacher. She didn't make it about math. A woman in her late fifties, she was about four foot nine and had short black hair. She didn't treat us like children or disrespect us like some teachers, but she expected respect. She was stern and direct with high expectations. Tenth grade Earth science was great, not because she was a great presenter, but because she made us work and find answers. She hardly taught, but she helped us teach ourselves. She also didn't just throw us into groups and let us fumble around until we learned something. She sent us into our books on discovery quests to find the meaning of everything from mitochondria to tectonic plates. I opened my textbook and really used it, more than in any other course. I memorized, I expanded my knowledge, and I aced tests. Some folks would detest this kind of learning, why I don't know, because I excelled in this class using her methods. It might seem like busy work, but this was the most active learning I had had in all of my years of high school so far and my grades showed it. My love for the natural sciences also wasn't extinguished by a bad experience.

My social studies teacher shouted for forty minutes in between sneezing fits where he'd walk right out of the class mid sentence to blow his honker. Then it was on to math.

My math teacher did the complete opposite from Ms. Marsolice. He ignored us and read the newspaper with his tenured feet up on the desk and a hot cup of tea in one hand.

Later on, it was on to English class where the woman would preach morals from the short stories and berate the men in the stories.

Even if the male character were a hero, she'd find something wrong with him. Her treatment of male students wasn't much better.

My study hall was spent out on the street smoking cigarettes and drinking coffee and then there was a lunch period in a large cafeteria full of popularity contests.

Mixed into the middle was a media arts class, which brought me a lot of joy. Mr. Luca was calm and let us liberally explore film. We created our own trailers for movies and some of us made mini films. Among the videos I made were a Just Say No to Drugs promotional, The Best of Freddy Krueger, and an eight-minute trailer for the Keanu Reeves and Patrick Swayze film *Point Break*. This class was the best grade I received in a long time. I could've made a day out of this one class, but unfortunately there weren't any other elective options for media arts. Cranky old folks had voted down the budget again and we were lucky to have any kind of art class.

Regular art class the previous year was a chaotic mess. The teacher was mellow in his Hawaiian shirts for about the first five weeks and then suddenly he flipped. He had had enough of the disrespect from some of the punks in the class. He tossed his hot coffee at Ryan Bailey and then flung a chair across the room before walking out of the room. He returned ten minutes later and everyone went silent. He picked out the four worst kids, walked them into the hall, and told them,

"If you ever come back to my class again, you'll be sorry."

I don't think I ever saw those kids anywhere around that room for the rest of the semester. I just minded my business and drew a lot of circles while I thought about things.

Round and Round.

I was terrible at drawing, but I used the time to sit and think. No one is going to stand over your shoulder and hound you in an art class. Just shut up and think.

Steven had surprisingly spent the year doing good too. He was busy with sports. Football was his love and always pulled him out of the dark place he had been the summer before. I hadn't hung with him since the summer and we went the whole year doing our own thing. At the end of the year we met up. It was just him, Elizabeth, and me. We sat on the bleachers in the park across the street from my house. The sun went down and the stars lit the sky. Our night was like a heavy metal song unplugged, stripped down and acoustic. We didn't drink or do drugs, but we got high on life and philosophical talk.

"Where are we all going?" I asked.

"Where have we all been? Have we been here before?" asked Elizabeth.

"Where are we now? Like really now. And why do we all react so differently to different situations?" Steven asked.

We didn't pretend to have any answers. We just tossed out a lot of questions and shared our wonder for this mysterious life.

It was one of the deepest conversations I've ever had. The depth made me think there should've been more talks like that with Steven—something I think we all longed for. It was heart to heart to heart, the three of us, my two favorite people under the stars. And then too quickly the night ended. It seemed like the last time I would ever see that Steven, as if he caught something bad that summer, something he couldn't recover from.

43

MY FATHER MOVED. He had packed it all up again, and after around a few dozen visits in five years, he was leaving again. He had a new family now.

I only saw his extended family at Christmas once a year out at my grandfather's Mattituck cabin. The year after I met my father he took me to meet his family— a long lost family I never even knew I had— A couple of aunts who I couldn't tell apart and their husbands, one very tall, one very short; Uncle Albert; a cousin; my grandfather and his third wife. I apparently missed out on the second one and never got to meet her.

Grandma Tortis wasn't invited to these events, so we had to visit her separately at her quiet little home in suburban Sayville. This was the same house where she raised four kids in poverty while grandpa was off making his fortune and marrying wife number two.

The gifts overflowed that first Christmas, with both grandparents. I had never received so much attention. I must have walked out of there with a whole backseat full of gifts. It was a celebration, a family reunion. They almost seemed to be trying to make up for all those lost years in one night. My father even said it too. "Don't expect as much next year. They were all just happy to meet you."

He was right. The second Christmas was tamer. I still didn't know some names and mixed up my aunts. I stared at these strange people

I probably wouldn't see again until the following year, my once a year family. I met my cousin Michael again, my aunt's son, who she had at fifteen. He was three years older than me and my father was a year older than her. Michael had been around all those years. He knew them all, and they all shared memories. The family photo album documented those memories, which I had no part of. Family amnesia. Missing child. What was I to them?

Michael was kind to me though. He never boasted. He tried to make me feel at home. As the years rolled on, he and I would sit and talk at family get togethers. He had a passion for music and really wanted to do something with it. I too loved music, so we had something great in common. But seeing each other once a year didn't exactly inspire a relationship and he lived too far away.

Uncle Albert was nice too. He seemed funny, but also tough. He was a cop, so he had a strong, good guy demeanor, but he talked with me and seemed interested. He wasn't like the male teachers and principals at school who pretended to be cops and lacked compassion. Albert seemed like he really cared about making the world better. He was far more optimistic than my father or grandpa.

Grandpa was serious and stern looking. His eyeglasses always hung on his nose. He hardly smiled if at all. Snow-white gray hair and sun damaged leathery skin made him look years older than he really was. He always seemed irritated. But if you showed up to see him for Christmas, you got a fat check in a card. If you couldn't make it, tough— you didn't even get a card in the mail— like the year when I missed his Christmas get together because it conflicted with my mother's family get together. Years passed and I never once got a birthday card. No phone calls. No "Hey, you want to get together?" By the time I was sixteen he had moved away to Florida to find wife number four and live out his remaining years sick of a weak heart.

My father moved to Florida knowing his father would be making the permanent move soon enough. We'll talk, he said, but we hardly did. Don't be a stranger, he said and walked out the door stranger than he was when I met him. More time to get to know each other gone forever. Down in Florida, he'd walk out on his second marriage and raise a son part-time. Some time is better than no time. I would have taken it. No, I wouldn't have.

44

I GOT MY PERMIT on my birthday in October of tenth grade, which meant I was automatically licensed on my birthday the following year after passing the road test that summer. In October of eleventh grade, I had bought my first car, a red 1989 Thunderbird. The car was a piece of junk. I spent my savings of three thousand dollars and the damn thing stalled on the way home from the bloodsucking used car dealership. This was the car that should have been a Mustang. Not that I had asked for it. I was fine with saving my Chicken Shack money and taking care of myself.

My friend Carlo and I were cruising along one Friday morning in late November of junior year. We had the whole day ahead of us. Winter was around a New York corner and we could feel it in the air. The sun shone down and melted the remnants of an early snowfall into dissolving chunks of gray matter piled on lawns, corners of parking lots, and dead ends.

We drove through the village heading for our friend Eric's place. Upon picking up Eric, we planned on getting some food to eat at the local IHOP, right after we smoked a big burly joint in the parking lot. We'd be so stoned that the pancakes summoned us. For about a month, this was a common ritual for us on Fridays. None of my friends ever worked at their part-time jobs on Fridays and I had just quit the Chicken Shack. We blew off classes, smoked joints, chowed down on heart-attack-provoking breakfasts, and ended up in some different place each week.

My blood-maroon colored Thunderbird drifted us down East John Street. Carlo had popped on one of his cheesy dance cassettes that had lyrics of love and heartbreak and the stereotypical chasing-the-girl theme. He claimed the girls liked his music and that was the only reason he played it, but I think he was the one who really enjoyed it. Disco, techno, girly 90's guido music, whatever they call it, I didn't seem to mind as it was spunky enough for driving around on a pleasant day with a little money in our pockets, a couple of joints and nothing to do.

The windows were rolled down in the Thunderbird to the uncanny scent of garden hoses— that watery smell when water is sprayed in the air somewhere nearby. Maybe it was just the smell of snow melting. I felt good and lit a cigarette. The smoke drifted out of my mouth so easily and the smell reminded me of times when I had not yet started smoking and someone would walk by with a lit cigarette to share the aroma, or when my father smoked around me.

An intersection approached up the road with yellow flashing lights and no stop sign on my side. On the cross road, a forest green mini-van came to a halt. As we came closer to the intersection I stared at the minivan with a concern and felt like I had seen this same scenario play out before.

My eyes zoomed in on the back passenger wheel. The tire spun spitting up leftover slush from the street and pushed the vehicle to a go. I knew it was going to be too late but I told myself differently. In slow motion— flashes of forest green, yellow blinking lights, and the road ahead. My fist pounded the weak horn on the steering wheel. I let out a yell of disbelief,

"No fucking way!"

Just as my vehicle entered the center of the intersection, the mini-van came smashing into the front driver side fender. The Thunderbird slid sideways down the crossroad and up onto the side grass. Glass shattered. Our seatbelts sucked at our chests; Good thing, because we foolishly didn't wear them a lot of the time.

"What the hell, that moron hit you," said Carlo.

"Oh man, oh man, oh man," I simply muttered.

Nobody had been hurt, nobody had died. Yet I knew everything had changed and there would be no turning around now.

My car was totaled. I got out and looked. Then I looked over at the minivan. A mother got out. She had just dropped the kids off at school. We probably looked at each other with the same wonder— what are you doing driving around these streets? But we didn't say anything other than "are you all right?"

I junked that car with a local auto body shop for a few hundred dollars. They would fix it up and sell it to the kid who had been living with Win. A strange coincidence, I suppose. He had moved in with a family a few blocks away and was trying to put his life together. But he would total the car again after only a few months after drunkenly driving off the road into someone's front porch.

I only had the car for a little over a month and had narrowly escaped several accidents. One particular night I slid off a ramp going 50 mph in the rain. My car was packed with four friends. I had lost total control, slid off the ramp, and opened my eyes to find us sitting in the middle of a grass field on the side of the road. We all looked around and knew we were lucky. Most ramps had guardrails, which would have reflected us back onto the road where another vehicle surely would have slammed into us. Too many close calls like that one.

After the accident that day, Carlo got his car back, which had been off the road for some time, but I stopped hanging with him. Something had been spoiled. You get into something like that with someone you don't really know that well and you begin to associate them with that experience.

I tried to think about why the accident had happened. Was it because Elizabeth and I were spending time apart? She was with theater friends who I didn't mesh with so well, and I was out getting into trouble again. Was I supposed to just acquiesce and break out in a random Broadway song? I didn't know how to fit in with that, and she was growing tired of my trouble.

Even though no one was hurt, I felt my ego had been hurt. I was no Randy Mckinney. Worse though, I was back walking the streets of the town to and from school and two miles to my new job at a grocery store. Maybe I needed the time to walk and think.

As for the accident, it didn't take long for me to figure out that well, number one, I really wasn't doing what I was supposed to be doing— out cruising around during school instead of being in class. Number two, I saw the rudimentary metaphor of life as a road with many intersections and even flashing yellow lights to tell you when to slow down. Years later, it would seem many of the kids I knew had never seen those same flashing yellow lights when they needed them the most. Number three, the totaling of this car gave me the insurance money to buy a new car, a more reliable one. The next car would take me to the new frontier and would become my shelter from the storm.

45

MY FIRST OFFICIAL JOB— that is on the books and legal, was at a grocery store, the same one Jane, Rachel, and I raided a couple of years back. I saw the safety of a legal job as a fine replacement to the dangerous chicken-cutting environment of the Chicken Shack. The turbulent environment there had been too much for me after a year.

Super Cohen's was one of the first supermarkets in the nation. Owned by the Cohen family, they grew from one location to a multi-million dollar empire of over forty stores across Long Island. While they weren't a super corporation, they also weren't a mom and pop shop, which meant lower pay. As a cashier I earned the minimum wage of $4.25 per hour. I worked as hard as I could. I wanted to prove myself, maybe even work my way up, and if this had been a different era I might have.

I was super fast at checking people out and greeted them in a friendly manner, something I knew even then at a young age, was missing from the shopping experience. Most customers here didn't want the friendly greeting though; they wanted in and out. They grunted when I said hello. They complained about prices and watched the screen with an eagle eye. You wouldn't believe the miserable customers who came through my line with their roast beef and milk and loads of other junk food to help clog their arteries. I could tell some of them already regretted the item as I crossed it over the scanner. They knew they had promised themselves or a loved one no more cookies or triple fudge ice cream and they were breaking that promise right in front of me. I was a witness to the crime. People like to dig holes. And sometimes they try to pull you in with them.

The company didn't care about being friendly either. They cared about dollars. You were just another empty-headed servant. The main store manager asked me why I was always smiling and happy, as if it were so terrible to smile. The beastly manager would bark orders.

"Get over here and clean up this mess," he would holler pushing a mop at me when business was slow. He would waddle away huffing and mumbling.

A younger manager joined the store at one point. Kyle was twenty years old and transferred in from another store where he worked since he was fifteen, perhaps before the era of work harder get less. He had moved up and was at the peak of his new career. He'd walk around with his chin in the air, with his shiny gold name badge that displayed his big title, Assistant Floor Manager. I couldn't believe the confidence.

The stock guys would put up a whole display just for him to yell at them to take it down.

"What are you doing? I told you to put that up in front of aisle three, not ten. What's wrong with you?"

"You said ten."

"Are you questioning me? Do you have a problem with your job?"

The boys would go right back to the drawing board only for him to bust their balls on something else later.

As young as fifteen and as old as sixty-five, all the workers were peasants to both the management and the public. The cashiers were mostly women. Some were young girls around my age, but some were older and busted up. One was missing teeth. One had huge goggle-like eyeglasses. Most were friendly, but some were angry at the world. The head cashier was a heavy-set woman with a knack for counting bills super fast. She was in it for the long haul. She asked me once,

"Why are you always smiling? What are you so happy about?"

I'll never forget one friendly customer though. Adam was a short, gray-haired, Russian-looking man with a mustache. He truly appreciated my service and thanked me for it. For Christmas, Adam gave me a bottle of Fahrenheit cologne. He knew I liked cologne because like all the other guys in this town, I poured it on sometimes, unaware of the offensive assault on others' noses. Whenever I felt down and thought the world was full of rotten people, I could always think of this friendly man.

When one of my great uncles died, I called in to take the shift off. Unfortunately, they were short a few employees that day and gave me the ultimatum: go to the wake or come to work. If I didn't go in, I was out of a job. I went into work the next week to pick up my final paycheck and didn't say goodbye to anyone there.

I helped Paul's father open up their restaurant, The Italian Garden. We set the place up for the grand opening. Once we were ready to open, they offered me a more permanent job. The timing was perfect for me since I was waiting to get my second car. I needed the money, but the time in work would also keep me busy and out of trouble. Elizabeth and I were back on. We couldn't stand being away from each other for too long. But because of my work and her chorus commitments, we saw each other a lot less.

I would run the counter, wait tables, bus tables, and drive deliveries using their delivery car, a beat up Mazda with wickedly crooked steering alignment. We all shared duties and shifted responsibilities on different days. Paul's sister Marie managed the place and was great to work for. Paul and I worked on two days together. This brought us closer and we started to hang on the weekends again. We hadn't seen each other in a while, so it was great to see him after so long. Things would be all right.

46

I WAS BACK ON MY FEET walking around town for a couple of months as I waited for my insurance to be settled. One day I saw Crazy John in passing. His hair was ratty, eyes red, and his face didn't look so well. Scratched and scarred. I remembered his face-tearing threats and wondered if the same had happened to him. He looked away like a beaten animal.

On the streets you seemed to run into people you wouldn't otherwise see on the road. You'd hear things too. I finally heard news of Vinnie the wrestler.

"Hey Jack, did you hear that Vinnie is back in town; he was thrown out of college for stealing computers," a friend informed me.

What about a future? What about his wrestling scholarship? It seemed like a waste.

Although Vinnie was back in town I still never saw him. I guess our paths just never crossed, but I still heard the gossip every so often. I heard Vinnie was getting into drugs. Then I heard how he had cleaned up and was driving a truck and delivering bread at four in the morning. I thought of how I wouldn't want to wake up at four in the morning six days a week to drive a delivery truck. Of course, there was nothing wrong with a stable job that made him an innocent living. It sure beat drugs and stealing computers.

At a party one night, someone told me Vinnie the wrestler had moved into a two-bedroom apartment with a guy my age. Gabe was a dropout, not really a troublemaker though. How the two met and why they decided to share an apartment is beyond me. Gabe abruptly moved out one day and filed an order of protection against Vinnie, who had apparently been abusing him for the whole eight months they were living together. Someone said that "Vinnie had beaten Gabe like a bitch" and that there had been some kind of sexual assault involved. I just couldn't understand it.

On my way home from the party, I came across a group of friends yelling and fighting with another group of kids. Most of these friends were football players, but I didn't recognize any of the other kids; they were older, Hispanic kids from the next town over. Even despite just hearing the lousy news about Vinnie, I still wished I had him by my side at moments like this.

One of my friends standing on the outside of the circle of conflict told me they were from the next town over. I peeked in at the erupting fight. A car was idle with open doors and a waiting driver. One monster of a guy pulled a sawed-off shotgun from the backseat. Before I knew it, people were ducking and screaming. But one person didn't budge. It was David Pace. He was telling the kid to put the gun away and just quit picking on them, that they didn't want any trouble, and that he didn't want to be in the kind of trouble for shooting someone. The big guy, big enough at about six foot five, that he didn't need a gun, said,

"I'm not going to shoot anyone..." He wasn't lying either.

"...I just want to fight."

Suddenly he struck David across the face with the butt of the gun. David collapsed. The kid struck him again in the face several more times. David's friends pleaded but no one was going to physically risk their life against this bully with a gun. The monster with the gun spit on a bloodied David and then got into the car and sped off. An ambulance was called and David was taken away. Of course, because there was a gun involved rumors went around that David had been shot by a gun when he had really been beaten by one. Of course, the gun and the severity of the beating also made this a serious crime and the police soon arrested Gonzalo Gonzalez for assault and battery. Word was he was in the same circle as Ricky Sharpe.

David lay in a hospital bed with his jaw wired and a high school football career put in jeopardy. We all sent get-well notes. We were relieved no one had been shot and David would recover after several months. The streets could be rough. There were beatings every week or so, but hospitalizations were rare.

Only a couple of years before this, seventeen-year-old Dean Zino was shot dead in the street after fighting with several other teens on a man's front lawn. Dean was out chasing down two younger kids, brothers Giorgio and Angelo Luzzatto. They were running fast on foot as Dean and his friends followed in their van. Afraid for their safety, they banged on the door of a corner house. The man opened up and the brothers asked him to call the police.

He replied, "I am the police." He went out front to confront the boys.

"Go back in the house, Clint Eastwood," said Dean. "This isn't your business."

"It's my business because you made it my business."

The man saw Dean shuffle around in his jacket and that was it. He wasn't going to take any chances with a punk in the street in front of his house. One shot to the face at point blank range and Dean was gone.

Numerous kids died in our teen years. One ran around his attic in a snowsuit until he passed out from creative suicide. One overdosed on pills and one on heroin. One was struck down at eighty miles per hour on Sunrise Highway. One collapsed out on the track training for the National Guard and had a heart attack at eighteen. But none were shot like Dean.

The man who shot Dean lived there for another few years before selling the house and moving away. This wasn't the first time the man had shot someone dead. He was a retired police officer who had shot someone in the line of duty in what was a questionable scene. When the former officer got off for self-defense in the street shooting of Dean, people protested for days in front of his house and held a vigil for Dean. And then they gave up and life went on.

Dean's parents were divorced within a year. The mother picked up the bottle. The father turned to gambling. Dean's younger brother Jeremy was only fourteen. By fifteen, Jeremy had left school and gotten into drugs. It would take him years to cope with the loss of his brother. The whole family might as well have been lined up in the street with Dean that night.

Police seemed more interested in giving out traffic tickets than doing any serious crime prevention. Cops in my town hung out in firehouses having get-togethers or they just hid somewhere out on the road to sleep their shifts away. At the time, my town had a rate of fifty annual violent crimes. Of course, many of the street fights were not reported. We also had an astounding annual rate of over five hundred property damage crimes. Kids I knew were making hundreds of dollars from stealing car radios parked at the train station before the age of "successful" car alarms. Other kids went out vandalizing just for kicks. I never got in with these crowds, at least while they were out doing their thing. I didn't see the point in destroying someone else's belongings like vandals had done to Don. I certainly knew it wasn't right to steal from another person, even though I had once stolen from stores. These punks made me look like an angel. I just wanted to be left alone now to do my own thing. I just wanted time and space. Fuck with me and you'll get it, like a tiger on your neck. Stay off my toes and you're cool. I didn't want to hurt anyone. But teachers didn't see this difference. I was the same as all of them, a no good punk.

47

THE STEROIDS made guys do terrible things—mostly to themselves. I knew of at least several dozen guys on roids and most of them went to the town gym ironically named *The Natural Body*. Some of them had roid rages, which caused them to beat someone up or break something. These rages were overrated though— I think some of them used it as an excuse to act how they normally would, but there was some validity to testosterone going right to their head.

Of course, they were all searching for something inside that was missing. All these empty guys. One guy named George filled up like a balloon from water-based roids. He didn't care. He thought the bigger the better, the bigger the scarier, the bigger the more respect he would get. And so in his quest for respect he ate like a truck driver, pounding down three or four cheeseburgers at a time. George did anything to try and forget the weak little dork he had always been. He ate and shot his way into heart attack alley, dead at twenty-two at 360 pounds from a dead heart. Another kid who hated himself named Brandon took an oil-based steroid, which killed his good looks. The oil leaked out of his pores and his skin boiled up with cysts. He was never the same after the skin graphs and infections— all for vanity and respect.

Vanity was their number one sin. The risk, if they were even aware of it, was well worth it. The guys in my town were obsessed with surface appearance and seemed to believe that power on the surface equaled real power. They worked out, not for health, not for their insides, but for the surface exterior to look good.

I guess my epiphany of this problem came from the fact I was smaller than most. In my early days I worked out incessantly and my closest friends called me Jacked Jack, but I didn't need to be him anymore. I had to face it, as we got older, other kids were going to sprout up past me. Even the biggest guy in town was still going to meet his match with a bigger guy from somewhere else. You're never the biggest, never the toughest, never the fastest, not forever.

There were more important things to strive for. Despite my size, I had a little martial arts and wrestling under my belt, enough to do damage and defend myself if necessary. I didn't need the huge biceps or ripped abs. Most people here didn't think this way though. They wanted to be tough, though most just wanted to look tough. It was always a contest. This competitive shallowness is nothing I wanted to emulate, at least not anymore.

We ripped open the plastic packaging and took out the syringes. Steven and I loaded our needles into the little glass bottles of Sustanon and then pulled back. On the street, you could buy it in vials or in pre-loaded needles. We certainly weren't going to trust some pre-loaded needle after hearing about all the stories— watered down, laced with addictive additives, or worse filled with vegetable oil. One guy we knew was shooting up mostly vegetable oil for a week until he was sick. No thanks. We were going to shoot steroids right from the source. The sealed bottles were shipped right from a pharmacy in Russia.

Holding the syringe upside down, we tapped it to make sure the air bubbles were out. I was paranoid about bubbles even though we weren't injecting into our veins. We plunged the needle into our shoulders. These were the short tipped needles, so a meaty place like the shoulder was the best place to go. There were nightmare stories about the long tipped needles that went into the buttocks. We knew a guy who stuck the long tipped needle into his ass and hit a nerve and couldn't walk for eight weeks. Another guy twisted the needle and it broke off in his ass. He needed surgery to remove the metal tip. So we shot it into our shoulders with short tips.

The liquid left the syringe and plunged into our muscles. The psychological rush caused us to let out our warrior grunts. We threw the needles down and flexed our muscles like the wrestlers we'd worshiped as kids— most of them now dead, addicted to painkillers, shriveled up, or broke. The ones who survived were Baptist preachers on late night television or lucky enough to still work in the industry behind the scenes. Hardly the heroes we thought they were. More like the bad actors they really were, acting like heroes. Now we were in one of those very acts that began their downward spiral.

Steven and I headed out to a party where we could show off our growing muscles that seemed to grow by the day. He'd end up putting his fist through the person's wall, and I'd end up wondering what the hell we were doing at some lousy party with assholes.

My mother had found a bottle of steroids in pill form a few weeks prior. She brought it to the pharmacist and had it tested and then yelled at me for an hour, threatening to send me to rehab. The pills worked, but not as fast as the juice, and there was risk of liver damage with the pills, so I graduated to the real stuff. It was a real epidemic in our town, so all you had to do was get to know folks in the town gym. I was far more careful with my liquid stash.

Gene and I shared a cycle too a few weeks later. He preferred to shoot it into his ass with the long tipped needles, and I stayed with the short tips. We did that same grunt-flex-wrestler act and then went out to show off at a spring party. Just picture two short stocky boys with more muscle than mind. We were clueless of how we might be perceived by others. Cocky jerks, talking shit, looking around. Barbarians at the table ripping flesh from bone, we devastated our meals. Food was another common problem with roids.

Just like George, who had eaten himself all the way to premature heart disease, we knew a guy named Vito who would work out and then stop at the drive thru for five burgers on his way home. Before long, Vito was so bloated on water based steroids and burgers that he couldn't fit into his Cutlass Supreme anymore. Rumor was he turned into the Walter Hudson type of fat fame where he wouldn't leave the house or even get out of bed. The depression that must have hit him when he realized high school was over and people in the real world don't give a shit about biceps or how much you can squat. Worse, was how he had literally taken off his eyeglasses one day a few years earlier and given up life as a good, grade-earning nerd to hang with the losers in the "popular" fun crowd. What a trade off.

Gene and I ate like pigs and then went off to meet one of his friends named Rex. They had plenty to talk about, but I was staying out of it. They talked of burglarizing the vitamin store at night. Rex had it all planned out.

"You sure you don't wanna be in?" Rex asked me.

"No, thanks. I'm good." The idea sounded crazy.

"Tommy said he's in," Gene told him.

"Great, so here's how it's gonna fuckin' go. We're gonna climb up the side. There's a way right up to the roof. On the roof is a skylight. We smash through the fuckin' glass, drop in, and stuff our bags," Rex explained.

"What about the alarm?" asked Gene.

"It's all good. We have plenty of time to get out before the pigs get called. The wire's only rigged to go off when a door is opened or a window is broken. The skylight is clear."

Apparently, Rex knew someone on the inside who had scoped out the alarm and timed a broken window alarm response. They knew they had at least twenty minutes after the alarm went off from the time they flipped open the back door to escape.

"You're just going to walk out the back door?" I asked them.

"Yup and if we're lucky we'll grab a safe and some cash too," said Rex.

And they did well according to Gene. They only got a hundred dollars from the register, but made out with hundreds of dollars worth of supplements they'd sell on the streets and use themselves. Not that Gene needed them. He had his steroids. But he thought the more the better.

I only did steroids one more time after that cycle with Gene. I reached under my mattress and stuck my arm up into the cut on the side. I pulled a pillowcase out of the mattress and opened it up—filled with syringes and a few bottles of steroids. I prepared to shoot one cc of Sustanon into my arm as I sat in my underwear on the bed. After loading it, I put the needle in my left shoulder, pushed in the clear juice, and then swore I heard the hiss of an air pocket. Paranoia struck me, the blood of anxiety rushed to my head, and I panicked. I imagined an air bubble going into my muscle and killing me right there in my underwear. I got dressed and hid all the paraphernalia. My heart pounded. My life flashed before my eyes. Of course, it would take more air than a little hiss in a muscle injection to cause harm, unlike the hiss of air that would spell death for the type of vein injections heroin users do. But I didn't care. I didn't want to OD or take something laced with poison. I didn't want to die in my underwear and have my mother find me like that. And what would Elizabeth think about me? I also knew too many guys with bad side effects, from roid rages to acne, and never mind the warnings out there about shriveled up testicles. It was all just wrong. After lying down to ease my anxiety, I awoke, bagged up all the drugs and needles, walked it out to a nearby dumpster, and never touched the stuff again.

Gene had done steroids a little longer than me. He got a little bigger, but also a little fatter, especially after he stopped shooting them. You either gained a lot or lost a lot of weight when you quit. I lost a lot.

48

I HADN'T EATEN ANYTHING in at least twenty hours. With a couple of days off from work, a paycheck ahead of me, and no food in the kitchen at home, I was hungry. I stormed through the cold hard hallways with metal lockers on each side, which made for a great punching arena when you got mad, or when a teacher got you mad. Mr. Mill, my fantastic (cough) former ninth grade English teacher, had stopped me for trying to buy breakfast in the cafeteria during homeroom. I had missed the appropriate café hours because I needed to scrounge up the two dollars at the door outside the building where I caught some kid who owed me. My stomach was a sour mess. If I didn't get in there and get something I'd have to wait it out in class for several more hours.

"You're not allowed to be in here now," he said at the doorway. He had caught me hungry and vulnerable.

"And you are?"

"You're supposed to be in homeroom."

"I'm going, but I needed to grab breakfast."

I threw the money down on the counter and the woman's hand froze when he told her not to accept the money.

"I'm hungry, man."

"I don't care."

"If you don't back off me, man, I'm going to eat you for breakfast," I threatened.

Mr. Mill backed away startled as if threatened by a real cannibal.

Realizing the woman was now afraid to serve me because of the teacher's intrusion, I grabbed my money and stormed out of the room past Mr. Mill. He followed at a safe distance. I stopped to toss over a trashcan on my way out, again to punch one of the lockers and then continued on right out the double doors. When I returned from the deli, the principal was waiting for me in the hallway with a suspension slip for threatening to eat a teacher. Eleventh grade wasn't turning out very productive. I was once again a magnet for trouble. Elizabeth and I had drifted once again.

While at the grocery store job, I had met a girl who worked the register and drove a fine looking blue Camaro. She told me she would be selling it soon to buy a Mitsubishi. I told her I was definitely interested since my first car had been totaled. She contacted me a couple of weeks after I was fired and offered the car to me for $3,300. I gave her three hundred down right away from my restaurant earnings. A week later I gave her my insurance check for $2,750. She gave me the keys and told me to hang on to the two hundred and fifty dollar cash balance until the end of the month. Two days later she called me back and told me she needed the money right away. I told her I had spent most of it on things for the car and asked her why she was changing her mind about the $250. She wouldn't tell me and demanded the money. She threatened to come back and take the car, since she still had another set of keys.

I bought new door locks for $25 and a $15 steering wheel lock. I spent an hour changing the door lock myself, and then slapped on the wheel lock. Later that evening from my window I saw her trying to get into the car to take it back. Unsuccessful, she huffed and drove off. This hysterical girl returned the next day to yell at me, scolding me for not paying my debts, even though she had given me several weeks to pay the small remainder. My mother came out and screamed her off the front steps.

A couple of weeks later, after receiving several nasty letters in the mail, I sent her a check. I could never understand what went wrong in her head, but I guess that just happens to people. Maybe she owed someone else money. Nevertheless, she had her money and I had a new used Camaro.

The interior was black and the steering wheel was a custom GT racing wheel. The seats were gray, but I put these funky wooly faux sheepskin covers on them. The bucket seats sank to the floor of the car. It felt good to be so low to the ground and the rear wheel drive really hugged the road. I babied this car— washing it, driving it carefully. I put in new louder speakers eventually. This car was all I really owned.

Later, when I would see some young kid obsessing over their car, I knew how it felt. Of course, once you get older you realize there are things more important than possessions. At that young age though, it was the only thing that gave me independence. Gas was only ninety-nine cents a gallon and so it was easy to cruise around just for kicks. I would take off and drive to some distant town and then turn around and go home. Long Island had a strange uncanny feeling in every town. Maybe all the towns had something similar about them. It was like you've been there before, even when you hadn't. I would also go park and sit by the water for hours at a time. For a while I felt like I lived in the car, and perhaps in a way I had. This car would take me to places I hadn't imagined.

By the spring of eleventh grade, things had gotten more hectic at home, so I was out a lot. Things were tense between my mother and Don and it was difficult to be around. With a mandate to take our shoes off at the door, Don seemed more concerned about keeping his carpets clean. I wanted to stomp through the house with boots after wading through mud.

My mother's moods were unbearable. She yelled around the house at a nerve-crunching decibel, not because she sought to scare us, but because she was scared. She was frightened out of her wits of what her life had become with Don, of where she came from, and the unknown of where she was going. Fear and anger was how she coped. She had become a different person. The littlest things annoyed her now. Whether it was my bothered mother, one of Don's fits, or JP bouncing off the walls, this home was overbearing for a kid like me. I did all I could to spend time away from the house from the age of thirteen. Now that I had a car again, it was easier for me to spend time out of the house.

I would drive around my town wasting time. I revisited all the old places I had once hung out, all those old escapes from home. I'd drive by Jane's house. She was long gone by now, but I liked the thrill of going down memory lane. Often I'd drive around the south shore, up and down past so many houses I once knew people in. These streets were rich with memory, like ghosts.

Sometimes those ghosts came alive. One day I was driving by the high school and I spotted someone I hadn't seen in a very long time. I parked ahead and got out to greet her.

"Jack Tortis?"

"Rachel Wright?"

"Wow, it's been a long time," she said and gave me a great hug. I was relieved she hadn't held Jane's turn on her against me too.

"At least a couple of years. Where you going? You want a ride?"

"I walked my little sister back to school and I was going to head home."

"What? Your little sister is in high school already? Geez, we're getting old."

"Do you want to go somewhere and catch up?"

"Yeah, how about the diner?"

The town diner was always a place to go. It was affordable and had great breakfast, lunch, and dinner. I opened up my passenger door and let her in and we took off for the diner.

Once there we took out seats across each other in a booth. The light hit her in a different kind of way. She still had the same smirk. She was happy. Free of that other world.

"You know, I'm sorry about what happened with…"

"You're not Jane, Jack. That's her apology."

"Yeah, but I didn't stop the fight."

"You tried. Besides, that's all over. I'm past it now. Jane is a long time ago. It's sad that my oldest friendship died like that, but that's life."

"Well, I guess we're both free now. Cheers."

We saluted with our coffee mugs.

Rachel proceeded to tell me all of her great plans. She was in a special alternative tech program where she could graduate high school while also gaining college credit and business skills. Her family was good. She didn't party anymore the way we had. And she hung with an entirely new crowd I didn't even know. After chatting for some time, I drove her home to that same old house.

"My parents are selling the house next year. So that'll be it," she said as we pulled up.

She would be completely free of this place.

"You should stop by sometime. My mother and father would like to see you. They always heard a lot about you back in the day."

"I'm sure all great things, yeah right?"

"Yes, but really we shouldn't go so long again."

I didn't tell her how messy my life was. I had gotten over Jane and met Elizabeth, but all my problems were still getting the best of me. I was trying though. I admired her rebellion from the town.

"Rachel, one day we're going to be far away from all of this. I'll see you soon," I said and drove away.

Although I drove past her house a couple of times after that day, as I passed through the neighborhood, I never found it inside to stop and knock. We both had different worlds now. I was happy for her. Rachel was gone.

49

SITTING IN ENGLISH CLASS, my teacher Mrs. Lumbrera called the roster. The woman was hard and athletic looking. Her jaw was square and her exposed arms were ripped with lean muscles. Her bleached hair was pin-straight and appeared sharp. She spoke in a raspy voice probably from smoking too many cigarettes. Here I was getting suspended for smoking outside and she was sneaking butts in the women's room, apparent by the stench and cloud of smoke that would follow her on her way out.

"Welcome back from the land of trouble, Mr. Tortis. You're building a wonderful reputation with the faculty here."

"I didn't do much," I said.

"That's for sure, but you certainly weren't suspended for being an outstanding student. But anyway, let's carry on."

"But…"

"That'll be enough, Mr. Tortis."

I sat with my head in the book for the remainder of class.

The best part of having the car back was being able to get to Elizabeth easier. She and I eventually started talking on the phone again, but since I wasn't spending much time at home this was getting difficult. And I couldn't afford to stand at pay phones and talk. With a car I now had the freedom to speed over to her house if I wanted.

It felt good being able to pick up Elizabeth and take her out and talk things over. We spent hours talking.

A few weeks apart felt like months.

We couldn't stay away from each other for too long. The year had been tumultuous for us. We had separated a couple of times, so I could sort things out, but things had only gotten fuzzier. Hormones were running wild. Caffeine and nicotine fueled my body with a constant rush followed by a sinking low. How is one to think straight?

Elizabeth smiled and leaned over to hug me. I grasped her tightly and she reciprocated. Tilting my head, I leaned in for a kiss. It was an unusually warm day and we were enjoying being back together. I know it hurt her family when Elizabeth and I took time off. They always welcomed me back and understood the complexities of an adolescent relationship with the knowledge that even the best relationships and the strongest love regardless of age is never perfect nor without its challenges.

"Ah, how cute," said Mr. Bundy standing over us.

We froze. Our lunch picnic was destroyed. Eleventh grade also reunited us with Mr. Bundy, who handled the ninth and eleventh grades. I couldn't tell who was worse, Mr. Panzram or Mr. Bundy.

"This is improper behavior for two kids your age and you're both cutting out of school."

"Mr. Bundy, we both have lunch this period," I tried to explain.

"And you think you can just leave school and have a picnic?"

"Why not? Is it illegal?" I inquired.

"No wise cracks, young man. Your behavior is atrocious. Elizabeth, you'll have detention for the next three days. Jack, I'll have to suspend you another three days for insubordination. Pack it all up."

Once again I erased Mr. Bundy's message from the answering machine, served out my time, and returned to classes just as I had so many times before. It seemed impossible to stay out of trouble, with or without Elizabeth. But she certainly minimized the damages.

Elizabeth gave me a peck on the cheek and departed for her own class. I turned to go into class and found Mrs. Lumbrera staring at me from behind her desk.

"That's your girlfriend?"

"Yes, why?"

"I hope you appreciate her, while she's still around."

"Yes, I do very much."

"I would if I was you."

I tried my hardest to ignore my teacher's crude remarks and went to the back to sit down.

It was as if she were trying to find a reason to send me right back to ISS. The class unpacked their books and settled in. Mrs. Lumbrera began class.

"The next few months we'll be reading such writers as Flannery O'Connor, Edgar Allan Poe, Shirley Jackson, and William Faulkner. We'll be dealing with the theme of life and death."

These writers were fabulous and I thoroughly enjoyed reading. My mother inspired a fine love for books and stories at a young age with *The Little Engine that Could*, *Grimm's Fairy Tales*, and so many other great books. From eleven to thirteen years old, I loved *The Hardy Boys* and read just about every single one of the one hundred fifty plus books in the series. Yet something about literature and this lady didn't mix. She ruined great writers, mostly because she turned their stories into a soap opera of death and because she refused to teach us. Instead she asked us questions we didn't know and waited for us to discuss something we read but didn't yet understand. There was no guidance or explanations. It was senseless. "Discussions" as she called them were gossip conversations where only the most extroverted aggressive students participated. I felt like I had an ax in my face. It was a battle between the loudmouth offensive lineman and the future salesman. When we weren't being stoned by their nonsense opinions, we had to sit and listen to her read an entire novel out loud in her husky voice. It was painful. I took some time off and went into isolation by cutting class.

After a week, Mrs. Lumbrera sent in her "illegally absent" referrals to Mr. Bundy. Not long after, I was apprehended in the hallway by Mr. Bundy.

"Mr. Tortis, you've been cutting English and I'm going to suspend you again. You just can't decide not to go to class."

"Yes, but I read the books already and know the…"

"Oh, you know it all, don't you? Believe me, we all think we know so much when we're young and foolish. Three more days, Jack."

Drag me out to the field and punish me, bury me alive in the wall, stone me, poison me.

On my way to the second day of suspension, I saw a girl vomit in the hallway. I walked with her, at a safe distance, and made sure she got to the nurse. When I showed up late to the suspension room, the director Mr. Horton stopped me at the door.

"You're late."

"I know, I was helping a girl who…"

"Two extra days, Mr. Tortis."

"But she was sick!"

"I don't care what she was. It's your responsibility to get here on time."

I sat down and dealt with it. It would be a marathon.

Mr. Horton sat behind the suspended students and watched over them. We sat in mandatory silence all day, staring out the window in between doing the assignments some teachers would send down to the room. Not surprisingly, Mrs. Lumbrera never gave any work. Instead of helping me or reaching out to me, she ignored me. Who was the child here?

On the morning of my fourth day of suspension, my health teacher Mr. Nicosia called me out into the hallway. The man was tall and athletic. He looked like someone who was sincerely healthy, which was great because most of the gym teachers didn't. He was always drinking water or those fancy health drinks, in contrast to the gym teachers who I'd see with their diet soda sugar fix as early as seven thirty in the morning. Mr. Nicosia was the real deal. He confidently entered the room, whispered something to Mr. Horton, and then waved me over. I got up and we went out into the hall.

"Jack, would you like to get out of suspension early? Today?"

"I sure would."

He waved me on to walk with him down the hall.

"Listen, an older teacher got a flat tire down the road from the school. If you come with me and change the tire for her, your time is done."

"Thanks, Mr. N. I haven't ever changed a tire though."

"Good then, we'll help each other and you'll learn something."

We walked out to his car and got in. The compact Toyota was fresh smelling inside and new. We drove down the road a ways until we came to a four-door sedan with a flat. We got out and Mr. Nicosia prepared the necessary tools. He handed me the wrench and told me to unscrew the bolts on the tire. When I got stuck on one bolt, he leaned over, took the iron, and wedged it loose himself. When I encountered another tough one, he told me to push down harder, and I got it myself this time. Then he handed me the jack and guided me along on how to jack the car up and remove the tire. I rolled the tire to Mr. Nicosia, and he rolled the spare back at me. I placed the spare on the wheel, leveled the car back down to the ground, and then tightened the bolts.

"Ok, that's it. That wasn't so bad was it? Follow me back to the school." He flipped me the keys to the teacher's car.

I followed him back to the parking lot, and I carefully pulled the car into a spot next to his. We got out and I thanked him.

"Thanks, Mr. N, I really appreciate this."

"Not a problem. You did a good job, Jack. Can I buy you a cup of coffee?"

"Sure, thanks."

Mr. Nicosia led me into the cafeteria. We ordered coffees and my teacher paid. He didn't say much, but he didn't have to. He gave off a sense of comfort. He looked down with piercing blue eyes balanced by a big friendly smile and handed me the coffee.

"There you go. Thanks again for your help. When the bell rings just go to your sixth-period class. I'll see you tomorrow morning in class."

At that moment I had wished every class was health with Mr. Nicosia. He had taught me a skill, a confidence, something I didn't get from a father figure in my life.

When the bell rang, Mr. Nicosia went off in his direction and I scurried off to my sixth-period class. I had missed fifth-period class legally— no Mrs. Lumbrera that day.

50

ELEVENTH GRADE was an up and down year for me. With Elizabeth, without her. With her again, then broken up again. In the months separated from my girlfriend, I was able to reconnect with friends, for better or worse. Despite my ups and downs with Elizabeth, I still loved her and my experience with her was a world away from the one Gene and I related to.

For most of high school I had really tried to stay away from his darkness, but we had addictive personalities. There I was on his doorstep again and again. Our negativity was like a magnet. All of the south shore boys seemed to find their way back to each other eventually, especially when we didn't have girlfriends or sports. We had all come from the same place, all went our own ways, sometimes spiraling out of control, sometimes finding ourselves, sometimes finding each other for a little while.

Once in a while I would get together with Gene for a "boy's night out" to smoke weed. We would start to talk about girls, but he didn't have much use for them.

"They're whores. You can't trust 'em," he would repeatedly say.

"All of them? That's statistically impossible," I would answer.

"All of them."

"You have issues, man. Girls are great."

I wondered if his present sentiments about females had anything to do with the distance from his mother who was in Florida. He had spent most of his childhood with her up until he moved up to New York. What happened there? Why did he decide to leave her and move to New York with his father? He never talked about it. We never talked about our families enough. Maybe we would've been in better shape if we had. Maybe not.

Steven, Gene, Andy, and I cut out of school one day in early May. We picked up two girls from another town out east thirty or so miles away. We went to a park and wandered around. We climbed a big hill and smoked joints at the top overlooking a meadow with flowers. Steven went back down the hill and got it on with one of the girls. After a while, I went down the hill to check on him. They were finished. Steven ran up the hill to go get high and the half dressed girl with swollen lips backed me up into my car and tried to get sloppy with me. I pushed her away. Her lips looked slimy and I wasn't sure what she had done with Steven only seconds before I came down the hill. I asked her to get dressed and went back up the hill to get everyone.

After driving around for a little more, I dropped the girls off. Gene was careful to get the girl's number, the one who had been with Steven. Later that month Gene borrowed his father's big boat of a car and traveled out there to get with her. Just as she was about to get into his car, a concerned parent intercepted. Of course, according to Gene, the concerned mother was just a crazy bitch. Because she didn't let her daughter get into a car with a strange older kid? He was lucky it wasn't some crazed father.

On the way home that day, Steven and I got in a tiff. I was driving and he was acting like a monkey. He was loud and distracting and I told him to calm down. He was in one of his hyper moods dancing and flailing his arms all over. One more time I told him to cut it out, but he continued to be rambunctious and laughed me off. I clocked him with a right hand jab as my left hand gripped the wheel. He sat for a moment stunned and then returned the punch. I should have been pissed but I laughed. Only Steven would dare to punch a person while they were driving the car they were in at sixty miles an hour on a highway. We all sat there stunned. Gene and Andy cried out from the backseat for us stop.

"You punched me. I've known you for so long and you..."

"And you punched me back while I'm driving!"

"Yeah, but you hit me."

"Like we never boxed. You had no problem hitting me then. You wouldn't calm down and let me drive. You trying to kill all of us?"

We bickered on for some time until we all went home that day. I knew he had become too much for me to handle. It wasn't fun to be around someone so difficult. If he wasn't wild like this, he had out of control fits of anger. I would've let him crash my car that day if he had been in real anger mode. When he was truly angry, the world stopped.

In the fall, Steven had always embraced football and was the star running back. At least he redirected this anger into a sport he enjoyed. During football season he stuck with his football brothers and cheerleaders. In the spring though, he had had no discipline, no bonds holding him to that group, and he fell in with the dirtbags. This was his downfall, which led to failing eleventh grade. He had no football mentors or coaches to look out after him and say, "Hey, what's going on? You need to get your act together." Where were these coaches who celebrated his touchdowns every fall? The truth is they were probably happy because they could use him to win games for another year, as long as he didn't lose total control. I wish I could've kept him to myself, so we could've looked out for each other, but there was no holding down Steven.

When he assaulted Ronnie I knew he had taken a path I wanted nothing to do with. Only a couple of weeks after our outing to the hill, Steven brutally busted up the kid. Ronnie had carelessly stepped right out in front of Steven's mother's car. She was out alone with

Steven's younger baby brother. She slammed on the breaks and beeped the horn. The baby had been shaken awake and was crying. Ronnie was irritated by the horn and didn't understand that he had almost caused an accident with a baby in a car. He spat on the car, kicked the fender, and told the woman to go fuck herself. One of Steven's friends witnessed the whole scene and told him who the kid was. Be careful whom you disrespect.

Ronnie was generally a good jock type kid. He and Steven had even played football together, but that didn't matter. In town one day Steven got out of a car, walked right up to him and hit him with a right hand everyone felt. One punch was all it took to cave in Ronnie's cheekbone, literally blasting apart the bones in his cheek and eye socket. Blood sprayed from his face and he crashed to the ground. His face swelled as he laid waiting for an ambulance. All that anger in one punch. Years worth, practiced on others, caused by others, but taken out on one.

Several reconstructive surgeries would be required to repair his disfigured, shattered face. The ordeal would involve criminal charges against Steven, and a civil suit would be launched. After being charged, Steven only got more violent and went on a summer streak of undefeated brawls, mostly knockouts, one torn lip, and one broken beer bottle over the head of a knife-yielding thug. He was lucky no one else pressed charges.

One afternoon, I drove Gene and Ryan to Tower Records where they wanted to steal some CDs. I waited in the car. So many years after being caught, I couldn't even think about stealing again. Besides, we were too old for this kind of behavior.

I waited and waited. A half hour had passed and I thought about going in to get them. At an hour into my wait, a police car pulled up to the front doors. I could see both of them led up to the front of the store by a guard in a blue suit. I circled the lot a couple of times, until from a distance I saw them being loaded into the back of the police car. I simply drove home.

Gene called me a few hours later and asked if I could pick him up from home. He actually had me get him at the corner because he didn't want his father to know he was going.

"My father's an asshole. He screamed at me for an hour and took my shit away."

Gene cried in anguish for a few minutes.

After a while, I turned and asked him,

"What do you want him to do, pat you on the back? You just got caught stealing and he had to pick you up from the police."

"Yeah, but he didn't have to be a dick about it."

"He's embarrassed. You're what, seventeen now? My mother was furious. Steven's uncle gave it to him good when he got caught. You think our parents should just let it go. We'd be like one of those criminal kids whose parents let 'em do whatever they want."

He was lucky he hadn't been caught for the vitamin store burglary, which would have had far worse consequences. I drove us to Burger King and treated him to a dollar menu meal. We smoked a joint at the dead-end and then ate our food looking out at the water. A sewage treatment plant was just to our west and so we called this spot Shit Point.

Nights at Shit Point had become a parking lot marijuana festival. Gene and I were over our steroids phase. The up was over. Enter a low. Gene and I would go to Shit Point for food, but we usually found more private parking lots where there weren't any signs of the police, like our old elementary school. Sometimes we even parked in front of people's houses if they had a nice set of shrubs along the side.

We'd park, get stoned, and zone out on old 70's music. Gene's pessimism would weaken and his anger would subside when he was stoned, so the more the better. But I could never keep the beast in him down long enough, so I would cherish any positive times.

For a field trip we'd walk out to our old elementary school field and sit on the bleachers under the night skies smoking pot and talking life. I thought back to the old days, running against Evan, backyard wrestling matches, heavy metal, such innocence, now all just stardust. There are so many stars in the northern sky, especially visible in a dark open field. We just hung out and gazed at the sky.

"You ever wonder why we meet the people we do when we do?" I asked.

"Yeah, like fate. Maybe there's a meaning, or maybe it's all just one coincidence."

"But what do you believe? Don't you have faith? You're the Catholic, right?"

"Yeah, but I don't know that my faith goes that far."

"I just think it's crazy how people come and go in our lives."

"It is crazy. I agree. The world is fucked up and crazy," he said.

So much philosophy of the world to discuss and so little time. There were some great moments out there, just the two of us, but time was running out.

Around this time, I had run into Andy and started to hang with him again. Andy introduced Gene and me to a jock named Gilby. He and I clicked right away and started to hang out on our own. Gene didn't seem to share the same fondness. Gil was too laid back and cool. He had plans to go to college. He wasn't angry and tough enough.

"I think he's a fag, Jack. Watch out. Gil's gay," he warned.

I began to question whether I was allowed to have other people in my life besides Gene. The possessiveness was eerie. Gene was sure he called me every day to make sure I wasn't going off with anyone else. He began to bad mouth Andy, our longtime childhood friend, in what seemed like a ploy to get me nervous about spending time with him. Just as he had done with Gil, Gene questioned Andy's sexuality. Maybe he assumed I was homophobic. As usual, the talk went on behind everyone else's back. In person, face to face with Andy or even

Gil, Gene was a friendly guy with nothing much to talk about, other than me that is, as I'd soon find out.

Lucky for Gene, Andy and Gil were invested in sports. Gene and I drifted back into the car routine for our weed parking lot sessions. We'd sit for hours stoned out of our gourds listening to music. This time we added 80s heavy metal and hot coffee rushes to our Friday and Saturday night excitement. Gallons of black coffee were consumed in order to wake us from our stoned-out dazes. Up, down, up, down. It sounds like fun, but it was tiring to waste away our weekends like a zombie in a dead-end parking lot. I had grown tired again. Up, down, up, down. It seemed our lives were stuck in this cycle.

Trying to stay positive was difficult when I was around Gene. His views on the world and girls were still extremely pessimistic. Music was the one great bond we had and we had both started to play guitar. I figured if we started to make music together it would take his mind off the negativity, or at least put it to good use.

Instead of true musical collaboration though, we were faced with yet another disaster. All the riffs I brought to our jam sessions turned into hardcore metal at Gene's direction. I just wanted to play fun rock and roll, but he wanted something darker and angrier. There was no compromise with his fast playing and low drop D tuning. Frustrated with the direction of the work, I stopped jamming with him. If only we had been able to compromise, we might have been the next best thing, but we couldn't even get past the song writing.

Gene obsessively called me when I disappeared for a few days, leaving message after message. After hearing one of his belligerent messages on the answering machine, I just couldn't call the guy back and take his offers to revise my tunes. I had never realized until then how much of Gene's vocabulary consisted of fuck prefixes.

"Fucking maybe, I'm fucking delusional....but I don't fucking know. I just fucking.... want to grab a fucking beer with you and fucking go out like two buddies. Let's just fucking forget about the fucking music."

Of course, I hadn't beat my mother to the machine on this one. She listened to it and then played it for me. Half laughing, she asked what was the matter with him.

I needed time away from him.

I needed to worry about myself.

Andy and I met up one Saturday afternoon. We went for a drive and then headed to a day party at someone's house. On the way, we picked up Evan Klause. After the brass knuckle beating, we didn't speak or even see each other for over a year. But more recently we had begun to bump into each other in school and at parties. The reason for this, you could suppose, was either I was hanging with a better crowd, or he was hanging with a worse one, or maybe the two worlds really weren't that far apart.

When I started dating Elizabeth I had asked her,

"So what was it like dating Evan Klause?"

"Well, it wasn't really serious dating. It was kid stuff. His mother didn't want me near him and he wasn't allowed to do much. My brothers used to tease him because they knew how much he was crazy about me."

"How's that?"

"Because I showed them the letters he wrote to me."

"Oh, do you do that to me too?"

"No, but his were funny."

"Funny? Why?"

"He was crazy about me and he knew I wasn't as into him."

"The poor guy," I said, gloriously knowing I had once again beaten my foe.

"Yes, I felt sorry for him. When I broke up with him he cried. He was *so* sensitive."

"What?"

"Yes, he had some issues. His mother was a bit overbearing and his father liked his beer. He had a speech problem when he was young."

"Wow, the speech issue sounds familiar. I always thought he had things so perfect because he was so confident."

"He wasn't as much confident as he was afraid. He really had self-esteem issues. But maybe he'll grow out of them like you did."

"Ah very funny."

For once I kind of felt bad for the guy. The Evan I had always known was the loud mouth bully on the field. If only we had talked and gotten to know each other better.

Evan got into the car and shook my hand. I think in an odd sense we were both happy to see each other again in better circumstances with a mutual friend. Andy spent time with him since they played basketball together on the team and both still lived in the same neighborhood.

"Let's party, whoa!" Evan yelled.

We were all wild and funny and it was a good time. Here I was, just a punk, hanging with two star basketball players torching up a joint. Andy only smoked a little since he was a little more health conscious, but he was stoned for sure. We drove around and listened to a Stone Temple Pilots tape. Evan loved it and knew the words.

"I have this at home, man. It's classic. Creep, Dead and Bloated, Plush— all so good."

At some point, when the joints were all burned down, Evan took out his pipe and we hit that too. We drove around for a while stoned out and then went to a party.

Once there we all went our own ways and mingled with different people. Andy and I found each other after an hour or so. After a while, we went to look for Evan.

We walked into a bedroom to find Evan sitting against a wall zonked out on something more than just pot. Only an hour before he had invited me into the room with a couple of older kids to "take a walk on the wild side" as he called it. I didn't know what specifically that wild side consisted of, but I knew it was nothing I wanted to be a part of.

"Hey, Evan. Andy and I are going to get going? Do you want a lift home?"

"No. I'm going to find one later," he said slowly and quietly.

"You all right?"

"Yeah, yeah, I'm great. Stone Temple Pilots, man!"

I said goodbye to Evan and left the party knowing he was visiting a place I'd already been. We all have our time there. And from where we're from, it's no surprise.

51

THE TWIN TOWERS were grand. I remember Don taking us to the World Trade Center one day in 1988. We entered the tower into its magnificent lobby. The room was wide open glowing with gold and lush red carpet. We entered the elevator and took the long ride to the roof. My ears popped and my head felt the pressure of a height I had never felt before. JP was acting up and I remember Don yanking his arm to get him to straighten up and quiet down. We arrived at the observation deck. The roof was the color of the sky. Don warned us not to throw anything, that from this height a penny could kill someone below and you would be charged with murder. The view was overwhelming. I looked out at Manhattan and to the rest of the world. And somewhere down there was the speck where I lived. I realized we were all just raindrops in an ocean.

In tenth grade, someone tried to bring those buildings down with a bomb in the basement. They must have disliked how small the buildings made them feel. They failed at their mission, at least this time, but it scared me to think about how crazy people had become, how everything we love and know could be taken from us in seconds.

My problems were nothing compared to others. A girl named Lisa in my grade was born allergic to almost everything around her. She was actually allergic to herself at times. The doctors had to shoot her up with steroids and so she was unusually bloated, but it didn't stop her from being herself. Lisa was so social and happy, and it's hard to believe that such a great person would be taken so soon. When she passed away at the end of eleventh grade, it reminded everyone there was no reason to complain about life. Of course, we did, but maybe a little less. The loss of Lisa was our local tragedy, and none of us could ever forget her.

Our school principal Mr. Shulman gave a short speech over the loudspeaker about Lisa's passing. He was the head honcho with three assistant principals working for him. He was a career politician decked out in a suit with politician hair parted to the side. His motto was "all students can learn" but of course everyone knew many kids didn't and wouldn't learn, certainly not in this school. They paid him about a hundred grand to show up four times a week and be the face and voice of the school. We sure needed it, but not from some Westchester yuppie who didn't know a thing about life on the island. Nothing went past face and voice. No heart. No soul.

Lisa could have used a tree, a bench, something permanent dedicated to her, but he was all talk and no action.

She was just a raindrop in the ocean.

Mr. Shulman preached about the importance of community.

"Be a part of a community," he'd say.

"Yeah right, man," I thought. Our town was the type of place where they'd all pretend to come together in a time of tragedy, and in the aftermath they'd slowly begin to cannibalize each other when there was nothing else left to devour. How do you pretend to be a community when the culture of the place is rotten?

Some of the kids and teachers were good at making their own culture inside a bubble. Maybe some were just good fakers. But they celebrated only two select groups and alienated all the others in school.

Forget about being independent.

Forget about being an individual and standing on your own.

Sign up and sign over your soul to one of two groups.

I wondered how many others like myself didn't know how to be part of a community that caters to jocks and honors students. A community that judges and keeps you down. If you weren't a super geek or super masculine, you were doomed. I had tried to be both, but I never fit in. So I lived in a kind of purgatory state with so many other generals, so many other punks.

I didn't want to throw around balls and have pissing contests. I didn't want to get toughened up by some bad breath, spitting coach. I was tired of competition. None of it really mattered in the end. None of it mattered to Lisa.

I didn't want to go on class trips to Fire Island with the honor society where I'd have to hear about some kid's father's boat or stare at all those brown boat shoes. I had none of that. No father. No boat. Certainly no boat shoes.

So what community was left for me?

None.

Who would reach out to the misfits and rejects?

No one.

So leave us alone.

Raindrops.

52

MY TEACHER Mr. Kelly sat down at his desk and asked me to have a seat. It was a quarter after two and school was done for the day. He held a stack of papers and ran his fingers through the corner.

"You know, there are some great things in here. You could polish this up and share it one day. Keep going. Just because you're done with suspension doesn't mean you have to be done with the writing."

"What, you want me to keep going?"

"Yes, I'd like to read on. Find out what happens."

"Honestly, I enjoyed ISS this time. I think I'm going to get it again soon."

Mr. Kelly laughed, "Now let's not let that happen. Besides, you're done with eleventh grade next week. Let's keep it clean for the next few days, eh?"

"All right, thanks. Maybe next year."

"But will you keep writing?"

"Yes, I will."

I went to leave and Mr. Kelly called me back.

"Oh, I almost forgot. Here."

He handed me an anthology of literature.

"Here's an anthology. Read it during the summer. Reading makes better writing."

I grasped the book, thanked my teacher and left the ISS room.

That would be my last suspension in high school.

Later I opened up the book and found an inscription on the inside of the cover that read Roger Kelly, Spring '87, University of Maine. This was one of his books from college. I felt honored, and it just about made up for all of the anguish I had been through in English class that year. All those miserable, mean-spirited high school teachers. Why weren't they replaced with teachers like Mr. Kelly, Ms. Marsolice, Mr. Luca, and Mr. Nicosia?

I spent the final week in school reading from the collection of stories, poems, and essays, and I finished off eleventh grade quietly without any further trouble. When I received my report card in June, I was both surprised and relieved to see a 65% grade for English, a poor but barely passing score.

53

THE SUMMER BEFORE senior year began. JP was growing up and getting into more trouble. After a stint in the state center, he still hadn't learned. The school year had been a disaster. After school was over for summer break, he'd ride his bike miles away to go hang with older kids, some my age or older. He was doing things well before his time. JP was only out riding around because his parents had told him to go get out the pent up energy. He could have become a pro cyclist with all the practice he got. It didn't make any sense that he had all this freedom and I would get grilled about being out too much. Throughout my teenage years, my mother would rant about "family time" and "family Sundays." But it didn't make any sense.

I know she meant well, but it bothered me to be with them, as many teenagers feel about spending time with their parents at that age. My trouble being around them was exceptional though. Don's embarrassing short shorts in the late eighties or his red Fila phase in the nineties didn't help. I just wanted to be separate from them. And I would get that wish soon enough.

My job at The Italian Garden was going great. The environment was so much better than The Chicken Shack or Super Cohen's. This restaurant made great quality food, no one belittled others, and the place was impeccably clean. The time there also reunited me with Paul. He had kept it pretty innocent for most of high school, which meant he wasn't spending time with a punk like me. So it was great to see him again.

The missing ingredient for the Roma family restaurant was location. Parking was difficult and the surrounding stores weren't doing so well bringing business to the area. We had survived for a little while, and then only weeks into the summer we had to close our doors. It was a shame because it was the one place where I couldn't complain about anything and I got great food on the house. Just when I had found a great job, I'd have to start looking for a new one. This was the story of my life.

In late June my father came back to New York to visit, but he couldn't stay long. He needed to get back on the road. He stopped in so I could do him a quick favor.

"Jack, could you do me a favor and sign this paperwork? You know, I'm sending your mom and Don money every month for child support, but I don't know if you're getting it. In a few months you'll be eighteen and I figure it would be best to cut out the middleman. That way you get the checks directly."

Money every month. Sure. Why not?

I happily signed the papers.

But of course, I never saw a dime. Child support would legally continue for several more years, unless the child signed off on it. I signed the papers and trusted him, happy just to see him, wishing he didn't have to run off again. And then he was gone.

54

I WAS KICKED OUT OF THE HOUSE at seventeen. The twenty-four hours leading up to being kicked out were uneventful. I was chewing on Twizzlers and watching a stack of Blockbuster rentals at Elizabeth's house, nowhere near as destructive as I'd been while we were broken up. Other kids in my town were out robbing car stereos, experimenting with mescaline, getting into roid-raged brawls, or getting stranded at stupid parties where another oblivious parent would go away only to return home to thousands of dollars of damage. Here I was now just minding my business. I was in love, but that made me a soft target for bullying, not by kids my age, but by my stepfather.

I had spent a year with Elizabeth in tenth grade. We took our share of time off in eleventh grade and I returned to my punkish ways ditching school and getting into trouble. By May it was clear that tenth grade had been a much more productive year than eleventh. The past year had ended up in a manic daze, and I had earned minimal credits toward graduation and barely escaped being left back. It was the summer before twelfth grade and I was trying to keep it all together, finally content with where I was in life. I had a plan to start out the year fresh. Then some kind of hell entered my life out of nowhere.

It was a night in July, and Elizabeth's parents were away on Fire Island for the weekend. We spent the evening watching movies, while her younger brothers hung out upstairs with a couple of their friends. Elizabeth's older sister was home from college and in her room listening to Pearl Jam. Shortly after 10 p.m., my mother showed up at the door, frantic.

She never popped in on me like this.

"Jack, you need to come home."

"Why? What happened? Is everyone all right?"

"Yes, everyone's okay."

"Then why would I come home?"

"Because it's late and you can't stay here."

"It's ten o'clock. I've been out far later than this and I've slept over here plenty of times."

"Don is upset and wants you home."

"Suddenly Don is Dad?"

The guy hadn't ordered me to do much more than stay away from his stereo equipment and take my shoes off so we'd preserve his pristine light-gray carpets. I had smoked cigarettes, been caught stealing, got into street fights, shaved my head with a Bic razor, smoked a glass bong in the apartment in his house with his employee, failed to do the right thing at school, and yet now he was suddenly concerned about my whereabouts and wellbeing?

Earlier that day he had dragged my brother into the house by the throat in a headlock. After gathering my things for the weekend, I ran into my little brother in the backyard on the way out. Don was inside the kitchen and yelled for JP to come in and explain where he had been. What was going on? Usually they were telling him to get lost. Why was Don suddenly inspired to be a parent? After sending JP off and neglecting him for so long, now he wanted him home? JP and I said goodbye and he kept kicking around a soccer ball until Don came out and dragged him inside. JP was crying and Don threw in a few punches to try to shut him up, but it only seemed to make him cry louder. It was a terrible scene and I felt helpless against such rage. I yelled at Don to calm down, but he slammed the door in my face and pulled my brother inside. I was on the outside, but my brother was still a prisoner.

"Jack, he's really upset," my mother said.

"Over what? Does it have to do with what he did to JP earlier?"

"No, he's upset because you're here."

"Here? At my girlfriend's house?"

"Yes, he says he doesn't want to get sued."

"Sued over what? Her parents know I'm here. This isn't a stranger we're talking about."

Elizabeth's parents actually preferred the extra company, especially if they were out. It wouldn't be the first time I stayed over and never had there been any commentary from my mother or Don.

"He doesn't want to get sued if you get her pregnant."

"What? This is crazy."

I couldn't help but think he had finally lost his mind. My mother's erratic behavior was scaring me and I didn't want any part of it.

"Tell him I said no, and if he wants to say something, tell him to tell me himself."

My mother left, upset and probably in the middle of something bad. I didn't want her getting hurt and asked her if she would be all right and if she wanted to come back here and stay with us. She denied any trouble, but I knew the risk was there. Don had had many fits and although he never punched or kicked or dragged her the way he did to my brother, he would resort to throwing objects at her— abuse her indirectly, so she could never say he hit her. And he'd break things like dish sets and glasses. One afternoon I listened from upstairs as he emptied the entire kitchen cabinet onto the floor in a rage. Glass by glass, it went on forever.

Don had these cycles he went through. My mother excused them and said they were due to medication or a head cold, but I knew better. The cycles consisted of outbursts of anger, then guilty disappearances, and then a make-up phase— all textbook-psychological abuse. Sometimes in his explosions he would lash out directly on my brother.

I got hit with a fist of psychological abuse from time to time, but JP got all the worst shit. Even if I was left out of it, just being subjected to the environment itself was enough to make me never want to be home.

Here we were again in one of those classic peaks of the cycle. I wasn't going back to that house and I knew it the moment my mother said goodbye. She called thirty minutes later to give me one final ultimatum— come home now or don't come home at all.

"Please think about this, Jack."

"I have. Tell him to tell me his problems."

He wouldn't talk to me though. Instead, he drove over to Elizabeth's house in the middle of the night and circled around the block beeping the horn like a lunatic. "I know you're in there," he must've thought. He did this for a couple of hours and then disappeared.

I'll never really know what his sudden obsession was. Jealousy? Loss of control? I can't even begin to go to that sad place in his mind. When he did finally call the next day, Elizabeth answered. He started to yell at her and told her he was going to shoot her parents dead when they got home and that I was never welcome back in his house. You'd think I committed an unforgivable crime. I overheard this madness and told her to hang up, but he beat her to it.

We immediately called 911. The officer arrived about fifteen minutes later and we told him the situation. The officer said the report would be on file and that they would go issue a warning to Don to stay away from us. He said if Don didn't listen to this warning we should call the police again and an order of protection would be granted. Don never called or returned. He didn't need to— he had already taken his license plates off my car in the middle of the night.

Originally my car registration was in my name, but to take some of the financial load off, my mother offered to insure it under her name and I would pay her. So legally, the plates belonged to Don. I was left with a car I couldn't drive and nowhere to go since I couldn't stay at my girlfriend's house forever. I hadn't thought this far ahead, but I knew I wasn't going back.

PART II
Unchained

The professor pointed to a visual of chained prisoners in a cave. The illustration of "Allegory of the Cave" showed the simple underground setting of the prisoners, the bridge behind them, and the roaring fire behind that.

He continued to explain: *The allegory is a dialogue between Socrates and a student, as relayed by Plato. Socrates explains the setting of how we're all born prisoners, and then he lets one of the prisoners go free. The prisoner is able to turn around and see the puppets and statues. But the problem is he thinks the puppets and statues are now the real tree, bird, tiger, lamb, so forth. Of course, we know the prisoner is still looking at just another layer of illusion. So Socrates takes him up another step to the surface where he must adapt to the sunlight after years in the darkness.*

The professor points around the room at everyone.

We are all prisoners, but we all leave the cave. When we first step out of the cave, the sun is bright and our eyes are blinded and we need time to adjust. The sun hurts our eyes. The truth hurts. It's difficult to deal with the truth at first. It's hard to face it. We must adapt to the new realities around us. This is a tough adjustment. Truth is a tough thing to accept, especially after you've been deceived with shadows. Eventually, the former prisoner's eyes adjust and they see the world for what it is. We must accept that the tree, the bird, the tiger, and the lamb we see before us is finally the true entity, and not the puppet we saw before and the shadow before that. We wonder if this is yet another illusion. Will we wake up years later somewhere down the road to find out this is all a dream and another farce? How do we live with such suspicion and skepticism? We question whether there is another level of reality, another layer of truth? How many layers can we peel back before we get to truth? Think about the layers in your life. The crowds you surf between. The lines and borders you walk.

Now our former prisoner is going to be a critical thinker. A true education brings us out of the cave. Whether it's self-education or a formal classroom, as long as it gets you thinking about the world around you. We're not going to live in paranoia, but we're going to ask healthy questions about the things we're told and the things we're expected to just accept.

This is like the Matrix film. How many have seen that film? Some hands go up. *At the end of the film you don't really know if he's in the real world or in the matrix. It's all about reality versus illusion. We're slaves bound to a society set up by others.*

This is the Wizard of Oz. How many have seen that film? Even more hands go up. *Good. It's good to see that old classic still alive.*

In the Wizard of Oz they're all looking for something they already have. They're on a journey to find the Wizard because they think he will give them what they need. The Scarecrow wants brains, the Tin Man needs a heart, the Lion desires courage, and Dorothy just wants to go home. They believe the Wizard will grant them their wishes. They're on the yellow brick road to find this grand godly wizard, who eventually sends them on a quest to find the wicked witch. Even after that wild chase for the witch's broomstick, they still believe. In the end, Toto the dog pulls open the curtain and reveals the wizard for what he truly is— just another human, a little man on a stool pulling levers behind a thick curtain and talking into a microphone to sound big and powerful. This revelation enables Dorothy and friends to turn around and see the shadows for what they are— statues and puppets. The wizard admits that all the things they had been seeking were right there within. You don't need to go anywhere to find those gifts. Brains, heart, courage. It's all right there inside of you. If you want to go home, all you need to do is click your heels. It's as simple as that.

They are drawn out of the cave and then thrust out into the light of day. In the end of the story, they all find themselves, and Dorothy wakes up from what we learn was all just a dream. Of course, Dorothy's whole dream was an allegory in itself.

You'll see the allegory of the cave in books and films. You'll see it all around you. Are you going to look?

The professor presses a button and the screen goes black.

55

I WAS BARELY LIVING SOMEWHERE. I dumped my black plastic garbage bag full of belongings in Paul's closet. It was home for now. After two weeks of sleeping in my car, at the beach, and a few nights at Elizabeth's house, Paul came by to visit. He had heard the news. Paul offered me the floor and insisted I stay with him. I couldn't refuse the help.

Paul's father, a tall handsome man with a thick black mustache and slicked back hair, welcomed me into his home. Mr. Roma had always seemed like such a serious rock. You couldn't tell if he was in a bad mood or not. But when he was in a good mood, he was a joyous man stuffing your mouth with food and wine, lighting up cigars, dancing to Italian music. And here he was opening his home. I had known his son for over nine years, back when he used to make me do push ups, so in a sense the man had seen me grow up. I saw him the day after moving in and thanked him.

"You get yourself together in the next few months and you'll be all right," he said.

He also apologized about the job loss because of the restaurant closing and hoped I'd find something else. I already had in the men's department at the local retail mart that took over the TSS where we all used to steal. The job was my ticket to getting the Camaro back on the road, but it would take weeks of overtime shifts at $5.25 per hour just to get up enough money to even chip away at the insurance and registration costs. Stocking clothes on shelves wasn't terrible, and it was legal, but the pay was poor and the store manager was abusive. These chain stores needed help because people frequently came and went. We were all replaceable cheap labor.

The manager would lock us in the store at night after closing time at 11:00 and would keep us prisoners until the store was the way he wanted it. Wasn't there a better management style to accomplish this? School the next day? Tough. A baby at home? Tough. A waiting ride? Tough. The last bus? Tough. Locked out of a friend's house? Tough. He didn't care.

The manager screamed and taunted us, circling the store isles like a hawk picking off each successful person at a time and ordering them to wait at the front for the others. The last few people always had it the worst because they felt like everyone else resented them for taking so long, and they were right, we did, but we were really all in it together. We still had it good compared to the Mexicans he'd lock up in the store all night for the graveyard shift to clean floors for half the legal minimum wage. I knew I would have to do better than this job, but with school starting back up I didn't quite know what to do.

As I walked home in the August night, I wondered where all those cars were going. No one walked anywhere anymore. If you walked, you were a poor freak. If you took the bus, you were old or disabled. All those middle-class cars trying to be nicer, something they really weren't. I just wanted my car back, not to join the rat race, but for my own independence.

I wondered if any of my family members were in those passing cars. Sometimes I would stop to sit on a curb by the highway and let myself become hypnotized by the headlights. Was my mother in one of those cars, out looking for me? Was my stepfather on his way to a job or a girlfriend's house? Were my friends out on their way to fun or self-destruction? I knew life went on out there. For me, everything was slowly freezing though. Nothing any of them were doing mattered anymore. I was alone, on foot, in a sinking town.

It took me three weeks in August to save enough to get the car back on the road. For those weeks, I walked three miles each way from work to Paul's. Some days, Elizabeth's mom picked me up or Paul dropped me off. I was thankful for any help I could get.

56

OUT OF NOWHERE, my Uncle Albert showed up at my job at the retail store and asked if he could speak with me outside. He led the way and I followed out to the parking lot. He lit a cigarette. He knew I smoked and asked me if I wanted one. I grabbed at any free cigarette I could get, even if it was one of his crumby Winstons. My heart warmed because it had felt like forever since I had seen family, and perhaps forever since family reached out to me.

"Jack, I heard about home and how you were kicked out. We're worried about you. Where are you staying?"

"I'm at a friend's house for now. I had to get out there anyway."

"How's that working out?"

"I'm sleeping on the floor and living out of a closet, but it's a roof over my head— most nights I get out of here on time."

"Most nights? What does that mean?"

"If I don't make it back before my friend's last sister gets in, I get locked out."

"Why is that?" he asked crossing his arms.

"It's not like they lock me out on purpose. They were robbed once, so the family now has a tradition where the last sister in for the night sets the alarm. When the light is turned out I know I'm on my own that night."

The first time the alarm was set at Paul's, Elizabeth stayed with me. We drove around for a while visiting all the old spots from the early days when nothing seemed to matter and adult life was still so far away in the future.

Now that world of adulthood was closing in us.

At two a.m., we went in for coffee at Dunkin' Donuts. After a while, I took her home. What else was I to do? I couldn't drag her down with me. This was no place for a classy girl you love. She snuck in the back door of her house and I drove off to sit this one out in front of Paul's house to wait for his first sister to leave for work and disarm the alarm. Every day and every night seemed to be a new challenge and my night shift at the store was wearing thin. Some nights I would walk out to the shore beach down the block. There was something calming about the bay— the sound of seagulls, the wind rattling a flag post, a familiar place that reminded me of my days in the south shore neighborhood back when I had my own bed.

"You know that's going to get harder once the winter comes," Albert warned.

"Yeah, I know. I'm going to need a new job before then anyway."

"What about school?" he asked.

"I don't know. It starts next week. I'll do what I have to. I just know I have to get a better job than this."

"What are your chances of getting a better job without school though?"

"I don't know"

"Well, listen, your grandma and I were thinking and we agreed we'd both be willing to take you in. It would be your choice— come live with one of us, finish school, and start over."

My mind went blank. I didn't know how to comprehend such an offer.

Live somewhere else?

Start over?

"Well, I'll think about it, but I really..."

"Think about it and just know the offer is always open. Give us a call. Your grandma definitely wants to see you soon to know you're all right."

"All right, Uncle Albert. Thanks for thinking of me."

He hugged me goodbye, and then I walked back into my lousy workplace.

Faced with the immediate stressor of getting my car back on the road, and keeping it there, I put the offer off. How was I supposed to leave everything I ever knew and start all over? What would I even do? I didn't know what was best for me. With all that was going on, I didn't know how to make rational decisions. My mind was swirling with confusion.

57

THEY ASKED ME TO STUDY, and the first time I just stared back at them blankly and shrugged my shoulders. I'll never forget the first time my mom and Don brought me there to meet everyone. The parents, his two sisters, aunts and cousins were all there. They were loud and overwhelming. They put me right on the spot and asked me questions "What do you like? What do you eat?" I felt like a nine-year-old specimen in a research lab.

Don's father was a tall man of Spanish descent. One December day on the way home from his Wall Street job he slipped off the platform onto the tracks. Another man jumped down, woke him from unconsciousness, and dragged him to safety.

"Thank you," he said as he awoke.

"No, thank Jehovah," his rescuer instructed.

And that was it. When Don's father got home that day he tore down the tree, gave out the last presents they'd ever get, and canceled Christmas. All future holidays were forbidden. Don was sixteen, and his seventeenth birthday the following month went unacknowledged. His parents became heavily involved in the religion and forced it on their two daughters, but for some reason Don never embraced the religion.

His parents had tried to coax me into the world of Jehovah on several occasions when they had me alone. They asked me if I wanted to sit in on one of their "readings" where they sat around the table and read from the Bible and discussed their beliefs. No interest. The next time they tried "the world is coming to an end" approach and asked me if I knew about the impending doom or the paradise world, which would be exclusively reserved only for people who worshiped Jehovah. I said quite frankly if everyone else died I'd rather die too.

Another time, Don's oldest sister Carrie invited me. Don was with me and told her that I wasn't interested,

"Leave him alone. He doesn't want to study with you."

Don had shunned the end-of-world rhetoric. I didn't know how his father had reacted to this, but I knew from what my mother had told me that Don had his share of issues with his parents. I could also tell by their interactions that there was a distance. I guess Don was smarter than my aunts made him out to be, and at least I had been lucky for that.

When my mother left Don for those couple of months in the early days, I think she tried to find faith. One night she brought me to a church. We never went to churches except for the couple of weddings and funerals we had attended, so this must have been an exceptional time in her life. I had messed around in religion class for a few weeks in elementary school before quitting, so my knowledge of religion was limited. We walked up to the statue of Jesus. She leaned over and kissed the statue's foot and then asked me if I wanted to. I was hesitant. I didn't know why we ought to, but since my mother did it I decided to follow. I kissed the cold hard foot of Jesus and then giggled about it in the car on the way home.

"Why did we do this tonight?"

"People just do this sometimes," my mother answered.

Maybe she was looking for something in that church that night. Maybe she wanted to give me the chance to make up my own mind and to see what else was out there.

Here I was so many years later, locked out of Paul's house because work let me out late again, sitting in my car prayerless, thrown out of the house into the wild, in some ways simply because I wanted privacy, the same privacy Don sought as a young man in his parent's crazy house, all which he no longer understood because his days of privacy were reduced to a safe in the bathroom and a trunk in the garage. I couldn't blame him for his jealousy.

He was a prisoner.

And I was free.

58

MY FIRST DAY OF TWELFTH GRADE was a blur, like it is
for everyone else. Who would remember such dreadful detail? What I
do recall is the inability to pay attention. Most people would relate to
a lack of attention in their senior year, but I looked around and saw
plenty of functioning peers going about their business. Maybe they
were good at bottling up all those senior emotions on the verge of
being thrust out into the world? Maybe they hadn't reached that point
yet? Some were in denial and it wouldn't hit them until they were out
of their parent's hovering shadows when it was too late and they were
all alone on some college campus in the middle of a perpetual party.
Some were getting ready for their last season of glory in football in the
fall or basketball in the winter or baseball in the spring. While some
prepared for college, many others were getting ready to do absolutely
nothing with their lives even though they had hustled for straight A's
throughout their six years in secondary education. And most were
probably like me— lost and scared. The days seemed to pile up.

Within days of school starting up it became apparent that my life
was no longer on track the way it had been. Elizabeth and I had a falling out. I guess I resented the whole situation I was in and although I
didn't blame her for my troubles, I couldn't shake all the helpless emotions. Everything was spiraling out of control. I felt guilty, and as my
hole grew deeper, I distanced myself from her. I told her we needed a

little space again.

"I don't want to drag you into this. Let me just sort things out."

"You'd be hurting me more by staying away."

"You don't have these kinds of problems."

"Jack, my family isn't perfect."

"What do you mean?"

"My family isn't perfect. We have problems. Every family does."

"I don't understand. Why didn't you talk about it?"

"It's not happy news. People are people. We're only human."

"You're very forgiving."

"My life isn't so white picket fenced as you thought it was."

"Yeah, but what about the family dinners, church...?"

"Having dinner makes a family perfect? Going to church doesn't hide problems."

"I'm sorry. I didn't know. But I still don't want to burden you with my problems. You have your own."

"So now that you know I have problems that's an excuse? You're not burdening me. Unless you just don't love me anymore?"

"I love you. I do."

"Then don't run away again."

"Listen, let me just sort this out and figure out what I'm going to do. I'll stay in touch."

"Promise me you'll touch base with me every few days."

"I promise."

And I would.

59

THINGS WERE TIGHT— financially and physically. Everything I owned was swept into one of Paul's two bedroom closets. I was fortunate to have this much though. Four or five shirts and several pairs of pants got me through. My bed was a space on the floor just to the side of Paul's bed. I joked around that I was his new dog, but I really couldn't complain. He treated me well. The family did too. They had opened up their home, gave me shelter and food too, though I made a strong attempt to be unseen and unheard as much as possible and this included avoiding the family dinners when they happened. Though if Mr. Roma spotted me he insisted I sit and eat. There were a few times I walked right into a family dinner. We'd eat, drink, and laugh. They were great people and I felt fortunate to know them.

Paul knew some nights I would stay out at other friend's homes, and I wanted to give him that time alone. Everyone needs his or her space. I knew this. He knew this. I tried. My breaks away consisted of other people's cold floors and sometimes a sofa when lucky.

Gene's dusty couch was one I often ended up on. I missed the old Gene and knocked on his door. He opened his arms and we rejoiced in our reunion. We agreed to let go of the tension left over from our failed music endeavors. Besides, we both needed a friend at this point. It was always like this. On and off for weeks, months, even a year at a time. I told him all I had done in that time and he told me his stories. Then once those stories were used up we always fell back into a cold world. We went right back to our old ways.

Gene was dealing and dabbling at the time, so I knew these nights would be a long ride. Some nights we would get so fried out that we wouldn't wake up the next morning. Noon would come and go. Eventually, I would pull myself up from the uncomfortable musty sofa and split before he woke. Other nights I'd sit there with him while he was all tweaked out. He was pushing quarter-ounce bags of pot out the back door and the larger quantities made him paranoid.

Ryan Bailey showed up one night looking busted up. His eyes were dilated and bloodshot, his speech slurred, and he hardly seemed like the kid we once knew. He needed the down of marijuana and Gene loaned him a bag. When he left, Gene told me Ryan had gotten into crack. I didn't know if this was just another story, but Ryan didn't look good. It was terribly disappointing to see Ryan like this, and I wasn't sure why Gene was feeding it with more drugs, but I guess a little pot was the least of his worries.

One night in late September, Gene became so obsessed with his paranoia and called all of his buyers to tell them his supplier had run dry and left town. He told them not to call anymore and then told his supplier he was taking a break. The white in his eyes was bulging out of his dark face and he was sweating bullets. He couldn't take it anymore. Who would want that kind of weight? I hadn't wanted the demand of dime-bags and couldn't imagine the "responsibility" of bigger ones. Gene was convinced his phone was tapped and that the FBI was watching his house in helicopters. He was done.

In a matter of two weeks he had gone from plenty of money and smoke in his pocket to dirt broke as he had always been before. This took a toll on his self-esteem and he sunk into a deep depression. Going to his house was like going to a morgue. It was always a cold dark place, but when he would get into these ruts it was agonizing and I would have to distance myself. He would go off and associate with new losers somewhere, which would excite him just long enough to get him out again experimenting with whatever they were doing. He went through an LSD phase, then a mescaline one, and of course a steroid one— all manic splurges of course. All he had now was some pot from his dad's allowance money, but at least he had a home, food, and a comfortable bed. Here I was working a job and living out of a closet and I was buying him Burger King meals. I couldn't afford to be friends with him at this point.

Steven was in a different crowd now. From September to December, he was in great shape because he had the structure of sports. I guess I had been like this too before quitting track— on and off seasons, busy and bored. Without football, he would've been completely doomed. What in the world would he do when school ended and he couldn't play ball anymore? He was an entirely different guy half the year. He even fell in with entirely different kids. It was as split as you could get. Doppelganger Steven. He'd come out of nowhere in the spring, but I wouldn't see him at all in the fall. It was like I didn't even know the guy.

Of course, last spring had taken a bite out of him and cost him a whole grade level. He would take advantage of this and play eleventh-grade football all over. Three years varsity football instead of two, if he could keep it together. I had heard from Paul that Steven had confessed to trying heroin during the summer in the aftermath of the assault. The words from that night three years earlier rang through my head, "I'll never do heroin, Jack."

Why would he tell me that at fourteen years old? Why was he thinking about that?

I called Steven in September and told him my situation. He told me to hit him up if I needed anything. Out of concern, I asked about his legal issues and he said there was some good news for him. The charges wouldn't be as serious as he originally thought and they'd probably wipe them out because he was still a minor. He said he might have to pay the medical bills though.

"That's great, you have a second chance here."

"I know. I'm going to do good. Hey listen, I'm sorry about that day in your car."

"Don't sweat it, man. I couldn't stay mad at you."

I told him to take up lacrosse in the spring. He laughed and said I should take up whacking off. He knew he went through a metamorphosis after the season ended, but he couldn't help it. I think he was so used to surfing between both crowds that he liked it.

A week after speaking to him on the phone, I had a dream I was on my way to visit Steven. I didn't realize where I was until I entered the gates.

The place is crowded. I find a spot to park and get out of my car to go look for Steven.

I walk upon the dewy grass. The sky is gray and it's cold out.

There he is! I spot my friend and call out his name.

I talk to him for some time. I reminisce about old times like when he was caught stealing the cassette tape in TSS and I miraculously walked right out the doors with a tape in my pants. Or the time he fist-fought his father in his driveway and nearly won. What about the time we boxed each other and he knocked me so hard in the cranium that my head ached for a week? What about the time Randy drove us around in his Camaro higher than ever? And what about all those house parties? Wild times! All we had were memories.

After a while, I get up to leave. Steven looks happy, but he isn't very conversational. I say goodbye and promise to come see him again. I walk away and Steven remains there, like always, but finally in peace. I should've said something that day on the phone.

I could only imagine how intimate he had become with a demon that took all the fight out of him. On his last day in this world he drove the spike in and then slipped away like the wind. In the darkness he saw a playground and heard the mad laughter of children and then that was it. I turn around for one more look at his tombstone. Then I awoke from this terrible dream.

60

THE WORK HAD PILED UP, after several weeks in twelfth grade. I gave up. How was I ever going to get caught up? I had already missed several days in the rut with Gene. How was I going to accomplish anything when I didn't even have a bed to sleep in? There was no choice left but to sign out of school. Teachers didn't know what problems we had and most didn't care. They had their job to do and I couldn't meet those expectations anymore. On October fourth I drove to school with a friend named Dennis, the same kid I used to get in trouble with in Mrs. Sullivan's middle school class and lunch period. We had both just turned eighteen. We ceremoniously signed ourselves out together. The woman asked me whether I was sure,

"Are you sure you want to do this, hon?"

"I don't have much of a choice. I don't know where I'm going to wake up tomorrow and I need to concentrate on making money."

"All right. Maybe you'll come back."

Hardly a possibility, I thought as I put the pen to the paper.

I was free of school but enslaved to work now. People didn't just drop out and hang out unless they were spoiled brats and there were some of those in this town. Most were like me though and had to go to work. I knew I needed a new job, but first I would celebrate my newfound freedom. Dennis and I went back to his house and got drunk on cheap, boxed wine.

I remember being on line in the cafeteria in middle school saying to some lost face how I couldn't wait to drop out of high school when I turned sixteen. I didn't care about what I was going to do with my life. This dangerous attitude was just a symptom of the terrible self-esteem and lack of direction I had. Too many kids feel the same way I did. Somehow, though, sixteen came and went for me. What else was there to do? Isolate myself from friends and go work? And yet here I was anyway, eighteen and done with school.

When Elizabeth heard what I was going to do, she hung up. Five minutes later, she showed up at Paul's front steps and tried to persuade me not to.

"I don't have a choice."

"Jack, you have so much potential though."

"Thank you, but I'll have to do something else with it."

"You told me you weren't going to run away."

"From you. Run away from you. I never promised I was going to stay in school."

"Please think about this?"

I coldly declined her suggestions and said goodbye. How much more help could I take from people? What could they do anyway? I was a burden to good people. I told her thanks for trying and that I needed to get full-time work.

Days before quitting school, I quit the retail job. My girlfriend, my job, how could they not expect me to quit school? I had quit friendships. I had quit sports. I had quit jobs.

I was a professional quitter.

I held the job partly responsible for my failure in school and inability to keep up, and it cost me one too many nights locked out of Paul's house. I wasn't going to stay with a job that had such consequences yet such little pay. I was walking away from everything, but I didn't know where I was going.

My first job as a high school drop out was in a shoe store. Leela, her older brother Jimmy, and myself all started at the same time for the grand opening of a new chain shoe store to be run by all high school drop outs. Leela had dropped out before tenth grade and Jimmy, now twenty-one, had dropped out years ago, never really finding his way. Their house in the north part of town was one of the first places I went once I was officially out of school. It was good to see her. The place brought back such nostalgia for the good old days.

Leela, Jimmy, and I arrived at the empty store and met the manager outside. A big rig was pulled up to the back door. First we unloaded the truck. This was the entire stock of a brand new store all in one load. We filled the backroom and then began to stock the empty shelves along the sides of the store, slowly inching our way to the inside aisles. We filled that building with shoes. After five days, there didn't seem like anything else to do except wait for customers.

After we pioneered the opening day, I was transferred to another location on the south side of town, closer to Paul's where I was staying. But I guess I lost my passion for shoes when I no longer had any friends to talk to or have lunch with. Alone in a new store with an overweight, depressed boss, I didn't know how long I could take watching customers ravage the shelves for the right look and fit. I began to drown in shoes— flip flops— boots— sandals—loafers— I couldn't breathe. At 12:50 on a Tuesday I told my boss goodbye for lunch and never went back. I called later and told him to mail my check— that something crazy had happened and that I couldn't talk about it. I didn't need to explain anything to him though.

A few days after leaving the shoe store, I quit a job at Border's bookstore. I loved books, and I was excited to get the job, but they placed me in the café department. This store location actually cooked food, burgers and such, with a back room infested with roaches. The vile bugs were frozen into the paddies. I was grossed out and pissed off that I didn't get to stock books. I didn't even wait for a lunch break. I panicked and had to get out. I weaved through the aisles making sure no one saw me as I slipped out the front door. I felt so free— rebelliously marching to my get-away car.

I tried one more restaurant. This was an Italian restaurant run by guidos but it reminded me too much of the Chicken Shack and not enough of the good old days in Italian Garden, Paul's father's place— a real Italian restaurant with real Italian food. This new place sucked. I told the guy I forgot my keys in my car, and then I split.

I tried to apply for another retail job, but I spotted Mr. Flinder folding clothes in the men's department. I certainly couldn't work with my old gym teacher, though it may have been interesting. He had been laid off and I guess there wasn't a huge demand for physical education teachers. I wanted to ignore him like he ignored me, but I said hello, knowing the acknowledgement was a bigger hit than being ignored. A year later I heard he was given a second chance and rehired. I hope he was better the second time around.

Depressed, I decided to check on Leela and Jimmy. They always cheered me up. She was still working at the shoe store, so she wasn't home, but Jimmy had quit and decided to study for the Series 7 test. While he waited for the exam date, he spent his days hanging around. In between my job search, I stopped by to say hello to Jimmy.

"Jack, you want to go to the off-track betting place with me?

"I've never been to one. What the heck! Let's go."

"It's a good time. Hey, you want to take your car? Mine's a little shaky right now."

"Sure, let's go," I said and we were off down the driveway past his car, which looked like it was collecting dust and going flat.

This was a gambler's bar. A weekday afternoon, grown men jumping up and down like children and then sulking down into their seats just a few minutes later when their wins were stolen by bigger losses. Each loss took more of their manhood. Some of them were handing over the titles to their cars. Some were on pay-phones begging their loved ones for another loan. It was a sad sight. I didn't play a single dollar and sat back and watched Jimmy bet away a hundred bucks before he called it quits. The place stunk like shit, piss, booze, and broken souls. It was time for me to get a real working job.

61

LIVING off the remainder of my last paycheck, things were looking bleak. Where was I? Why did this happen to me? Where was I going?

One night Gene and I went out for some brews. We met at The Dragon, a local sports pub where they didn't bother to inspect our fake IDs anymore than a quick glance. We had a couple of beers like the *men* we were. Beer never satisfied me though. It just made me full and gassy and made me feel like I was drinking piss.

"Hey, can you hook us up with some weed tonight?" I asked him.

"Yeah, but fucking, I don't have any money."

"Don't worry, I'll buy a bag," I replied fully aware this was no news.

"Sure, let's go over to my sister's friend's house."

We got up to leave, but we noticed a girl we knew. It was Kara from the house party several years ago. She and I had seen each other here and there through the years, and I couldn't help but think of that day when she was spread out on her table. I really tried, but she was branded, maybe like all the rest of us in some strange way. The mission was to not let her know what I was thinking. Treat her the way I would want to be treated.

"Hi, Jack. Hi, Gene. How are you guys?"

She leaned in and gave us a hug.

"It's been so long," she said softly as she leaned in.

"Hi, Kara, yeah it's been a while."

Gene starting talking to one of her friends I didn't know so well. I nodded hello to her.

"Where have you been? I don't see you in school anymore."

"I'm done with that place."

"Oh, Jack, you didn't drop out, did you?"

"Yeah, I've been busy working."

"We all have our own paths I guess. Maybe you can always go back later."

"Yeah, how are you?" I asked quickly changing the subject.

"Good. Things are going really well. We're meeting someone from the softball team here and going out later."

"Do you still play on the team?"

"Yes, I love it. It's given me a real sense of home. I feel like I belong."

I wish I had felt that way somewhere in that old cold place, but I didn't.

"I'm happy for you, Kara. That's great."

Smiling, Gene stuck his tongue in his cheek behind her back.

"Oh, are you ready to go, Gene?"

"Ah, yeah, let's get going. Bye ladies."

"Bye Kara."

"Good luck with everything, Jack. Maybe I'll see you again soon."

We waved and left The Dragon and headed over to his sister's friend's house. Gene went in with the money I had given him, and I waited in my car. A few minutes later Gene came out with the bag of marijuana and we went down to our old elementary school to smoke a joint.

When we were good and stoned, we went back to his house to watch television. Looking around for snacks in his kitchen I couldn't find anything I'd enjoy, which is pretty hard for someone stoned. He never seemed to have anything good when I was over. I think he always hid away the good stuff in his closet to hoard on later. For himself, he cooked up one of those disgusting potpies. No thanks.

So we sat and watched television. At around ten o'clock, Gene's older sister came home. Michelle was great looking and always captured my attention when she came home, which was rare. She worked a lot and was saving her money for a house, which is why she still lived at home instead of renting an expensive city apartment. It was always good to see her wild brown eyes. She was always so cheerful about something, which contrasted sharply with her younger brother's demeanor.

Gene had gone to the bathroom, probably to shit out the horrid potpie, and I was in the living room when Michelle came home.

"Hi, Jack. That was cool of my friend to let you guys have that bag."

"What do you mean?"

"You know, the freebie. I just talked to him and he told me you guys dropped by."

"Oh yeah, that's right. I'm stoned."

"Don't smoke too much, you crazy guys," she laughed and walked off to her room downstairs.

This was beyond belief. Gene had received a bag of pot for free and had kept my hard-earned money for himself. I only had sixty dollars left in my pocket and nothing else coming in.

Cheap, lying, scumbag. I was pissed.

Gene came back from the bathroom and I confronted him.

"Where's my twenty dollars?"

"Huh?"

"Your sister came home and told me. Where's my money?"

"Oh yeah, man, I forgot all about it," he laughed and shrugged it off. "Let me go get it."

Gene came back from his room and handed me my money and after a brief uncomfortable time of watching more television I left. There were no more words to say to this guy. We nodded goodbye and that was it.

Angered by Gene's behavior, I called up Andy to vent.

"Shit, that's low," he said.

"And you know what he's been saying about you…"

The words had slipped out. It was too late. I had needed this outlet for a long time anyway, and so I told him. I told him all about the gay theories and accusations and when I was finished he had some to tell me.

"He said you probably had AIDS because you were sniffling."

"What? Sniffling? I probably had a cold. You kidding me?"

"No, he said it."

"He joked around about something that serious?"

"Yep. You know none of us take anything the kid says seriously though."

"Why didn't you say anything about it?" I asked him.

"Why didn't you? Doesn't he talk about all of us?"

I was shocked but I shouldn't have been.

Of course, I never forgot the things he had said about Ryan years earlier when we were all just a bunch of little punks. I wish I could've forgotten about it like Ryan. I wish I could've shrugged his words off like Andy.

But even Andy needed some distance from him. After the gay accusations he felt strange being around him. Jeff still talked to him from time to time. Paul and Steven had stopped talking to him a long time ago at this point. The three of them hadn't clicked in a while, and Gene talked badly about them behind their backs as usual. In a sense, Gene saw Paul and Steven as competition, as more popular kids with more going for them.

The last time I heard from Gene he left one of his *fucking* messages on Paul's family answering machine. Mr. Roma heard it but blew it off.

"That's how this kid talks now. He did well, I guess."

"Come on, answer your phone. Anyone home in that big house? Well, Jack, fucking, at least fucking call me back. You're my fucking good friend. You're like a fucking brother to me. Well, I'll fucking be here. You know where to find me."

I should have learned my lesson a long time ago. I kept hoping. I kept falling right back into the same patterns with him. I should have left him where I found him crying on the floor in the fourth-grade hallway. Then again, maybe in a strange way I had.

That night I had a dream I was back in high school as if no time had passed. Everyone is the same, but I am aged with gray hair and slight wrinkles. No one recognizes me. No one seems to know me except the teachers. All of the teachers I ever passed in the hallway are now passing by in rapid succession showing me a look of recognition. I snapped up out of the dream knowing my reality had been so far from recognition.

If I were forced to do it all over again from the beginning I would have been a different person in a different circle— the dork or geek I really was. Fuck all that popularity, all that weekend hype, gossip and melodrama, the silly competitiveness. None of it mattered.

But there I was, known by most as the punk, with no opportunity for redemption. It was too late, like the girl who sleeps with the whole football team, just too late. But I thought about Kara and how she had turned it all around. I didn't know how. What was her recipe? Even if I tried to turn myself around, I felt tainted by past associations with all those people, all of them, just about everyone I ever knew.

62

I JUST WANTED TO BE by myself. I drove down to a park near the water. What was I doing, I wondered. Sitting there all alone in a parking lot staring at a fence. I watched the sun go down on the other side of that fence and then the darkness enveloped me. I had taken a few red hot hits out of a portable metal pipe I carried around in my glove box. My mind was foggy but racing with thoughts. What was I going to do? How had I fallen into such a position? What was I going to do to get out of it? Though it was a nice escape, the pot only seemed to be complicating my thoughts. After a while of sitting there listening to music, I decided I would dispose of the stinky pipe. It made me feel crackish, like Win's dirty glass bong had. This would be the first step in freeing myself from this distraction. I also felt better about not having to worry about being pulled over and caught with paraphernalia. I tossed the pipe to the bottom of a steel trash bin in the parking lot.

From now on if I smoked any pot I would smoke it like they say the natives smoked it, in an old-fashioned paper joint. This would limit my high and how much I smoked. Not smoking it out of an instrument somehow made me feel more natural. I would roll the joint, bite the end off, and spark it up. The smoke would fill my lungs and then I would release it into the night sky out a crack in my window. But not tonight. The pipe had me blasted enough to last the rest of the night, and I was starting to think maybe I could be completely clean for a while to get my head straight. I always followed up my pot smoke session with a cigarette.

Music was a necessity in my ritual. I had to have the right rhythm. The lyrics had to capture my state of mind like a soundtrack. I let the tunes take me to another place inside myself. The self-titled *Candlebox* album was on heavy rotation in my car—

"Change"

"Far Behind"

"Cover Me"

"He Calls Home"

The entire album reflected everything I was feeling and would become the soundtrack of my life. I popped in the cassette tape and lay back for a while.

I had been out late and time got away from me. The Roma house was locked and alarmed. With nowhere to go, I resorted to Dunkin' Donuts. I had a couple of dollars to spare so I bought a donut and some hot coffee and made myself a seat at the counter with a paper. Opening up a newspaper on the counter, there he was. Arrested for throwing his mother down the stairs. She didn't make it, and now Nicky Ulrich was facing murder, charged as an adult since he was now eighteen. There was no word about a step-father.

I couldn't believe what I was reading, but I guess it wasn't a surprise ending. The kid had been a lunatic. I had actually had a future murderer sleep on my floor in my room. I decided it would be better not to tell Paul about this because even though he knew me well enough to know I'd never hurt anyone, I knew him well enough to know I'd never hear the end of his jokes.

At 2:30 a lumbering tall guy came in and I noticed him from the corner of my eye. His large presence made me nervous, but then I heard him.

"Jack!"

It was Jim Hirsch who I hadn't seen in some time. We had become friends and apologized for our fight back in the day. Later he had even consulted me on fighting Ricky. He ended up fighting him and was beating him pretty good until Ricky's friend Alan knocked him out from behind with a flowerpot he took off of someone's front porch. I would've intervened if I had been there.

Jim smiled big, jabbed me on the shoulder, and then gave me a great hug.

"Hey you, great to see you," I said. "Where have you been?"

"You too, pal. I'm living in the next town over and finishing up school there. I don't come over here much anymore, but I was over Jason's house tonight. Remember him?"

"Oh, how could I forget him!"

Jason and I went to elementary school together. He was a classic class clown. Erasers at Ms. Giano's bald spot when she was turned around at the board. Desks flipped over. Fist fights with Sean Norris. Being dragged away from those fights in a full nelson by the principal. Jumping on top of the gym teacher as he went over the horse yelling "Bam Bam Bigelow!"

"How is he?"

"Good, he's calmed down. He's finishing out twelfth grade at home. How about you? Hey, let's have a seat."

We sat down, ordered some fresh coffee, and I told him how I'd been kicked out of my house and signed out of school.

"Great news, right?"

"Just hang on there, buddy. You're going to be all right," he said.

"Hey, look at this news story," I showed him the article about Nicky.

"Oh man!"

"Yeah, after seeing that, things are looking pretty good."

"I agree. Do you know who I saw the last time I came to town a few months ago? Ryan Bailey. You knew him right?"

"Yeah, I grew up with him on the south shore."

"Oh yeah," he paused out of hesitation. "The kid was strung out bad."

"Yes, I saw him a while ago and he didn't look too good."

"I tried to say hello, but he could barely speak. His words were all broken up and his teeth were disgusting."

"Yikes."

"I'm sorry, man."

"No, for what? This happens. Hopefully he'll pull out of it."

"You said you're living with Paul and he's good. How's Andy and Jeff?"

"They're good. Andy's been doing good with basketball. Jeff's been in the skater crowd for a while and still loves music."

"What about Gene? You still hang with him?"

I spent the next hour telling him the Gene drama.

"What a tragedy. Well, you have to worry about yourself. There are a lot of knuckleheads out there."

"Yeah, I wish him the best and hope he's all right, but you're right, I have to know what's good for me."

After we exhausted our catch up, we said goodbye. It was great to see Jim and have somebody to talk to. I told him to tell Jason I said hi next time he talked to him. He reached over and gave a large hug and he was off. All these people who flash through your life for a moment and then they're gone. I guess their spirits live on inside of you. But there were some I could do without.

It was five o'clock in the morning and I so headed to Paul's to wait for the opening. I stopped at a red light and noticed a bizarre scene on the opposite side of the road. It was Vinnie the old wrestler pacing around in the brisk November morning air in boxer shorts and a wife beater. I hadn't seen him in years. He had dramatically aged. He seemed worn and wild-eyed.

Over his head, he held a sign that read: WILL WORK FOR FOOD.

The light turned green and I sped off with the brim of my hat pulled down low. As I drove on, I swore the sign had read WILL WRESTLE FOR FOOD.

I'm sure he pulled through, but I'll never know. This was the classic cliché of popular successful kid in school falling from grace in the real world. Why do so many kids fall like this? Why do they seem so confident like Vinnie, yet they fall apart post high school? Vinnie still fared better than his best friend Hal, a rambunctious antagonist who had been arrested and served time for sexually assaulting a boy with a stick. Two demented minds, friends for so many years, probably battling their own identities, and masking themselves with all that masculine, tough-guy, bullshit.

63

I DID SOME CLEAN UP WORK with a friend of a friend for a couple of weeks. He drove us into Queens where we cleaned out apartments for a landlord. Many of them were likely evictions. I imagined a few had fled the city from the law or worse. The buildings were decrepit and the apartments were harsh to the eyes. Purple paint, twenty-year-old shag carpets with unimaginable stains, stenches of death and despair. We gutted these places, throwing out left behind belongings and even some furniture. We found the oddest things like a piece of volcano rock and a piece of coral reef. Imagine that, of all places, in a ghetto apartment in Queens.

Work dried up after two weeks and good thing because it was depressing. I needed a stable job and it had to be better than a shoe store or fast food. I heard there was an ad out for carpet cleaners, so I called the friend with the info and then called the number he gave me. They told me to come down for an interview the next day. They hired me and told me to come back on Monday morning at 5:30. We usually got started on the first job by 8:00. After our first one, we'd hit another two to three homes. We'd head in around three and hope to be home by six. Long tiring days. No more late nights. It was a good thing and Gene wouldn't be around anymore to distract me. I was free of that world. But free yourself from one thing, tie yourself to another.

A Joe Pesci type guy named Carl in his late forties met me in the lot. My new partner showed me around and then took me to our white work van filled with a tank of water, soap, and a reel of hoses.

"Jump in. We'll stop at the roach coach on the way in."

Twenty minutes later, we stopped at the side of the road to buy a cheap breakfast from the vendor truck. Some mornings we'd go to the deli for buttered rolls or bagels. The stops reminded me of when my father would pick me up and we'd make our cola stops after a day of fishing. The commute was an hour, sometimes an hour and a half, depending on how far west and north we went into the city. Nassau county jobs were a treat. I experienced some beautiful Suffolk County homes out east in the Hamptons the first week during training, but those permanent routes were only for the elders. They wanted to show us what we could eventually attain. First we needed to work our way up in the gorges of Brooklyn and Queens.

These homes were plagued with poverty. I had been teased with all the wealth during the training week.

Come into our world and see what you can't have, taunted the wealthy homes.

Come into our world and see the way we live and suffer, cried out the poor homes.

It was a depressing scene. People gave us city issued payment certificates. Others counted change to pay the bill. Most of these apartments could only afford one room at a time and the carpets were beyond cleaning. Carl and I sometimes felt guilty taking money from these people. Many of the carpets were so old, stained, and torn that they probably could've gotten a new carpet for another twenty dollars if they knew better or had the money, but that money was food for a week for these people. On more than one occasion Carl and I glanced at each other with the common understanding that we were going to do more than what we were getting paid to do— a good deed— even if the cleaning didn't do much to salvage the sludged carpets. At least we knew, and they knew, that their carpets were cleaner than before.

Hope.

In more hostile places we arrived to, we went in and out, pretending not to hear the crying, the screaming, the spanking, the domestic chaos. No extras.

Hopeless.

The day before Thanksgiving was spent cleaning a couple of roach infested apartments in Queens. We climbed four flights up; there were no elevators in this part of town. The building was decrepit and probably days away from being cited for fire code violation. After that one we went down into a dark basement apartment that never saw the light of the sun. The mold was too much for us and we retreated. It was a grungy day.

"What are you doing for the holiday," asked Carl.

"I guess I hadn't thought of it yet."

"You probably spend it with family, right?"

"Yeah."

No. What family? Where were they? Who were they? Who was I?

Flash forward to the future. I was excited to get to see him again. I finally found him after many years and was relieved to know he was indeed alive. The stipulation was I had to go to him. No problem. Anything to talk to the guy again and know he was all right.

I enter the long hallway and they close the metal door behind me. I walk with my head down ignoring the stares, screams, and taunts. I am led through another big metal door and brought into a visiting room. I sit at a picnic bench, but this is no picnic. Steven enters in shackles and is placed in the seat across from me and told to remain there. The guard says "fifteen" and then walks out.

"My god, Jack it's great to see you, but what are you doing here?"

"Good to see you too, Steven. I wanted to know if you're all right."

"All right." he laughs. He laughs louder. He can't stop laughing.

"You wanna know if I'm all right? I'm far from okay. I'm living a life sentence behind these bars. You want to know why?"

"No... unless you want to talk about it."

"Talk about it." He laughs again. "I'm in here because I took someone else's life. I didn't set out to do it. Shit just got out of control and I was pissed off. Pissed off at this world. Pissed off at where I come from. Pissed off at everyone I've ever known. And of course, they got me with guns and drugs too. It's real pretty, Jack."

"No, it's not."

"Is this what you came here for? To see me at my worst? To make yourself feel better?"

"No, it's not like that, Steven. I just wanted to tell you I still care."

Steven leans forward.

"It's a little too late for that, Jack. A little too fucking late. No one ever cared. No one ever... ah fuck this. You know what's crazy? I wish I could give back that guy's life and trade it for my father's. He's the one I should've put in the ground."

"I'm so sorry, Steven"

"You're not sorry. You're just sorry you came here now. Don't feel sorry for me. I got my own survival in here. I got skills. This is life. Remember we used to talk about growing up? This is what I grew up to be."

"I'm sorry...I'm so sorry. I should have."

"You should just get out of here now. Go back out to your world. You don't belong here. Get outta here... get outta here."

Steven starts to pound on the table with his fists. The guards rush in. Two scoop him up and lead him away. Another guard motions me to follow him out. The last thing I see is Steven's back with a prison uniform with a big red number on the back— 19— his old football number. I awoke on Paul's floor feeling nauseous.

64

I LEFT EARLY in the morning on Thanksgiving Day, so no one in Paul's house would put me in a position. Paul and Marie had already asked me about my plans and I told them I might be working overtime cleaning the vans. I didn't want to intrude, so I split out.

I ventured out east on the north shore to a beach my father had once taken me to. I remembered liking the place and feeling good there. After some driving around, I found the beach and sat there for a while just thinking. I had stopped at a 7 Eleven on my way there to pick up some food and drink. In the beach parking lot I sat and gnawed on a buttered roll while sipping hot coffee. The Long Island Sound was in some ways far more beautiful than the south shore. It was quieter and cleaner there. It was rocky along many parts of the shoreline and the water seemed a brighter color.

Here I was celebrating the holiday and what my life had become as a high school dropout. But I was actually grateful. The past several days had gotten me thinking about things. I knew there were kids out there with so many more problems, some didn't have a car, some didn't have the ability to work or even walk, some didn't have food, some wouldn't even make it to eighteen. I was lucky. We're all lucky, every day.

I watched the sun set. It had been a remarkable day alone, just me and my car, my cigarettes, and my music. They were always there for me. Elizabeth was too, but I couldn't hurt their feelings the way I could hurt hers. She invited me to the holiday dinner at her house, and even though I know it hurt her that I didn't come, I also knew I couldn't face her family in this state. I needed to do something. I was losing her. I was losing everything.

I looked out at the water. I wondered if my grandmother, my mom's mom, was looking out at her view of the water from her large warm house. Did she even know where I was in my life? Did she wonder? I hadn't talked to her or anyone else in some time. What was the point? They knew where I was. They knew how to contact me if they needed to. They had Elizabeth and Paul's numbers, but no one called. My grandmother was off in Italy when I was kicked out and by the time she returned to the states it was fall and I was out of school. What was the point in driving over there in the shape I was in? I was worn and she was well. You don't make nice company when you're not feeling so nice. I'd rather be alone than take someone's pity.

Going to my grandmother's house as a kid was like a trip to Mars. Back then I would pretend it was all mine. I would act like the rich kids I saw on television— fucking Silver Spoons— yet I knew deep down inside that it was all a lie. As soon as I got back into the car to go home I was back to being low-class trash. I was on one side of the fence and they were on the other— blood or not. But like Mr. Luger's fancy real estate office where I emptied his garbage, like my grandmother's house for the holidays, and her even wealthier sister Judy's house in Bridgehampton, all gave me something to dream about.

The night had escaped me, and I drove back to my town, despite knowing I'd be locked out. I drove to a parking lot and set up camp. I broke out the Mexican blanket and put on a heavy sweatshirt Paul had given me. I would start the engine up every so often, only for a little while, since I'd run out of gas if I kept the motor running too long. I shivered in the November night. The temperature outside was getting colder. As the night progressed I drifted off.

A stuttering little boy spells out the word butterfly for the first time.

My brother's smile.

A faded black and white photograph of six smiling friends, a world ahead of them. The Kennedy brothers on each end. Steven and Paul to my left. Gene to my right. Me in the middle.

Wrestling. Guns N' Roses. Running free on the track.

The beach. The bay. The birds.

Long Island in the shadow of the city.

The nineteen eighties crashing into the nineties.

A girl in a Catholic school dress stands there laughing and talking with her girlfriends. She doesn't see us, but I see her. She has long straight brown hair, eyes the color of a forest, and a smile that captures me. Something inside feels funny.

A horn blared and a light flashed——

—My swollen eyes stretched open. My face muscles were numb, my lips were tight and chapped. A layer of frost covered my hair. A car approached and its window opened. I struggled to roll my window down.

"You gotta go. Can't stay here. Get on now."

"No problem. Thanks," I said.

The security guard couldn't even let me stay in the empty lot, but I didn't complain. The guy had saved my life. Another hour or so and I would have frozen to death for sure. I turned the ignition, cranked the heat, and then drove off to the safety of the twenty-four-hour diner with twenty dollars in my pocket and several hours to waste before the rest of the world woke.

I sat there in the diner drinking coffee and picking at a muffin thinking about where I really was when the security guard woke me. It was a nice dream. A great place full of the best memories. I wanted more of those. I wanted to be in that place.

65

JEFF CAME BY Paul's one Saturday. I was surprised. I hadn't seen him in a long time. He had been in a different circle of friends than his twin brother Andy, but I'm sure he gave him the run down on what was happening to me. He asked me if I wanted to take a ride and I agreed.

"Where to?"

"You want to go visit an old friend? Then we'll grab some lunch."

"Sounds good. Who'd you have in mind?"

"Remember Scott?"

"Yeah, wow, that's a blast from the past."

Scott had been a kid we knew back from our days in elementary school. He only went to our school for a year and then moved to the next zone over, which meant we'd see him again in junior high. Many of us didn't though. It was just the way circles worked. Jeff and all of us always circled back around to each other, but we never saw most other kids again.

"He lives in here."

Jeff pointed to the entrance of a trailer park community and pulled onto the dirt road.

"What's this guy been up?"

"He dropped out last year and just works."

"Sounds familiar," I laughed. " What does he do?"

"I don't know, I think something with construction, but he's married and has a baby."

I didn't know what to say to that. Eighteen, married with a baby.

We stepped up to the door and knocked. Scott opened the door looking worn and dirty from a day's work. I hadn't even seen him in probably five or six years. Here we were all grown up. Here he was really grown up.

"Hey, guys, great to see you. Damn, Jack, it's been so long."

"Good to see you too, man," I answered.

"You guys remember my wife, Danica?"

Danica, the girl from math class. I couldn't believe it. We all said hello and she went back to cleaning the counter.

"Hold on guys, I'll be right back. I'm just going to change out of these work clothes."

Jeff and I sat at a small round kitchen table and observed Danica scrubbing the kitchen floor. She was barefoot and wore shorts and a scant shirt. Back and forth she scrubbed really digging into something. A stain. A tarnish. A mistake. On her hands and knees, her ass pointed up, but I couldn't have the same feelings I had had in math class so many years ago. Not here, not now. After a few minutes, Jeff and I looked up at each other with a look of understanding. An understanding that we were both experiencing the same kind of reality dose— and it wasn't like we were judging them— maybe their life was better than ours, but it was just so grown up so fast and so soon, like a rushed meal that isn't finished cooking.

Scott returned and asked us if we wanted a beer, but we both declined. He opened one for himself and we sat there for around forty-five minutes. He didn't talk much about himself, nor did he ask what we were up to. We talked about little things from the past, and Danica went in and out of the room to check on the baby. Jeff excused us after a while and told him we needed to get on our way.

We all said goodbye, and Jeff and I left. We were silent all the way to the car. On the way out on the dirt road, Jeff turned to me and said, "Whoa…Reality." I echoed these sentiments. Perspective can do wonders.

66

I ARRIVED at five a.m. and met my partner as I had done for the last five weeks. We climbed into the van and went off for a day of carpet cleaning in the city. Some of the homes were well kept, but most of them were poverty-stricken disasters. We would suck up as many roaches as we could and scrubbed over the hopeless grease and grime as much as possible, but still our efforts did little justice for these homes. Maybe it still made the people feel like their homes were cleaner— something new and fresh in a world of staleness. After a full day of this, we would battle our way home in the hard traffic.

"How long have you been doing this?" I asked Carl.

Brake lights lit up for miles ahead. Horns honked. Smoke drifted from the exhaust pipes. Thousands of headlights lit up behind us like votive candles in a cathedral aisle.

Nowhere to go.

"Eleven years now. It's been a while. I don't know where the time went."

"Are you going to stay here?"

"Yeah, as long as I have a job that pays the bills, hell yeah."

My mind raced with memories of people. I thought of Elizabeth and wondered where she was. I thought of Paul and my other friends and wondered what they might be up to in school. Then I thought of Mrs. Ravitch and her sweetness. Mr. Nicosia and how he taught me more than just how to change a tire. Mr. Kelly and his suggestions and encouragement. Glimmers of hope.

School.

School had been my life, but it wasn't anymore. Being back there was the only thing I could think of out there in the cold, dark world of traffic and roaches, carpet grime and chemicals. I imagined eleven years into my future— the same white van, the same highway, the same apartment buildings in the city. It was honest work and my partner was content. But something didn't fit right with me. I wanted something else. I didn't want to get my hands dirty cleaning up after others like my mother, my stepfather Don, my aunt's husband, my neighbor, or my father. All these cleaners. What were they cleaning? Here I was following in their footsteps. I didn't want to clean anymore. I wanted to get dirty and mess things up just to be different.

School was a way out of this, an escape to a better life. But why hadn't it worked out? Why were so many people against me? Why didn't I have anyone to show me the way like other students had? Why weren't there more people like the few who had made a difference? Why weren't they all like those good ones? I guess that's just the world we live in.

There in the cold December traffic, I realized there was something missing from my life— something I had been seeking all along— a greater cause. I shuddered at the thought of cleaning carpets, an honest and admirable job for many, but not something I wanted to spend the rest of my life doing. I had other dreams. I remembered being a child who loved to get lost in books, who enjoyed playing teacher and cop with his friends, and loved the mysteries of science and nature. I wondered how I had drifted so far away from my hopes and visions of the future. And I knew now.

I made up my mind right there in the carpet cleaning van on the Long Island Expressway heading east in rush hour traffic— I was going back to school.

PART III

The Education

The professor stares out the window. His back is to the class and no one can see his face. No one can read what's going on inside.

You see, once the former prisoner is out of the cave, he can't really go back. You can't go back to high school. You can't go back to middle school. You can't go back to childhood. You can't go back to old relationships, most of the time.

Plato describes how the former prisoner, so excited about the new world of reality, wants to go back down into the cave and share this truth with his family and friends. What do you think happens?

The professor turns from the window and faces the class. His face is serious and he projects his voice across the room.

When he gets there and tries to tell them that what they're looking at is merely a shadow, he is met with resistance. He is ridiculed. He is violently opposed. Instead of acceptance, he is alienated. 'Who do you think you are telling me that what I see right in front of me is not reality? You left the tribe and now you come back here like some kind of big shot?' He can't go back to the old neighborhood, the way a millionaire can't go back to the poor neighborhood they grew up in, the way a rock star or rap star can't go back to the streets, not without being torn to shreds. The former prisoner is shunned. Once this happens, you must go forward.

67

ON MONDAY MORNING after a night of zero sleep, and after calling in sick, I went down to the school. It had been just over two months since I last stepped foot in the building, two months too long. First I decided to talk to my guidance counselor. Unfortunately, Mr. Priestley wasn't in. He had checked out two weeks earlier by way of heart attack. I explained my situation to the secretary and she suggested I go and speak to one of the principals, being they were the only ones who had the power to let a student back into school. Set on my goal, I walked down to Mr. Bundy's office and knocked on the door with confidence.

"Hi, Jack, what can I do for you? Didn't you leave school?"

"Yes, that's what I wanted to talk to you about. I was wondering if I could come back somehow."

"Change of heart?"

"Yes, I realized how important it is to me. It took a lot, but I learned."

"Well, unfortunately I can't let you back in until next year because we're right in the middle of things. Come back next summer if you'd like and we'll talk."

"Next summer? That's eleven months away."

"Sorry, there's nothing I can do right now. You can always sign up for the GED or try again next year," he said under his bushy mustache.

I walked out of Mr. Bundy's office feeling discouraged. I briefly considered coming back next year as he'd suggested. I thought about how I could graduate with Steven and how he wouldn't be left behind after all, but he had been left behind, and he didn't need me when he had the football team and others. I couldn't wait.

The following day I returned to the school and found Mr. Panzram in the hallway.

"Hi, Mr. Panzram. Listen, can I ask you something?"

"Yes?" he said in his strange, muffled Brando *Apocalypse Now* voice.

"I was wondering if there was any way I could sign back into school."

"No, I'm afraid not, Jack. You should just forget about school."

"No. I really want to come back and do good. I was never that bad to begin with."

"No, it's all over for you. Go take the GED or get a job. You're not going to graduate, not from here," he said with a devilish grin as he shook his gleaming waxed head.

I walked out of school feeling just as hopeless, but then suddenly remembered something. There was one more principal to seek out. What did I have to lose? I walked back into the building. Mr. O'Connor was the twelfth-grade principal. I hadn't thought of him because I hadn't seen him since seventh grade when he was last my principal. Many boys disliked him because a lot of girls visited his office. It didn't really seem to bother me that he liked good company. I had been in trouble with him before, but for some reason I had no grudge. I guess he had a way of helping us own up to mistakes. I had not spent enough time in twelfth grade to reacquaint myself with him, but he recognized me right away when I knocked on his door. He waved me in with a big smile as if he had been expecting me.

"Hi, Mr. O'Connor. Could I talk to you?"

The principal was an older balding man. He wore a brown suit that accommodated his rounded abdomen well. He had a big smile with big teeth. His round cheeks were cheerfully rosy.

"Yes, come on in, Jack. Have a seat. What can I do for you?"

"Well, I dropped out in October and I realize now I really want to be here. I want to finish and graduate. It's important. I was wondering if there was any way you could let me back in."

"The places we find ourselves. Hold on a second and let me check your file."

He left the room for a minute and then returned with a folder. He sat and opened it.

"Well, you missed about two and half months. I see you also failed tenth and eleventh-grade history. Hold on."

I remembered what they told me at the jamboree so many years before—it's too late.

Mr. O'Connor typed something into the computer and scanned through his records. I stared at him intensely.

"You know what, here's what I can do for you."

I leaned forward.

"I just happen to be the ALC principal too. Come back to start in January after the holiday break and promise you'll be here every day until June, and then I'll let you graduate on time. You'll need to go to school at the ALC in the mornings and then night school four nights a week in Brentwood to make up those other two classes. I'll assign you new teachers and have a talk with them about it, if this is what you want to do. It's a lot. Do you think you're up for it?"

"Absolutely. I really want to."

"All right then. Deal?"

"Yes, Yes! I promise I'll be there every day. Thank you, Mr. O'Connor. You don't know how much this means. You were my last hope."

"Well, we go way back and I believe in second chances, sometimes third."

"Thank you."

"You're welcome. You'll get your schedule in the mail next week. So until January, have a great holiday."

"Thank you, you too."

I walked out of Mr. O'Connor's office reborn into a fresh world of hope determined to graduate in June.

I thought of Dennis, Leela, all the others who dropped out and never went back. They had their own new lives and would be all right. But I needed this. I wanted this now. I wanted to lock my graduation into history. I wanted the accomplishment. I needed a way out of the life I was living. The paper certificate didn't do much for me. The walk down an aisle, a handshake, and the tossing of a hat didn't do anything either. It was the sense of accomplishment and a belief in learning that I wanted. I knew I couldn't wait any longer. I finally had plans for once in my life.

I called Elizabeth and told her the good news. I told her I would take up my uncle on his offer for me to live with him. Then I called my uncle and he gave me directions.

"That's great, Jack. We really need school these days. I'm glad you made this choice. It'll only be a forty-five-minute commute and I'll be happy to help you out with money as long as you're doing the right thing."

"Absolutely. Thanks so much, Uncle Albert."

The following day I couldn't bring myself to go back to cleaning carpets. I called them to tell them I wouldn't be coming back. But it was December. I needed to get by for a few more weeks and have some holiday money. I went around applying to retail jobs and a pharmacy store called Rock Bottom hired me on the spot. The name was appropriate for where I'd been.

For the next three weeks, as Christmas approached, I stocked shelves in Rock Bottom, and I dreamed about my ascent to the top.

The place was carefree and a manager seemed absent from the scene. I didn't care though. They could've talked down to me like the managers at Super Cohen's or harassed me like the Chicken Shack managers did to others, and none of it would've mattered. I was going back to school.

Feeling better about myself now that I had a plan, I went to go visit my mother's mother. I pulled up through the tall hedges, down the long driveway that rounded right up to the front of the house. The middle lawn in front was full of frost. The pond was almost frozen over. It was so great to be back here. All the good and bad memories. The bad didn't matter anymore. I rang the big loud cowbell out front and stared down at the familiar slate floor. The blue door opened and my grandmother's face peered out with a big smile. She looked so vibrant. She seemed to have only gotten younger since I had seen her a year ago. We hugged for a long time. She knew I had had it rough, yet she didn't know half the story.

My grandmother made us lunch and we sat and ate looking out at the view of the bay. I had wondered if I would ever see the water from this window again. The wild cold winter waves sloshed around out there. The giant frame of the Robert Moses Bridge was faint in the distance.

"We were so worried about you, Jack."

"Well, it's good to be back to life."

"You know I would've let you stay here with me if I had known. You know how Andre feels about people staying with us though."

Why say anything I wondered.

"It's all right. I found a home."

I did understand her husband in a sense. I probably wouldn't have wanted to take in a punk with such a history, especially if I really didn't know him that well. That was perhaps the crux. Knowing each other. Knowing your own family.

My grandmother and I spent a few hours together and it was nice to visit with her. When it was time to go she told me to come back soon and handed me some money. I guess she felt bad. I took the money, but it didn't change anything, just like how none of the flaws and mistakes ever changed the way I loved my grandmother or anyone for that matter.

My grandmother gave me one other thing that day. I had told her I still needed to work part-time and wanted something in a positive environment with flexible hours. She told me her friend at a health food store was waiting for me if I wanted a job. It seemed enticing, something different, so I went to check it out. The place was called The Healthy Alternative. It was right on Main Street in Brightwaters, a few miles away from where I would be going to night school to make up two failed classes, and also a few miles away from where I was born. Everything was lining up.

In a dream that night I was back in my hometown in the Super Cohen's supermarket. I'm on line and the checkout girl starts mixing up my order with the person behind me. She hands me the receipt and tells me it's all in the bag, but I stop and check the bag before leaving. I ask her again and she blows me off. We start to argue. Someone from behind me pipes in,

"You giving this girl a hard time?"

I turn around and it's Gene laughing. I hadn't seen the guy in fourteen years.

We end up back at his Dad's house, but it isn't the same house and his Dad is gone. His room is bigger and overlooks the woods. He sits on a windowsill and I stand looking out the window down at the forest. A winding path leads out into the woods and disappears.

"Hey, you ever take a walk in those woods?" I ask.

"Nah, not really."

"Why not? You want to go?" I want the adventure.

We head out on the path, but just as we enter the forest, the darkness of the woods envelopes us. The wind picks up and suddenly it is raining. Leaves from the trees blow around us. Thunder rumbles and lightening flashes around us. Gene runs back to the house, but I continue on through the woods. The run is just about to begin and the weather is clearing.

68

I THROW MYSELF into the wave, in my mind. Maybe the wave could be interpreted as the hard times I had just gone through, but I also thought of the wave as a good thing, like the cleansing process I was about to go through. I stood on the cold beach looking out at the Atlantic waves crashing in. The world was big, bigger than most of us realized. My world was expanding now. I was about to say goodbye to something. I was about to live in a new town on a new part of the island, in the middle, away from the pull of the ocean. The new town had a lake, a lot like the old town I lived in before my mother remarried.

A calming return to innocence.

The day was cold but clear and sunny when I arrived at Albert's house for the first time. I had been to his house many years ago when I was about eleven when my father still lived in New York and rented Albert's upstairs apartment. It was a two-story house with a deep driveway on the right side of the property. The small front yard to the left was boxed in by a fence. The house was the third on the block from the corner of the expressway service road. The noise wasn't too bad though. The barrier walls worked well. In fact, those first few nights were some of the most peaceful nights I have ever had to lie down to go to sleep in this world.

Albert met me out in the street and walked me up to my new

home. He grabbed one of my two bags— the only surviving belongings. Everything else had been lost or thrown in the garbage by Don. My uncle led me into the country style living room and then down the hall to the guest bedroom— my new bedroom. The dresser was an old relic from my grandma's house and the bed was an old leftover from my father's last days at his mothers before he left to become a man, after he had already left my mom and me. The wood floors creaked a little and the bed's metal springs came to life when I sat on it, but it was all so perfect. It was a bedroom— shelter! The room even had two windows— one a view of a tree and the other one peered out to the backyard where an above the ground pool sat in the far corner. The view was calming.

I placed my bags down in my new room and Albert showed me around. Next to my room across the hall was his bedroom. Next to my room was the bathroom. For a single guy, the house was pretty well kept. The kitchen was clean too. A wood molding and a pantry cabinet full of food were the only things that separated the living room and the kitchen. He told me to help myself to the food in the pantry and anything in the fridge. I promised to contribute for food once I started working again. The first week I remember popping open a can of string beans and eating them in one sitting. I felt so nourished and healthy again. No more donut dinners and scraps.

Albert worked the night shift four times a week. I had entire nights to myself to relax, think, and reflect. Even though I had vowed to keep my head straight, life was so dreamy. Maybe that was the problem. I had been on such a rush for so long that I forgot how it felt to be stable and clean. Everything was happening so fast. Moving in— Going back to school— living in a new town where I was a complete stranger— it was surreal. Albert did everything to make me feel at home and help me get on track. He didn't try to act like a father. But he treated me like he was my guardian.

The basement is where we would smoke cigarettes on cold winter nights. We agreed that this would be the only place where we would smoke so the rest of the house would stay clean and fire safe. We shared a big glass ashtray that sat on the workbench piled with random tools. A few feet away sat a large vertical shelf loaded with a collection of 1980s Playboy magazines. On the other side of the basement was a dark unlit area with his locked gun collection.

I felt safe. I felt like I was experiencing the closest thing to living with a dad— something I had never felt before. Here was a guy I had met only a hand full of times, yet he was my flesh and blood— my father's brother. Did he really want an eighteen-year-old living with him? Was he doing it for my father? Or out of spite for him? Had my grandma sent him? It would never be clear what his intentions were, but the time seemed right for both of us. We needed each other. He had recently divorced from his first wife and was left with alimony and a lonely three-bedroom house. Maybe he was just as lost as I was in an odd way. We made sure we shared at least a couple of meals every week and got together on Saturdays for a cheap breakfast at the local pancake house. Good talks interspersed with long yet comfortable stretches of silence.

69

ELIZABETH AND I had reconnected and we went to my grand-ma's house for Christmas Eve. I didn't want to be away from her any-more. I wanted us to have a life. She had been there for me through all those times, even when I pushed her away. She was persistent and devoted. Now we were going to get a second chance. I was going to get a second chance. One lucky guy.

Uncle Albert met us at his mother's house. The four of us sat at the table and ate pasta and talked about the plans. Although my grandmother offered her home, I ultimately took Albert's offer to move in with him. Something had drawn me to him, perhaps that desire to be closer to a man in my family, after so many years of being around women. I also hadn't seen her in a while. But I realized the instrumental role my grandma had in assisting my metamorphosis. There wasn't a thing she wouldn't do for family. Being with her and Albert again made me feel like I had known them my whole life. They felt like family.

When my cousin Michael dropped out of high school a few years before me, Uncle Albert and grandma offered him the same deal. He declined. Albert asked him again and again, but he wasn't interested. He wanted to focus on music. I think everyone scoffed at his dreams because he didn't like to talk about it with the family. At some point, his mother met a man and ran off to Texas, abandoning Michael and his stepfather. His real father was unknown and his mother seemed to vanish leaving him to fend for himself. Michael and his stepfather lived together for another year and then that was it. Michael disappeared off the map. I hope he managed. But I wasn't going to take any chances without school.

On Christmas day, Elizabeth and I spent the day with her family. I felt so fortunate to be there with them. We laughed and ate good food. The house was full of abundance, like my grandmother's at Christmas when I was little. For a little while, I disappeared downstairs with her brothers to play video games. Later on that night, we sat by the fire and her dad told us funny stories about a wild firehouse he worked at in the 80s before transferring to a quieter one. The guys were real jokers. They pranked one guy into thinking they had all collectively won the mega lottery and the guy nearly had a heart attack before realizing they were putting him on. Another day they replaced the tuna with cat food for those trying to steal leftovers from the fridge. Despite all the fun and games, they'd pick up in a moment's notice and run out and save lives— breaking down doors, climbing stairs and fire escapes, carrying three hundred pound people downstairs— right near where I had been cleaning carpets.

Her parents treated me with a few gifts that Christmas. The most memorable was a big blue and green plaid blanket. I would never be cold again.

70

ON JANUARY THIRD the alarm clock went off at 5:00 am. I popped up in bed and slid out of my blankets. The wood was cold when my feet touched the floor. I sat there for a moment with a smile.

After a quick breakfast of oatmeal, and a warm shower, I dressed and prepared for my day. It was my first day, so I wore something that made me feel loose and comfortable, yet warm.

The cold January air hit my face when I opened the front door. I walked out to the street and got into my car and warmed it up. After a few minutes, I pulled away and hit the ramp onto the expressway heading west. All the cars advanced, paused, advanced. I exited after a few exits onto a parkway that ran south. The flow brought me back out onto another parkway heading west where the traffic wasn't as thick, not yet. I drove along, full of gratitude. After forty-five minutes, I pulled into a parking spot in the street. I was back.

I would arrive at school early every day because Uncle Albert told me during lunch one day it's always better to be early than late.

"I'd rather sit and wait around than rush to get somewhere."

This made me think of my father, and I didn't want to be the late person.

In the winter months, I would stare out at the field of snow in front of the school building as I waited for school to begin. I watched all the teachers arrive. Some days I watched the sun come up. The snow on the lawn was so clean and sleek looking. Little drops melted into the street where I was parked. I realized this would be my last winter in school. I arrived in the heart of winter and the season seemed to give way to spring right before my eyes. I knew it would be the last spring but I also knew that a new season was about to begin in life.

Known as the ALC, the alternative learning center was in a separate building several blocks away from the high school. It contained four classes from ninth to twelfth grade and had about ten to fifteen students per grade. Ninth grade had the most students. By twelfth grade most of the real crazies had already been ejected from school; some went off to jail, a few had overdosed, one took a gun out to his father's car and took his own life in the driver's seat. By twelfth grade the only ones left were the survivors, the fighters. Maybe we were the lucky ones who didn't have it so bad after all. We knew we had made it this far. Why not keep going? Maybe these teachers weren't so wrong— that high school could give us a foundation. Maybe all my twelfth-grade peers at the alternative school had gone through the same exact epiphany I had experienced that day in the work van.

The building was right across from a cemetery, where Lisa, the one allergic to herself, was buried. It was a subtle reminder to look out at those stones and know our lives were so fragile and some short. The cemetery forced us to look at the end. We all knew we were living in the moment and those stones signified the end of everything. We had to hang on to life, fight for it, and keep it close. It was do or die.

Mr. O'Connor had set up an appointment for me to go and meet the teachers before the holiday break. I walked into the front doors, stopped at the secretary's window, and introduced myself. The gentle woman told me to wait a moment and then called someone. A minute later a familiar face entered the hallway with a warm smile. It was Mrs. Sullivan from seventh grade. How things come full circle sometimes.

"Jack, it's good to see you."

"Mrs. Sullivan, good to see you too. Wow, it's been a while."

"I'm glad you made it. I hear you're here to finish up a job."

"Yes, ma'am."

"Just as Mr. O'Connor said, show up every day and work hard and we'll help you every step of the way."

It was great to see Mrs. Sullivan. She had always been so stern with me, but kids like me needed that. She never crossed the line and disrespected us. She knew how to do it the right way. My fond memories of her social studies class gave me something to look forward to.

We went into an empty classroom and the other teachers joined us. Mrs. Shelley was the English teacher. Mr. Gongolski was the math teacher. Mr. Bissell, the track coach I never had the chance to run for, was the science teacher. I had heard good things about all of them through the grapevine. A nice social worker named Ms. Wells also joined us. I'd be seeing her every couple of weeks to check in on my progress.

We all introduced ourselves and they gave me a rundown of the policies and what to expect. My schedule would be seven to eleven thirty a.m. I told them I was ready.

I would start with social studies. Because this was the only class I had a state test for at the end of the year, it was critical I did well in this class. I knew with Mrs. Sullivan's structured teaching I would do excellent. She pounded us with readings, study sheets, and lessons every day.

English was more casual. Letter writing and a little bit of reading. Mrs. Shelley let us enjoy words without stuffing them down our throats.

Math was very general— practical business math, which was all right for me as long as I didn't have to do any of the theoretical stuff that didn't mean anything to me in the real world. Mr. Gongolski was a soft-spoken, kind man. If you had trouble with math or even behaving yourself, he knew how to turn it right around and talk you into good results. In fact, all of the teachers were great at this and made us all feel at ease.

The last academic class of the day was science. Mr. Bissell was a bit kooky. His classes were fun and sometimes dramatic. He really wanted us to think about the world of science, and he succeeded.

If only I had had these teachers for every class every year of school.

After science, we had a class period that rotated with physical education, career explorations, and social worker meetings. Ms. Brotton was the gym teacher. She let us explore different exercises and yoga. We also talked a lot. I told her stories from my glory days of track. She suggested I get running again.

Career class was with Mr. Schuhart. He was a nice guy and we just talked about different options. He asked a lot of questions and gave surveys, which got us thinking about graduation. I told him all about my carpet cleaning adventure and how I had decided to return to school. He loved the story.

Ms. Wells was difficult to talk to. Not because she was a bad social worker, but because I was an eighteen-year-old and she was pretty. She was short with short dark hair and she had dark eyes. She had a way of holding her neck with her hand, as if she had a neck ache. I would stare at her pretty hands while talking to her because if I looked her in the eyes for too long I got nervous and my words would trip out of my mouth. She asked some tough questions to get me thinking but didn't pry too much.

Everyone was exceptional. I didn't know where they had been hiding all those years in high school. My stomach problems were gone. I felt good. We learned. We laughed. We were relieved to be past the anguish the ninth, tenth and some of the eleventh graders in the ALC were still going through. To contend with those kids, the teachers should have been paid a million dollars a year. They were real heroes of public service, there by choice, there to make a difference, and they did make a difference.

I distanced myself from the other dozen or so kids in my classes. I knew some of them for a long time and didn't have any problems with any of them. Some of them were funny, which made for good classes. All of the terrible kids were gone. We were the survivors. I was glad these folks had made it too. But because of where I had been, I couldn't get caught up with anyone. I was there to do a job and to worry about myself for once.

71

AROUND FEBRUARY I would learn my father and stepmother were getting divorced. He told me over the phone. She was suddenly an evil demon out to destroy him— All simply because she didn't want to do his laundry anymore. He moved his belongings out into some roach-infested apartment complex and came home one day to an empty apartment. They had stolen everything. All they left was one lone sock. He blamed it all on her of course. She had arranged the burglary as revenge, just after she wiped out their savings account, at least according to my father.

Albert ripped on my father after the news.

"You know, you'd think he'd learn after one divorce. I did. You do what you have to. Just keep her happy."

Albert always seemed angry at his older brother, even judgmental, maybe for his own good reasons; I don't know. I couldn't imagine them growing up. They were night and day.

My father had told me stories about Albert: the hippie who wandered the country high in a bus with his best friend, the lost guy who mowed lawns until he was twenty-eight, the kid who jumped out of his brother's car and beat another kid for making a stupid face at them, the cop who busted a man's face with a baton just because he felt like it. My father was filled with imagination, so some or all of his stories were most likely fiction.

The only reason my father left my mother, according to my father, was because he had come home and found her having dinner with the mailman. Of course, there's no single shred of evidence. My mother laughed hard when I told her. Either he was a prophet of truth revealing everyone else's lies or he was a hyperbolic storyteller. He could have made millions writing books with all the stories he told.

Albert often talked about his work over lunch. The domestic violence house calls. The rainy day when a crossing guard would call in sick or the traffic light that would black out. His area was wealthy and his calls seemed to be more of a nuisance than a danger, but I knew there was always danger in his job. Free gun laws enabled thugs, like some of the people I once knew and worse, to buy whatever weapon they wanted along with cop-killer bullets. Then there's the meth heads so cranked up they don't feel the first few bullets. I respected Albert's job and knew he was always lucky when he got home from a shift no matter what neighborhood he worked in.

One night I was down in the basement smoking and flipping through Uncle Albert's old *Playboys*, thinking how relieved I was to feel like I finally had a home. Albert had come home at some point and called someone on the phone. He didn't know I was downstairs, but I could hear him talking. I was about to head up and go to my room and didn't mean to eavesdrop, but then I heard my name, my father's name, something about my father not taking care of me, something about needing to clean up after him again. He told the person how it must be tough for my father to know his younger brother was taking care of his son. I heard a sense of triumph in Albert's voice. He had done good, no question. Why he was helping me didn't matter. I just loved having a roof over my head and the safety of a home. I had never felt so secure.

I had another dream about Steven. I haven't seen him in three years and he's changed. His dark hair is dyed with blond highlights.

His voice is older and raspy. His skin is pale. We give each other a grand hug and clink our bottles together.

"What's going on, brother?" he asks with joy in his eyes.

"Man, it's been so long!"

I step back to look at him.

"What are you doing these days?"

"I'm visiting this old town. I've been away at college. How about you?"

"Great, man. I got a big offer from the University of Arizona to play ball there, but I didn't take it."

"No? Why not?" I ask.

"Oh, it was too far and I just wanted to work awhile and make some cash."

"Well, that's good then. I took some time off too. You can always go back."

Another guy steps in between us and pulls my old friend by the arm.

"We got to go, Steve," he said.

"Yeah man, I'll be right there."

The man walks away and Steven turns back to face me.

"Sorry bud, but I have to go, but stop by the house sometime. My mom would love to see you."

"Yes, I'll do that."

"I wish I could hang out longer…"

"Why not. Can't you duck out? Let's get out of here and take a drive. We'll go explore somewhere else, go sit by a lake."

I imagined us driving out to the end of the island, as far as you could go, where the ocean meshed into the bay at the tip of land called Montauk Point. We would sit there and talk some more— Get out and walk to the edge— look out to the horizon knowing that we were looking into the past— that on the other side of the ocean was the old world, the place of origin, so far away. When you get that far away it's hard to go back.

"No, I can't, buddy."

"Tell him something came up."

"You have to go alone. I'm sorry. You have to go alone."

He hugs me goodbye and he is off. I sit back on my bar chair feeling bad. He's leaving me the way I left him. I hear a familiar voice and look around. Evan Klause is in the corner. He had walked off the basketball court in his senior year the way I had walked off the football field years earlier. Better things to do now.

Evan yells out to me,

"Hey, Jack. Stone Temple Pilots, man. Where you been?"

"Not around here. You take care now."

I don't want to be in this sad town bar anymore. Why am I even here in the first place?

I leave the bar, and on my way out to the lot I spot Steven behind the alley. He's with his new friends and probably doesn't see me. I look away, but the building is on fire and the flames bring my eyes back to the light. I turn away and walk in the shadows until it's all behind me.

I am at the lake where I used to live with my mom. Steven is gone. I am alone. I walk the old path from school to the house where I used to live. I've gone home.

72

THE HEALTHY ALTERNATIVE was a healthy place to work. My day classes ended at eleven thirty and then I would go to work on Monday, Wednesday, and Friday. Monday through Thursday I had night classes at the nearby high school. The classes ran from six to nine, so my days were full and busy. I would do homework at the public library or in my car on Tuesday and Thursday in between day and night school when I didn't work. On Fridays I worked the whole shift until closing. I luckily had weekends off to spend time with Elizabeth, relax, and do more homework when needed. The days flew and I was busier than ever, but I had purpose.

Jerry was a bulky man with shiny black hair that reminded me of Phil Scarpa, but he was nothing like the chicken boss. He was gentler and kinder. He told me he had had some debilitating rare disease and he was only brought back from his deathbed with herbs and alternative remedies. I didn't know if I believed the story entirely, but his passion to help others was moving.

The back of the store was a shop that sold vitamins, herbs, supplements, books and other educational materials. The front was both a full-service and self-serve restaurant that served lunch and dinner. Many people just came in for their daily protein shake or shot of wheat grass.

I stocked shelves but I also made shakes and wheat grass. I made the wheat grass shots from a pad of grass that looked like sod. I cut the grass and stuck it in the juicer. It smelled and tasted like lawn grass, but there was something healthy and fresh about it. I stayed away from food prep and serving, which was a nice change. Of course, I still got a free meal on the days I worked, which was helpful. I couldn't believe such healthy food tasted so good.

One afternoon I found a couple of hundred dollar bills folded up on the floor under one of the tables out front. I went to Jerry.

"Finders keepers, I guess," he said with a smile.

This would help pay for the senior prom in early May. I was relieved because I had been worrying about how I was going to pay for a nice night out for Elizabeth and me. We decided to go only a few days before the RSVP date. When we checked with our old friends it seemed everyone had already made their plans. Paul had a full limo already. The Kennedys had tickets to a sold out show afterward. We got a few invitations from others, but they all seemed complicated. We decided to go alone.

I hired a driver with a Lincoln Town car. Before we left we took dozens of pictures on Elizabeth's front lawn, together and solo. I held one side of my tux open and gave the camera my eyes. It was fun, and she looked beautiful. Her brown hair now had red in it. Her dress was white and black and matched my tuxedo. We did all kinds of poses and then carried on our way. We arrived at the event like it was the red carpet.

At the prom we sat with a bunch of smart kids whom we had never really gotten to know. All our old friends were elsewhere. All the troublemakers were nowhere to be seen. It felt like we walked into a prom full of strangers. These smart kids were all nice though. It was like we all knew each other forever, and I regretted not getting to know them in high school. It all seemed like a lot of wasted time, but here we were with one final chance on our way out. One final chance to start anew.

73

AT THE END of the school year, I was invited to the annual graduate awards dinner and presented with "most improved" student of the year. I was also given a small but generous scholarship from a local member of the community. Elizabeth and I went and sat at a table by ourselves. Again, it seemed like we didn't know anyone in the room. Even the people we sat with at the prom weren't at this event. It was all of the top honors kids, the top 1%, and all of them would be going to college in the fall. Their turtlenecks came off on this night, and we all looked the same for once in our black ties and white shirts.

When my name was called, I headed up to the front stage. As I made my way to the front, I heard some chuckling and spotted a couple of kids pointing and laughing at me. I could just hear them, "Look at that…What does he think he's doing here…He's not going to college…" I guess not all of the smart kids were nice ones.

Six months earlier, I would've been over that table in a second and all of those dorks would have been sorry, but I wasn't going to let them ruin my glory. They didn't know what I had been up against. Here I was eating in the same room as them, and I was the lucky one with a beautiful young woman by my side and an amazing experience behind me. Laugh it up, boys.

74

I GRADUATED ON THE HONOR ROLL. The six months had flown by. In June I shook all three assistant principals' hands at the ceremony. Mr. Panzram didn't look me in the eye. Mr. Bundy acted like nothing had ever happened. With a big smile, he shook my hand and squeezed my bicep, the way Vinnie the wrestler used to. I was his pal suddenly. It's okay though. It's going to happen to everyone in life. People are going to prove you wrong once in a while. They're going to bust through that illusion.

I spoke to Andy the week of graduation. He was upset because he had flunked one of his state tests and the head principal Mr. Shulman wouldn't let him walk in the ceremony, even though he passed all his classes and would graduate in August after retaking the exam. He and several others would have to take a test prep class that summer in order to retake the exam. They would receive their diploma in the mail. What an insult. Here was a good kid, a star on the basketball team, and never in trouble the way I had been, and yet he was being denied that once in a lifetime moment. I realized then that the day didn't matter much.

The handshakes.

The speeches.

The pictures.

None of it really mattered much. It was where you had been and where you were going that mattered. A new stage for my life was beginning and I would have new opportunities never imagined. I didn't realize it then, but for every one of my stories there are thousands who don't make it. Some of them end up just fine, but most of them struggle.

After the long line, the handshakes, and the handing off of a rolled piece of paper, we took pictures.

My uncle Albert and me, big smiles.

"Thank you, Al."

"For what?"

"You know, giving me a place..."

"You did all the work though and you worked hard."

"Well, thank you anyway. You..."

"Don't mention it. You're quite welcome, Jack. This was so worth it and it's only the beginning."

Albert seemed to distance himself from me for the rest of the day like an animal does when their offspring is ready to go at it alone. Maybe he sensed this would be it for us and I would be moving on to find myself elsewhere.

My father surprised me and drove up for the day. There's a funny picture of the two of us looking at each other laughing. We look so much alike, yet we're night and day. No grudges— it just is.

My mother and JP were there too— it was great to be reunited with them. Don stayed home— he wasn't invited. I was still worried about them. JP was reaching the age I was when his father came into my life and took me away from my home. That age where things can go wrong.

In the parking lot, I bumped into the Valedictorian. I recognized him from the speech.

"Todd, great speech up there."

"Thank you, Jack."

I was taken back that he even knew who I was.

"Thank you. You spoke for all of us. Congratulations on everything."

"Yes, you too. I saw you at the awards dinner. Nice comeback," he said.

"Thanks. You take care of yourself."

"You too. Best wishes."

We shook hands. Here was the smartest kid in the class, eventually on his way to medical school, and he was as personable as any of the popular kids, yet so sincere. I wished I had known him a lot sooner. He reminded me of Judd, the smart kid I was friends with in elementary school. I wondered how my old smart friend was doing in his other world.

In my dream that night the crowd receives me well. I jog up the stairs, wave as I cross the stage, and stop at the podium. An older looking Mr. Kelly greets me with a hug and then introduces me. I smile at the crowd and step up to the microphone.

"Thank you. Congratulations graduates! You should be proud. This is the first chapter of your lives and you're about to write the final page. There are so many other chapters to come."

The crowd cheers. Mr. Panzram, and Mrs. Lumbrera, now an assistant principal, look on from the side, all smiles. I look out at the crowd of nearly a thousand.

Four hundred wear black caps with tassels dangled over the right side.

"I graduated here many years ago and I'm pretty fortunate to have attained the success I have achieved, because I wasn't always successful. In fact, I barely passed. I even dropped out in twelfth grade before returning to graduate."

More cheers.

"Along the way, I realized the world could be cold and full of injustice. People are judged by how they appear on the outside or the mistakes they made in the past or the hand they're dealt. These judgments become your reputation. Once a reputation is created, it's so difficult to redeem yourself."

The principals and teachers on the side stage applaud. I notice a tall man out in the crowd clapping. He is thinner, balder, grayer, and the mustache is gone. I stare out at the former assistant principal who only recently returned to teaching English. Our eyes meet for a moment and he lowers his. Mr. Bundy and I have a common understanding.

"That's the world, sometimes. But sometimes we can change this. Sometimes we get back on our feet and accomplish the presumed impossible. Maybe some of us can do this all on our own, but with just a little bit of help and a little bit of compassion, we can all achieve our goals. I had help from some very special people along the way, and I thank them deeply. What we need in our schools are more people like the ones who reached out to me."

The crowd applauds. I look out and see Mrs. Sullivan, Mrs. Shelley, Mr. Gongolski, and Mr. Bissell. Like most of my great teachers along the way, they have all retired, but these four have returned for this special day.

"This is a school. These children are the future leaders of our world. There is no room for cruelty or injustice here. There is no room for judgment or permanent reputations. There is no room for people that are going to fail our children, fail our future, and fail our existence. Everyone deserves a second chance. Everyone deserves a helping hand."

I see a proud Mr. Nicosia on the side. He salutes me.

In the front, I spot Ms. Wells with a hand on her neck. My mind stretches from distraction back to focus.

"You have all achieved something special. Now take this victory, walk into your futures, and don't ever let anyone try to keep you down. Congratulations and best wishes to all. You may now turn your tassels to the left."

Black hats and shouts of celebration fill the sky. The principals and other administrators move up the stage and huddle around me. As the cameras flash, they reach out to shake my hand with wide smiles. Mr. O'Connor is not here. He passed away shortly after retiring, but I feel him all around.

75

WHEN I HEARD PLATO'S TALE for the first time sitting in Professor Mariel's university English class, it reminded me of where I had been years earlier.

All of us live in a bubble of a cave. We don't see what others on the outside see. We don't always hear or see the signs that symbolize meaning in our life. We don't really feel. It might be the relationship we shouldn't be in. It might be the good one we take for granted. Instead, our senses are caught up in immediate gratification— the pizza on the table, the small town chit chat, the list of things we need to buy, and even a false desire for immortality. We have no recognition of what goes on on the other side of town. We don't even know what's going on in the next room. We walk outside and it's a rainy day, but there are beautiful things happening all around. Our senses fool us. To see the truth, we would need a microscope or a telescope to zoom in and out.

We see the world for what it really is only when we step out of the bubble. Sometimes we are dragged out of the cave against our will. Other times we make a conscious choice to stand up, break those chains, and exit the cave. Sometimes we stumble out on accident.

We experience the cave in our personal lives all the time in our relationships. Sometimes when we meet people we think they're great, and then we're disappointed when they steal from us or ruin our lives. We judge other people before we even know them, and some end up saving our life or being our best friend. It can work both ways. Illusion versus reality.

No one is out of the cave for good. Just when we think we're out of the cave, there's new darkness to stumble into. No human can know and feel all. Coming out of the cave is a perpetual journey. Again, there is no going backward. If we try to go back down into the cave, we are shunned. We are alienated, cast away without a home to go back to. We can't be part of that family anymore. We've left the tribe. We must go forward to the light, the sun, the truth.

The people back in the cave don't want to change. They are comfortable and sit safely on the sofa of tradition. That's fine for them. They have the right to do so. We won't judge them.

We only break those bonds when we have the motivation to change, when we want to grow. Or when we get lucky enough to have an opportunity to do so and recognize it. The allegory is often used as a metaphor for education, not necessarily formal education, but just the act of learning and opening your mind to something new— bettering your life. Once we are cured of ignorance, the lost bliss is all but nostalgia.

76

I AWOKE ONE NIGHT when I was five and no one was home. My mother had stepped out. The lamp was flickering, so I got up and went to fix it. I went to check the plug and it zapped me with a shock. The electric moved through me and I felt the adrenaline race through my body to counter the electric. My heart started to pound. I left the light alone, which had stopped flickering, and climbed back onto the couch. I curled up and my body shuddered as I fought my way back to sleep.

A wise old Native American told me years later that when the lamp shocked me it filled my soul with electric. The energy from the shock would flow forever and it would be up to me how and when to use it. Maybe it was this electric that kept me going on the coldest nights.

I wanted to be far enough away where I could become somebody new. Others moved away too. But most stayed. Some even still live in the same houses they grew up in, driving on the same streets, going to the same deli, seeing the same people year after year. I can't imagine it, but maybe their childhoods were different. Not to say mine was the worst. So many kids have it far worse.

That past— Sometimes I want to forget all of it, but I don't know if I will. Sometimes I find myself wondering how they are— Steven,

Gene, even Evan. I guess the people you grow up with are always a part of you, for better or worse.

These days, at least twice a year, I like to share "The Allegory of the Cave."

Examples of Plato's "Allegory of the Cave" are all around us, historically, sociologically, psychologically, intellectually, and personally. Think of a time when you came out of the cave. Maybe you crawled or fought your way out to the top, maybe you stumbled out of the dark and into the daylight, or maybe you were dragged out by someone else. How did this logical realization change your former views of life and the world around you?

Did you go back to tell others about your epiphany? What were their reactions or resistance to your great experience?

Remember, the experience must go beyond finding a new belief in a concept, person, or faith because our abstract senses often deceive us. The experience must be concrete.

Discuss Plato's allegory as it relates to your own experience. Make a connection and refer to the Plato text. What are the parallels or possible applications of the lessons contained in the dialogue where the philosopher addresses the difference between light, darkness, and shadows, or knowledge, ignorance, and belief? Be sure to explain how this ancient piece of writing continues to be relevant to us in the 21st century.

This is a creative piece. Leave me with something to think about.

Any questions?

I look forward to reading your stories.

The room on this last day of the semester is usually quiet following my retelling of the allegory, with everyone feeling reflective, looking forward to writing their final essay, and moving on to their future. But one day a hand went up and a curious student asked,

What's your story, professor?

Acknowledgments

There's a lifetime of people to thank, which wouldn't fit on this page, so here's an abridged version. Thank you: Loyola University, Apprentice House Press staff for their outstanding help, Kevin Atticks, Caroline Tell, and Rachel Kingsley, Carmen Machalek...my MFA peers... my colleagues who give so much to the teaching of writing... Denise DiMarzio...to those who read early and later versions of this book...Andrew Wetzel...Ben Shaberman...Ray McCarthy...all of my teachers and principals—the good and the bad...James Connolly... Joan Tschopp...all those who kept asking about the book...Kevin... my family...Julie and Landon...

and *all* of my friends from childhood, who still mean so much.

About the Author

Billy Lawrence was born in New York and grew up on Long Island. He has taught at various colleges around the U.S. This is his first published novel.